THE

GREAT DIVIDE

H. L. HARDING

Copyright © 2025 by H. L. Harding

First paperback edition November 2025.

Cover design by Angelika Brewer.

ISBN 979-8-9932372-1-3 (Paperback)
ISBN 979-8-9932372-0-6 (eBook)

Published by H. L. Harding
Instagram @ H.L.Harding
Facebook @ H. L. Harding - Author

To those who never stopped believing.

"There goes the neighborhood."
R.L.K.

CHAPTER ONE
COSTLY DECISIONS

Everything has a price. Everything you have, have had, and will have cost someone. I lose myself in the thought, wondering if those who came before me realized how much it would cost us in the 2200s. If they even thought about how the consequences of their actions would impact the generations that came after them. Leaving what they called "the *United* States" a broken mess, a shell of what it once was, divided into four different divisions as the result of The Great Divide; a war that started and ended less than one hundred years ago, yet still impacts us daily.

The war came about quickly, due to a pandemic and bipartisanship drawing a line down the middle for people to choose one side or another, on top of the overwhelming hatred of people based on things from race to sexuality to religion that have been around since the beginning of time. There wasn't any gray area that was acceptable. You had to choose. Families were broken apart, based simply on differing opinions. People used these differences, yet again, as a reason to hate. If someone didn't agree with you,

you were immediately their enemy. The war cost so many lives, and in the end there was no winner, simply a once mighty country divided into five parts, with land separating all of them. Five very different parts: The West, The North, The South, The East, and The District.

The West believes in extreme freedom; during the divide they wanted to make The United States a place where there are limited laws or policing, making citizens responsible for their own behavior. They don't have one leader, but an entire board of directors who help to manage things. They only have three major laws: do no harm, do not steal, and do not betray The West. For the people living in The West these things are a non-issue because they know not being civil with one another could be the cause that they would need more strict governing. Occasionally someone will come from out of town and attempt to take advantage of their system. The West has a small military that they set up for times like these; they are almost never activated and have jobs that they do when not active. Their military is similar to the Reserves in The East. Those who come to The West and threaten their way of life are taken in quickly and locked away until they can be tried and potentially sent back to where they came from or otherwise jailed in The West to serve their sentence. In The West less houses are abandoned because there were many people who fled here when the division began, due to fear of losing their freedoms.

The North has stayed true to the bipartisan democracy which had been the way of The United States since the late 1700s.

Every two years they vote on whether or not they like their President and if they can stay for another two years before their major election. If the current President is determined to not be fulfilling their duties, then at the two-year mark, they are replaced by their Vice President who finishes the last two years of the term, until the next election takes place. The homes here are completely full, even more than in The West. People don't enjoy change; the unknown scares them. It was natural for so many people that didn't have a strong feeling towards making changes to the United States to head to The North with the least amount of change. The North is kind of like a time capsule in the sense that things haven't changed there in over one hundred years, they liked the way that life was when the divide began, so they kept it that way. It was the only thing that they could have control over, and people tend to cling to that kind of thing.

The South rules with an iron fist. Everything you can think of doing has some kind of regulation. Want to cut your hair? It must be within the guidelines. Want to buy groceries? Only certain ingredients are permitted in The South. Need medicine? You had better hope that it is one The South allows, and this is just scratching the surface. Total control. I love being a leader but could never get behind this type of leadership. Typically, those who went to The South were radical in their thinking and those that call The South home are complete opposites of those living in The West. Next to The South, The District might be the most difficult place to live.

Though I have never been there, my mother told me all about it. Before it got too bad in The District they would take the school children there on a field trip, staying in the bus even then. They took an armored bus and barely drove into The District, staying as close to the exit as possible. This was a way to show them how well off they were living in The East, a form of keeping everyone in check.

The District is where the government used to be housed for what was once the United States. Great big statues and enormous white mansions remain standing here. These buildings are now home to those who wanted away from it all, or those who were essentially banished here, the outcasts of our society. The windows are boarded up; the bigger buildings are home to large clans of outcasts who have chosen to work together. In most places, belonging to The District is almost as bad as belonging to the enemy territory. Families who have family members that have ended up in The District do not discuss them, and if they must some will even go as far as pretending that they are dead, not daring to mention that they went to The District.

Here, people have no leader, and unlike The West they don't even work together toward a common goal. No, The District has no laws, no leadership, no goals. The people here just want to do what they want when they want, without any consequences and that's completely acceptable in their society. Here, looking at someone could get you shot, and no one would bat an eye as your body dropped to the ground. Children are the only exception; it is

4

a silent agreement that is passed on to every new member of The District. Children are left out of the chaos which our ancestors created. If a child is ever harmed everyone takes part in punishing, likely killing the offender. Only the strong and smart survive here. My father always says that strength isn't always determined by muscle size. The North and East are constantly using The District as a reminder to The West as to what can happen when people are left to rule themselves, without laws or consequences.

The East, where I'm fortunate enough to live, is in the middle ground of the views of The North and The West, wanting people to have a say, but also having rules and leadership in place to avoid total chaos. Here, everyone's voice counts, there is no such thing as an electoral college, like there had been many years ago and still is in The North. There are not many people living here though, because people were afraid to bring forth any ideas that could disrupt the peace. Both The West and The South just piggybacked on the ideas of the extremists who had been living in the United States at the time of the division. Although many people chose a division to live in, there are still a lot of homes throughout the country that are abandoned due to people fleeing the country in masses and killing each other off throughout the course of the war.

In The East, there are loads of abandoned houses everywhere. It was a larger area that was built up quickly, destroying much of the surrounding greenery. The only good thing to come from there being less people now is that some of the greenery is coming back. Just down the street from my apartment are abandoned row houses. They have become overrun with vines in the last few years since I moved here to the military housing after Graduation. The members of the military without families or who are lower ranking live in these apartments, those who are married with children are allowed to move out into houses. My brother lives on the same floor and frequents my apartment for dinner; just the other night, while on my balcony eating, we spotted a wild deer. This was the first he or I had seen so close, without being in the forest for training. The sight even caught my dog's attention; Jethro's ears perked up at the sight of this large foreign creature. Jethro, with his large body and shaggy fur the color of coal, looking like a wolf with floppy ears, terrifies anyone that comes across him, not knowing the sweet being he is, yet this deer perplexed him and caused him some alarm.

The only other place you see animals, other than dogs or cats, is at the farms who breed animals to supply the grocery stores and military food storage. Maybe this deer was a sign of a coming rebirth, that things are going to get better for all of us. Maybe there is a time coming when I can enjoy a book without looking over my shoulder, expecting an attack. That is the dream, but right now it is entirely too much to ask for. I have a military to run, simple pleasures like curling up with my dog and a good book must wait.

Today everything will have to wait. Today is day three of Graduation. We have already spent the last two days watching the intellectual and physical portions. Just like every year since I graduated myself I will attend to scout out the new talent and potential recruits to join my team in the military, out of two hundred Graduates. With a knock on my door, I am snapped out of my daydream of wild animals, greenery, and time to read.

"Margot! Let's go! Major Generals can't be late!" My brother, I can't help but roll my eyes, of course he's here an hour early. The drive to Graduation should only take half an hour.

"Hudson! Why? Why are you here, so early, banging on my door!? Either let yourself in or wait quietly out there." I don't have the patience for him right now.

As if he was waiting for those magic words, I can hear the key in my lock, the tumblers moving obediently to the key, and the doorknob starting to turn. This of course gets Jethro up in arms, ready to take on whatever or whoever is about to walk through that door. Lucky for my brother, Jethro realizes it is him almost immediately the second the door opens. He melts into a puddle at my brother's feet to receive pats and his standard greeting from my brother.

"Hiya boy! You want belly rubs? Let's go get you a treat!" My brother has a special voice he uses for Jethro; one he'd never let any of our soldiers hear. No, he reserves his deepest, most commanding voice for them. Every time he's here I have a laugh at the sight of the six foot four, burly man walking into my kitchen with his fifty-pound shadow prancing behind him. Every bit of Hudson is rugged, from the curly dark mess of hair on top of his head that matches his overgrown beard, to the torn jeans and shoes that the sole has separated from, looking as though they are trying to speak with every step he takes. My brother, followed by a needy Jethro, plops down next to me on the couch with a box of crackers for the three of us to share. This is the real reason he has shown up so early, to raid my cabinets for snacks.

Suddenly, Hudson turns towards me, "So, do you know what you're looking for today? Maybe today you'll *actually* pick someone."

"I'm not sure there's any way to describe it, but I'll know when I see it."

My brother simply shrugs at me, "Hopefully it's not a dud year".

Every October, Graduation means new people coming into the workforce, and specifically for us, new recruits to join our ranks. This is a chance for us to continue building up our military. When it's time to head to Graduation Hudson and I change into our official military uniforms. Hudson offers to drive, which means that he will listen to his music, and make no effort to have a conversation with me for the entire drive that should take us about thirty minutes depending on traffic. This leaves me to reminisce on previous Graduations, including my own, which completely changed my path and where I thought I would end up.

Graduation determines your role in society, most importantly how you will contribute to the coming war to protect our way of life. The most common assignments that people talk about are teachers, medical professionals, and soldiers. Even though these are the most common there are still plenty of other jobs that need filled: sanitation workers, retail workers, farmers, entertainers, the list goes on and on. Every role holds importance in our society. Even though we are focused on the possibility of war at all times, we still have times where we're able to actually enjoy life even though it's on guard.

While a lot of the old entertainment venues are now abandoned, we still have some restaurants and an old bowling alley with pool and pinball. There's even an abandoned arcade where we can sometimes get the old games left behind to work. Even the people working at these establishments are respected, because they allow for much-needed relief from the stress that the state of where we live brings about. I thought for sure I would end up being assigned to a teacher role, and I guess I was kind of right. I teach how to be the best soldier that The East can offer. I have to keep track of a whole herd of people and make sure I don't lose any of them, which admittedly would be a lot easier if they were schoolchildren.

CHAPTER TWO
GRADUATIONS PAST

In The East students attend primary school until they're about eighteen, after that they attend secondary school for the next four years until they reach Graduation; this is mandatory for all children. In Secondary School everyone is required to take a history class on the events leading us to the broken mess we are in now. Our schooling covers the major events, though probably told in a completely different light than in the West, North, and South. Somehow major events continued happening in the Twenties. The 1920s brought the roaring twenties, prohibition, the end of World War I, and the Spanish Flu pandemic. The 2020s brought about a new pandemic, which led to the largest political divide, in what was once the *United* States, has ever seen. All of it leading up to the 2120s and the war that led to where we are now, The Great Divide. These events ignited the fire which is now ablaze in 2227. This fire created a new kind of civil war. Not a war about what is right and wrong, like the Civil War in the 1800s, but a war of *who* was right. One person's ideas and opinions versus another's. The fighting and arguing changed the world my Great Grandmother was born into and led to me having to live my life in a constant state of survival.

Secondary school covers many subjects we would never need, because once you graduate everything you learned is basically of nonimportance, unless you become a teacher. Most of us are twenty-two when we reach Graduation, some a little older, some a little younger. Graduation is not a celebration, but a life sentence, this is where your next move is decided. Where your future is decided for you. Graduation means a three-day aptitude test, during the first weekend of October, that determines what your contribution to The East and the inevitable war will be; whether you will be a soldier, a doctor, a teacher, etcetera. Although you can interview for other roles than what you are placed into, the majority of people just stick with the results they are handed. The aptitude test is not a normal test with questions you have to answer, and results quickly after based on how you answered the questions. No, these tests are designed to test you in every way imaginable. To make the entire Graduation even more daunting everyone in the division is required to come out and watch days two and three, other than some of the medics and soldiers who must stay at their posts.

Graduation consists of three parts: intelligence, physical strength, and emotional strength. Graduation takes place over a long weekend, Friday to Sunday, all but day three's testing is done at the same time as at least a few other students, in alphabetical order, and each portion of the test is given on its own day. Sunday's testing, the emotional strength portion, is completed one by one.

The first test, to test your intelligence, is administered on Friday, in two parts. Each part is three hours long and is divided by a lunch break. Lucky for us, lunch is provided at least. Intelligence is measured by performing a number of tasks and tests. The first half of the day consists of pen-to-paper tests that cover an array of subjects, including math, science, and history. These tests have right or wrong answers, there is no middle ground. The second half of the day focuses more on tangible intellectual tests, like puzzles and escape room riddles. For the intelligence portion of Graduation you earn a score out of three hundred. At least this section of the test allows you to study for it, at least a little bit. On this day we are all in a large gymnasium together sitting at individual desks. This portion tests us, mostly, on what we learned during grade school, although they do enjoy throwing us curve balls.

Part two of Graduation takes place on Saturday, it tests our physical strength. Unfortunately, for some, this portion of Graduation is not something that you can study for. Sure, you can run after class or lift weights on the weekend, but that can't make someone have the coordination or drive to excel in this portion of Graduation. This portion includes an obstacle course where they shoot you with paintballs as you try to complete it. You are not only judged on how you work to dodge the paintballs, but also by how many or how few paintballs stained you by the end of the course. Last year one of the graduates finished the course completely covered, head to toe, in bright green paint. The poor guy looked like a swollen grape the following day due to all of the bruises.

Part three, the emotional strength portion, is the most challenging. Remember, they are testing us in order to determine what our contribution to the approaching war will be, emotional strength can make or break a person and determine their outcome in the war. The ability to run from danger and fight off a foe is important along with having the smarts to make a plan, but the emotional capacity to continue on when all you want to do is stop is everything. Technology is a large component during this portion of testing, through the use of virtual reality headsets and four-dimensional sensory devices. This portion takes place on an old professional football field, so there is no worry of bumping into anything, or anyone. Then, the horrors begin. Your goal is to get you and your virtual team to safety all while being attacked by members of a virtual enemy army, the end point is notated on a map that you are handed at the very beginning. It probably wouldn't be as bad if it wasn't for the four-dimensional sensory devices, they are what makes you feel like you are in the middle of the terrors of combat. Where running through a virtual swamp soaks you to the core and being attacked leads to a blood-like substance being on your hands. Not to forget that the entire time the entire division is watching your every decision from the stands above the field; judging you during testing and every day thereafter for how you act during Graduation.

Six years ago, during this portion of Graduation a graduate, Lincoln Hart, was being attacked by six others. The entire division watched him *kill* his attackers with a knife he had found earlier in the course. He managed to make it through almost the entire course with his whole team *alive*, before losing them all in a final ambush attack before he reached the finish line. This was a feat within itself. It was rare for someone to even have half of their team survive past the first wave of attackers, but of course all that many in the division remembered were his brutal *murders*. The division criticized him, even though he was given top marks and had been asked to be a leader in the military. He lasted four months after Graduation before going AWOL. The most common rumor was that he made his way to The District, but no one has seen or heard of him since. He was a year above me, but I never really knew him. My first time learning of him was at Graduation, after that all I knew were the rumors and the pictures of him plastered everywhere for propaganda.

My year's Graduation had a standout as well, but fortunately not in the same way as Lincoln, because my year's standout was me. It has been five years, and I am still greeted with unwelcome stares everywhere I go. The first two months after Graduation I was haunted by my picture popping up everywhere I went with the words "Graduation standout-follow Margot to a brighter future" flashing across every screen they could find and everywhere they could hang a poster. The worst were the life-sized cardboard cutouts of me stationed in random places. At least my mother insisted I look presentable for Graduation. While I still got my way in putting half of my hair on top of my head, my mother presented me with a green ribbon, to put in my hair to compliment my curls along with a fair amount of makeup. Mom reminded me, thankfully, to go with the waterproof option. She thought of everything that day, even down to the color of the ribbon that she had me stick in my hair, supposedly meant to compliment my green-blue eyes and my dark blonde hair.

My year I didn't dazzle them with my strength, I was average, and that is being generous. My marks during the intelligence portion were good enough, I scored above average. By most standards I had top marks, if I had been able to focus more and keep my head out of the clouds and with the book I was currently reading that I had even brought with me in my backpack, I am sure I could have scraped up at least twenty-five more points. No, what made me the standout this year was my performance in the emotional strength portion. I had a strategy going in; I had been able to imagine at least ten different scenarios, based on previous graduations, and how I would go about handling them. Of course, this only did me some good, because once you are in the testing zone all logical thinking goes out the window and your fight, flight, or freeze instincts kick in.

My emotional strength portion of testing started just like everyone else's; standing in the middle of what used to be a professional football field. The entire division filling the stands, including my family, watching me flail around with a virtual reality headset on, and the images displayed on the giant televisions around the stadium. The second I put the headset on I was transported to the middle of a war zone, with the objective of getting me and my team out alive. This was the same for everyone, but the things that happened to you between putting on the headset and getting to the finish lines varies from Graduate to Graduate. One minute I'm standing there with my virtual team, alone, the next minute brings an onslaught of soldiers wearing The South's uniforms, ready to kill every one of us. Every part of me felt as though it went numb from confusion and fear. Freeze. The next moment I was running as hard and fast as I could away from the danger, leaving my entire team behind. Flight. I made it about twenty paces away before screeching to a halt, remembering that a major part of the objective was to not only get myself out, but my team as well. Fight.

Lucky enough for me I was able to play off running away as looking for higher ground, which I found rather quickly. There was a hill not too far away, and between it and myself was some kind of gun. Surely I was bright enough to point the thing and pull a trigger, even though I had never held a real gun. Only ever a fake one at the abandoned arcade. I got to the top of the hill with the gun just in the nick of time. I was able to take out nine of the ten attackers before any of my teammates were touched. This feeling was a feeling I had never felt before. Shooting a gun and taking people, though virtual, down was a rush. I think the feeling of being the protector was what did it. All of my life I had relied on my brother to protect me. In this moment I had power that I had never had before, the power to protect, to fight, to take charge. From this point on I would never go back to being the bug I was before, always being stepped on by others and allowing my brother to fight my battles for me.

After witnessing me take out the rest of his team the remaining attacker focused his sights on me. At this moment he pegged me as the biggest threat in the field. It was now or never; I took aim and took out the remaining attacker. I quickly ran to my team, directing them to search the attackers for anything that could be useful to us as we made our way to the safe zone. This type of power fueled me even more than the power I had felt taking down those attackers. I was meant to be a leader, and I had finally been given the chance to prove myself. I had never been given the chance to lead before; I think I was always overlooked for the bigger and less friendly people, those less likely to be taken advantage of. There at that moment I was a strong and powerful leader, even though it was to virtual people. This was my chance to prove myself.

My team was quick to trust me and follow my lead which was beneficial to my final score. Once we had collected what weapons we could find we made our way to the safe zone, the finish line. Along the way we encountered countless other traps and enemies. The first trap was a tripwire; I had to dive to stop my teammate from setting it off; she was less than five steps away. The proctors were impressed by my willingness to do whatever it took to keep my entire team alive, and I continued to do this through to the finish line. My entire team and I made it to the safe zone with only minor bumps and scratches which were unavoidable when you are fighting your way through the desert, then the jungle, and finally the rain forest. All of these places were filled with their natural vegetation and predators, along with some enemies of the human variety. I was the first graduate in over twenty years to successfully complete the emotional portion while keeping all of my teammates alive.

When I took my headset off the entire division was on their feet clapping and cheering for me. The next thing I knew I was being tackled by my brother and sister with my parents trailing not too far behind them. My brother, Hudson, had just graduated the year before; he did well, but I definitely surpassed him with my performance. His score in the physical portion alone put him straight to the top of the military's list of recruits, where he'd just completed his first year. My sister, Eloise, had her Graduation two years after me, and I certainly set the bar higher than our brother had. Compared to our brother she is the complete opposite, with me in the middle as a mixture of the both of them. Hudson towers over Eloise, her perfectly fashioned hair makes his look even more disheveled than it would have without her standing nearby. Since grade five she has had the same shoulder length, straight hair as blonde as a sunflower in the middle of a July day, that she often fashions into two buns on the top of her head. She ended up doing well, much better in the intelligence section than Hudson or I did. Due to her results in the intelligence section, specifically the sciences, she was invited to become a doctor at our local hospital, following in our mother's footsteps.

It was the time for my results; they wait until after you have taken all three portions to tell you all of your scores, followed by your recommended placement. The recruiters use that information to then request that you join them for an interview. For the intelligence section I scored two hundred fifty out of three hundred, in the physical section I scored two hundred twenty out of three hundred, and for the emotional section I was nearly perfect. I scored three hundred ninety out of four hundred. One of the proctors took off ten points, because they thought I was trying to make a run for it at the beginning. He wasn't wrong, but I will never admit that to anyone. My scores had the proctors recommending me to either join the military or become a teacher, putting me on the short list of recruits for the military. When I chose to join the military I was immediately put in their fast-track leadership program, which is how I got to where I am today. Of course, my parents were overjoyed by me doing so well and insisted, like they had after my brother's Graduation, to take family pictures. Our family always looks like a strange bunch when we get together to take pictures. My brother on one side of me lumbering over everyone and my sister on the other so much shorter than the rest of us, myself in the middle with hair that is in between the dark black of my brother's and the sunshine blonde of my sister's. Our parents each have qualities that can be seen in each one of us, like bookends that make the collection come together and make sense. Now the stadium where my life was changed five years ago is in front of me once again.

CHAPTER THREE
GRADUATION PRESENT

Walking up to the stadium today feels like every other time I have walked into it. A rush of emotions and adrenaline. I've always found it exciting to see how people react during their tests, of course we only get to watch the physical and emotional portions, but seeing the reactions to people's intelligence scores is also interesting. Being Major Generals means that we enter through a separate gate from the rest of the division, military members are allowed to have their weapons, while everyone else in the division has to go through the security gates and metal detectors. Anyone caught trying to bring in weapons, of any kind, are immediately detained. Unfortunately, some have tried to use Graduation as an opportunity to attack us, while we are all confined to one place. Those living within the division had even tried once to use it as an opportunity to try and overtake our way of life and change it from within.

As I enter the field I take a moment to stop and look around. I know my dad is somewhere in the stands, as retail workers are required to come. Dad owns a restaurant in the division, which is always closed for Graduation. He's always enjoyed watching Graduation, so long as it wasn't his children participating in it because that brought him stress. My mother and sister, Eloise, haven't been to a Graduation since Eloise's Graduation due to them both being doctors at the hospital and not required to come since their work is essential. Seeing these stands completely filled always makes me wonder about the way things used to be before the division began. This massive stadium used to be a place where people came to watch and enjoy professional athletes competing against each other on a regular basis. Now, we come here once a year to watch a bunch of twenty-one- to twenty-three-year-olds be judged to determine their path in life. I wonder what it would be like to sit back sometimes and watch people throw a ball around for fun. Today I have a lot riding on the results of Graduation, so watching is a job and there isn't any sitting back involved.

As Major Generals, my brother and I must attend Graduation and watch each of the Graduates going through their tasks, clipboards in hand, taking notes on each of them. Final scores are important and taken into account, but sometimes through watching you can find a diamond in the rough. Hudson and I have both found that you can't always trust the final scores when it comes to choosing people to join our ranks, as previous team members have shown us. Personally, I love to see an underdog exceed during the testing, and if not during Graduation then after when they finally get into their designated career.

Hudson, of course, enjoys trying to find people that he thinks will be the best soldier, right along with that he wants people that he thinks he will get along with and trust. The military is a big family, so finding someone to join is personal to him; they could be the best soldier, but a lousy person, and that kind of tradeoff is not what my brother is looking for. His best friend, up until this last year, was one of the greatest soldiers The East had ever seen, but he broke Hudson's trust and completely changed who my brother is as a person. The light-hearted, trusting man he once was is now long gone. I have my own reasons for not trusting people, and this last year has added to the list. It caused me to adopt the mindset that if you trust no one and suspect everyone, then no one can hurt you.

Along with watching the Graduates to see which we would like to consider for our team it is also a part of our duty to corral them, getting them from place to place during their testing. Watching is the interesting part, moving them from place to place is frustrating and much like trying to herd cats. This year's Graduate class is quite the mix of people, including our cousin, Michael. Hudson and I knew going into today that he would be here and already knew that we wouldn't be choosing him to join us. We know he has no interest in the military; teaching is where he wants to be. Even though he isn't going to be a prospect for us we still make sure to pay special attention to his testing. Doing so allows us to learn more about him and sell him to the teaching recruiters, being highly regarded military officials means that other recruiters respect our opinions, so if we thought he'd make a good fit as a teacher we'd make it known. Michael is all of one hundred twenty-five pounds soaking wet and he has no interest in anything that has to do with exercise or even the outdoors. No, he would much rather spend his time reading and devouring new information. He is a firm believer in the notion that a day not spent learning something is a day wasted. As a result, his physical score is abysmal.

Our cousin isn't the only one here that is related to someone of power in the stadium. Bartholomew Stevens is one of the graduates this year as well, the son of one of the wealthier families in the division, whose mother just so happens to be one of the examiners here today. It is no surprise that all of the examiners ended up giving him extremely high scores that were not deserved. Even though his mother isn't allowed to participate in evaluating him there is no doubt in my mind that she had gotten to all of the examiners even before Graduation had begun. Every parent wants their child to do well at Graduation; some have the means to ensure that they will and are willing to do anything they can to get their child ahead. You see, if your child fares well during Graduation it looks good on your family, and your family is more likely to be favored going forward. Unfortunately, this kind of corruption is everywhere, and The East is no exception.

During a break I find myself looking around the stands at those in attendance, when I notice that the President is there. This is not the part that catches me by surprise, she is always in attendance at Graduation like every President before her, and I have seen her here the past two days as well. Something about her seems off today though, her face looks too serious, too concerned for the environment which we are currently in. Graduation is a fun and exciting time for those not directly involved. I notice a man next to her, someone I have never seen before, sitting all too close to her. Her husband isn't in his normal seat to her right, instead there are guards surrounding her, again men that I don't recognize. The guards are generally people pulled from our military forces and assigned to the President's detail for the length of their term, so not recognizing them is concerning. I find myself frantically searching for Hudson. Something is very wrong here, but I don't want to draw too much attention to myself or my realization.

I am concerned by what I have just seen for a number of reasons, and living so close to The District means more danger lurking around every corner for us here in The East. It doesn't help matters that none of the other divisions are behind The East's ideology that change is needed. Even though The North and West are more willing to listen, they don't want to have their way of life changed and be forced to conform to another division's ways. They would rather have everyone follow their example and mold themselves into their division's way of life. I finally spot my brother and move quickly towards him, while trying not to draw any attention to myself. I make my way to him, fortunately, without drawing attention to myself.

I get close to him, facing the same direction that he is and begin speaking to him in a low whisper without making eye contact, "Did you notice what's going on with President Madden? Something is off here, and I don't like it." I follow my brother's eyes, head unmoving, as he looks up into the stands, quickly spotting her. He takes a moment to take everything in and then drops his gaze. We have been trained to quickly take in as much detail as possible without being caught staring at a person. I know that during that short amount of time he was doing the same thing that I did when looking at them, taking in every detail as to be able to describe them later on.

"Not here." That's all Hudson says to me before walking away. I know better than to push him further here. Those two words told me everything that I needed to know. They confirm that what I had seen and felt was real and there is something very strange going on here. Possibly dangerous. I know this is something that we will discuss later in the safety of our car or home, where there aren't prying ears and eyes around, people we don't know or trust. I force myself to stop thinking about the events that just occurred and attempt to distract myself by focusing on the testing that takes place in front of me. Then, I notice him. Why didn't I notice this Graduate before now? Obviously more pressing matters had my focus, but even yesterday during the physical portion when I didn't have this situation with the President, I don't recall seeing him. He must not have been a standout yesterday, because I'm sure Hudson would have pointed him out to me had he been someone with great strength or athletic ability. Right now, our team could really use some more muscle, especially after losing two of our stronger teammates.

This boy, a young man, looks strong, like he might be an athlete or lift weights in his spare time. I can tell exactly what kind of person he is, a thinker, a work smarter not harder type. Someone like myself who takes the time to analyze everything around them before acting. He looks like he could probably carry a wounded soldier from the battlefield, but would find a less strenuous way to do so, like fashioning a cart to pull the person along with. I continue to watch him, his focus is on everyone but himself, hyping those up around him when they are getting ready to go into their emotional portion of the test or as they are coming back from completing it. This is a rare thing to witness in our society, especially today during Graduation. The majority of the students here today are doing everything that they can to make themselves stand out, even if that means making those around them look bad on purpose. He seems like he wants everyone around him to do well, and doesn't seem to mind that it might hinder his own performance. He is the one that stands out to me today, he is the one that I want to bring onto our team.

Now it is his turn to enter the virtual battlefield. Right from the beginning his performance is a beautiful sight to see. He reminds me so much of myself on Graduation day, although my performance was to hide my cowardice, his actions seem genuine. Throughout his test he makes his team the first priority. Even though they are virtual he has stopped several times to tend to his wounded teammates, taking his time. He has even gone as far as to say a quick prayer over those who are dead or severely wounded before moving on without them. This kind of behavior is unheard of. Especially because these *teammates* he is caring over aren't even real! They're all just a part of the virtual reality he is currently in. This is exactly why my team needs him, all of us are guilty of getting too wrapped up in ourselves.

I quickly wave at my brother to have him come over, I can tell the young man is almost at the end of the course, and I want Hudson to see him before his turn is finished. Hudson clearly has written him off, because he's not even watching his attempt anymore, just flipping through his notes on previous Graduates when I get his attention. Hudson half walks, half jogs over to me, probably thinking that I have noticed something else regarding the President. Time to prepare myself for the complaining from him that it's not any kind of emergency. He reaches me quickly.

"What is it? Something with President Madden?" His words are breathy with nerves.

I knew that this would be why he thought I had called him over, he wouldn't have thought that it'd be that I'd picked my own recruit. Every year before now he told me to find people for the team, but I've never found someone that I wanted to pick as my recruit. Until now I have allowed him to choose whoever he wanted, I just usually either met the person when they first came in for their interview, sometimes even sitting in on the interview.

"I want him for our team." I watch as my brother glances up at the tall, bulky, unimpressive looking young man in front of us. He wouldn't stand a chance against Hudson if they ever got into it. Maybe he is thinking the same thing, because then the laughing starts.

His words are full of laughter, of course Hudson wouldn't be impressed by someone who doesn't look like a born fighter, "You can't be serious. First, you call me over here, making me think that something important is going on. Then, this is what you have to tell me?" He scoffs and rolls his eyes, "You haven't had the desire to pick someone since you took this job, and *this* is your first pick? You have got to be kidding me, Margot!"

It figures that the one time I find someone I'm criticized for it. "Nope, not kidding. This is who I want, you can have the remaining picks." I motion towards the graduate, "Just look how he interacts with the others around him. Not a selfish bone in his body, that's who we want having our six." I take my eyes off the graduate for a moment and look at my brother, watching the gears in his head turning this idea round and round.

"Fine. But if I don't like him when he comes to the interview, then he's out."

"Deal. Hasn't that always been the rule?"

"Yeah, but you've never wanted to bring someone to the interview, so I just wanted to make sure everything was clear."

"Crystal." I roll my eyes. Some days working with my brother is frustrating.

Hudson takes this as his cue to leave. He can tell that I am irritated by his arrogance and mocking. This is exactly why I haven't chosen anyone in years past, I knew this is exactly how he would act and I've never felt strongly enough about anyone to feel like fighting him on it. We may be the same rank, but he still holds seniority. It's like he forgets that we're not kids anymore. This takes me back to school when no matter what I did I was picked on by someone. It makes it hard to be your true self and speak up for your beliefs when people do everything that they can to tear you down on their way to the top. Hudson always has my back when it counts, but his attitude about my pick triggers me to go into defense mode due to the bullying I suffered in school. Luckily Graduation and my career success since then changed that, for the most part. I like to think that being treated so poorly in school helped me to become the person that I am today.

I feel like this mystery candidate may have gone through something similar to me, like he has something to prove too, which is what's drawing me to him. I find myself walking towards him, even though he's clearly engaged in another conversation. He's nudged by someone standing beside him, someone who's noticed me approaching. I'm not sure though if this other person is a friend or just someone near him in the alphabet who was about to take their turn or had just gone. Either way this person takes my walking in their direction as a way out of the seemingly forced conversation and leaves.

The moment I'm close enough to reach my hand out, the young man quickly returns the gesture, while saying "Major General Briar". The fact that he knows my name takes me by surprise, it's rare that someone not in the military already knew the rank, let alone the name of a soldier. He either studied before today, has family amongst our ranks, or is up to something. I refuse to believe the latter yet, based on how he had acted during his emotional portion. If I get the chance to interview him this will definitely be one of my first questions.

"Pleasure to meet you. What's your name, Graduate?" His handshake is firm yet gentle, not like some men who act like they are trying to rip your hand off when you're shaking it for the first time. There is no effort here to exert dominance.

"The name's Theodore, but you can call me Theo." His smile is warm and inviting, something seems so familiar about him.

"So, Theo, do you have any expectations for your results? Is there any career path that you're hoping to follow?" I silently hope he's going to say the military as I wait for his answer.

"I probably haven't put as much thought into it as I should have, if I'm being honest. All I know is that I want to be somewhere helping people, if I could I would really like to-." Just then his name is called to reveal his scores, but I miss hearing the last name as someone walks by and greets me in passing. His intelligence score is higher than I have seen all weekend, two hundred seventy-five out of three hundred. Next up, his physical score, no surprise here this score is underwhelming, one hundred eighty out of three hundred. Hudson is going to be even more irritated with me inviting him to join our team after seeing his physical score. Lastly, his emotional score. *Wow!* An impressive three hundred seventy-five out of four hundred. Caring can earn you a lot of points, depending on the proctors. I know it made me want him on our side. I look at his face as he takes in his scores, he is beaming with pride, this is a genuine guy who is proud of himself for doing so well. His family will be pleased with these scores as well.

"Congrats on those scores! Wow, they're incredible!" *Oh gosh, I'm probably coming on way too strong,* "If you have the time and are interested, I would love the opportunity to interview you this coming week. It'll be a chance to get to know each other a little better, and I can tell you about how joining us in the military could be the right fit for you." I can't help but stare at him, while waiting to hear his response. *Why is he taking so long to respond? It shouldn't take this long, especially if he has any interest in joining us. Maybe he doesn't want to join us and is finding a polite way to decline.* I find myself down my own personal rabbit hole of doubt, but suddenly he's smiling up at me, a full teeth smile.

"I would be honored to have an interview with you! Was there a day and time you had in mind? I'm currently just working for my mom, so I can make time anytime to come and see you." His response sounds so much more professional than my over eager invitation.

I quickly consult my calendar, "How about Tuesday around 10am?"

Theo doesn't hesitate, "That sounds good!"

"Perfect, here's my card. It has the address on it for where to meet, I'll see you then."

He takes my card, all the while still giving me a toothy grin, and walks away towards a large group of people who I can only assume are his family. I don't watch long enough to see who they are, it's too hard to make out who they are in the distance, and someone will probably notice if I'm staring too long. I still can't believe that I *actually* chose someone for the first time and that they agreed to come to the interview! Hudson is my only obstacle now, but I'm sure after seeing his scores in intelligence and emotional intelligence he might see things my way. His physical test scores may be a point of argument from Hudson though. I am excited to find someone I can possibly relate to and take under my wing. I saw so much of myself in him while he was testing and I look forward to seeing what kind of soldier he will become, that being if he agrees to join us.

CHAPTER FOUR
THE INTERVIEW

As we make our way to the car I know the ride home isn't going to be as quiet as the ride here. No doubt Hudson will not only want to discuss what is going on with President Madden, but my recruit decision as well. Surprisingly, Hudson starts right away with my recruit decision.

"Are you sure he's going to be of any value to us? Sure, his intelligence and emotional scores were great, but his physical score was horrible! How do you expect him to be a soldier when his score was complete garbage?" The entire time he keeps his eyes on the road, not looking to me for my reaction.

"I think he is going to prove to be a great value to us. Why are we talking about this anyways? I thought you might want to talk about what's going on with the President..."

He is still staring at the road, but I can see his hands tighten around the steering wheel.

"I thought we would start with the easy stuff first and then move into the daunting stuff." He pauses to see if I might react. "Something is definitely going on with the President, and the fact that we don't know who the people surrounding her were makes me feel even more uneasy. All I know for now is that something is off, and we cannot trust anyone but each other." His knuckles are turning white from gripping the steering wheel so hard. Hudson has always had a temper, but he's been reaching his boiling point a lot faster since the betrayal.

"We need to remain vigilant, something is definitely going on, and we need to get to the bottom of it. This is the first time in a while that I've had a bad feeling like this." Unfortunately, my gut hadn't picked up on our recent betrayal, something I still haven't forgiven myself for.

"Agreed. We need to keep our heads down and our eyes peeled." His voice is almost a growl, trying to keep his anger in check. "We need to be careful where we discuss this and who is around us, you never truly know who your enemies are. If the wrong person finds out we have any suspicions or doubts it could be very bad for us, our family, and our team."

All I can do is silently nod in agreement, staring down at my shoes, there's nothing more to say. We sit in silence for the remainder of the ride home, and when I finally decide to look up, Hudson is turning into his parking space. I need to get upstairs to Jethro, today was exhausting and I know he is going to be excited to see me. The sooner I take him outside; the sooner I can go to bed and sleep off the stress of this weekend. Luckily, we have tomorrow off to recover from the weekend, and then it will be time to dive into recruit interviews and to make our final selections for our team.

Tuesday morning comes so quickly that it feels like I didn't even have the day off on Monday. The exhaustion from the weekend had taken over me yesterday and I did nothing but sleep and take Jethro outside. At least today isn't going to be too strenuous at work and I'm even able to bring Jethro along with me. I always like having him there during interviews. Jethro is a great judge of character, as all animals are, and he is very quick to let me know if anyone who comes in isn't welcome. As I grab my lunch from the fridge I hear my brother's familiar knock on my door, followed by him waltzing in, as though this is his apartment too.

"If you're going to barge into my apartment, make yourself useful and get Jethro ready to go." I shout at him from the kitchen as I angrily shove my lunch into the bag. I thought adult life would be different, especially living on my own, but working with my brother and living in the same building as him means that he is barging through my door just as much, if not more, as when we were living at home. I love my brother, but man do I need privacy...maybe I'll change the locks and not tell him. I start giggling to myself and it's met with a dirty look.

"What!?" He sneers.

"Nothing, just thinking of something funny, you wouldn't get it though, something from my book I'm reading."

Hudson rolls his eyes and walks toward the front door, Jethro in tow, since he already got him leashed up and is holding on to his leash. As he makes his way to the door I grab my bag and head for the door as well. Hudson decided to drive today, I don't argue as I'm still exhausted from the weekend. As we make our way to his shiny black pickup truck, his pride and joy, I find myself looking around a lot more than normal. I am usually looking around to make sure everything checks out, but after the strangeness that took place over the weekend involving the President I am more worried and observant than normal. I can't help but look for clues, anything out of place, this time I come up with nothing. Finding nothing is both good and bad; good because it means that we are okay for the time being, bad because it means that something is coming.

The ride seems like it's going to be uneventful and luckily without my brother's annoying antics. I choose to use the ride as a chance to eat breakfast, if I don't eat now, I might not get to. I don't know when or if I'll get a break today to do so. Jethro decides he needs to monitor my every bite. I end up giving him half of my bagel just to get him to stop breathing in my face while I'm trying to eat. Next thing I know we're about to park with a minute to spare before we should be in for the day. This means that I have about an hour to prepare for Theo's arrival for his interview.

Driving to Headquarters will never get old. It's located in the downtown area on a main road, so we have to park in a lot designated for us a few doors down. Our building is the width of a city block and so deep that the back doors open to another, less busy, street. This also happens to be the street that our large garage door opens to. Our building has several stories that extend both above and underground with many front doors to enter through depending on your reason for being there. Our down time between arrival and Theo's interview is of course accompanied by Hudson's irritating questions about my choice.

"So, are you really sure about this kid?" He has the audacity to ask me this while sitting on the floor petting *my* dog!

"Yes! For the last time, yes!" Let the eye rolling begin, anytime I speak up and challenge him he rolls his eyes, it's been like this since we were small. "I don't understand why you can't just accept my decision and give him a chance!" I notice my brother's face suddenly flushing with color, something that doesn't often happen here at work, but since it's just him and I his guard is down.

"I worry about making these decisions now ever since the incident with Ryan." *This is it; he is finally going to talk about this with me.* "I don't want to make the same mistake-"

The chime on the door rings as it swings open, silences Hudson; pushing it open is Theo. I've always found it interesting, and sometimes impressive, how people present themselves for their interview. Theo's appearance doesn't surprise me at all, the way he's presenting himself gives me the feeling that I was right inviting him here. He is wearing a full suit and clearly took the time to make sure his hair was combed neatly, he even brought with him a briefcase that looks like it has been handed down for a few generations. The leather looks worn, and it even has a last name etched into it. *That last name! That's how he knew who I was! He's a Flynn.*

Both his grandfather, General Demani Flynn, and his father, Lieutenant General Lewis Flynn, had been impressive during their time in active duty. Even though his grandfather is now retired, he still frequents political and military events, even coming around occasionally to give us encouragement and tell us his stories. His father oversees operations and currently outranks me. We don't see him much because he works out of a smaller office with the elite and highest-ranking officials. I didn't catch Theo's last name at Graduation, or I would have understood everything immediately. At least this bit of information will hopefully make Hudson feel better about my decision. I realize that I'm caught up in my thoughts and quickly stand up to walk over to Theo to shake his hand and introduce him to Hudson. Moments after I make my realization, Jethro is bounding towards him with excitement, a promising sign. Luckily, Theo is just as excited to meet Jethro. Jethro knew to retreat when I walked up, and to stop trying to lick Theo's face off.

"Theo, so great to see you again! I'm glad you could make it." I gesture in Hudson's direction, "This is my brother and Major

General, Hudson Briar. Hudson, this is Theodore - Theo Flynn." I can't hide my *gotcha* grin, I'm beside myself that I might have actually proved my brother wrong for once. My grin widens even more as I see the look on Hudson's face as he realizes who my recruit is. It is taking everything in me not to laugh out loud. As they shake hands I see Hudson's cheeks redden with embarrassment, especially since he had been doubting me wanting to bring Theo in for this interview. As they go through pleasantries I find myself thinking of all the stories Theo's grandfather has told us over the years. He is the reason I have continued to push myself and got to this position, I want to make an impact on others' lives as he has mine. I find myself smiling when my thoughts are interrupted by my brother elbowing me in the arm.

"Were you planning on doing his interview today, or would you rather sit around dreaming all afternoon?" He knows I'm a daydreamer, and there is absolutely nothing wrong with it, but it is still embarrassing being called out on it in front of my recruit.

I glare at him before I turn to walk towards my desk and Hudson heads off to work in the armory, allowing me to handle a majority of the interview on my own, knowing that he'll be watching and listening the whole time through our intercom system, "Come along, Theo, we can go ahead and do your interview here at my desk." He eagerly follows behind me like a little puppy excited just to be near someone. As he takes a seat, I notice his pants raise up just enough so I can see that he is wearing brightly patterned socks with his completely monotone suit. I smile, thinking that the suit is who he is on the outside because he's a Flynn, but that the brightly patterned socks are who he really is on the inside. I study him, attempting to figure out just who he might be, separate from his prestigious family and the front that he might put up during our interview. People often leave out so much with their words, you have to learn to read between the lines.

"So, tell me about yourself, Theo." I begin cracking each knuckle on my hands, mindlessly. "Based on your last name I'm almost certain you were raised in a military family, so tell me more about how your upbringing made you the person you are today." He takes several breaths before starting to answer me, clearly trying to decide how to go about answering this question. Searching for the right answer.

"Well, as you've figured out, I do come from a military household, but even without that I think I would still want to join the military." He inhales deeply while looking around as though searching for his next words, "I'm the youngest of four, and always have someone looking out for me, whether it's my parents or my siblings. I think that that made me want to care for people and look out for those that weren't able to do so themselves." As he says this, I think about the way that he had acted during the emotional portion at Graduation, and it all makes sense. It didn't matter that those teammates were virtual, all he saw were people that needed his protection, and he stepped up to do so.

"Good, it's an important step in becoming a great soldier to know why you're here and what you're doing it for. Without a why, there's no reason for the what. Now tell me, did you enjoy school? How did you do there?"

This answer comes a lot quicker, no calculating how to respond; probably because it isn't about his high-ranking military family. This answer won't affect anyone but himself.

"Um, I really enjoyed school. I think that it was somewhere that I was able to set myself apart from my siblings and make a name for myself. I really enjoy anything related to science, any science really, but I guess my favorite would have to be chemistry. I got to learn how to make fireworks, and I still use that knowledge to help the division make them for special events." This is a skill we can use, if he can make fireworks, what else can he make? "I've recently started learning about biology as well, and hope that I can combine my knowledge of biology with chemistry to do good for others."

"Well, you're in luck. Our team has several people that incorporate science into their roles here. You'll be able to shadow them and learn from them before we make your final placement. Sometimes it ends up being something totally different than what people come in here thinking they're going to do. Maybe you'll even quit science and join me and become a strategist." I throw in a semi-forced laugh to make sure that he knows I'm joking and not trying to jab at him for enjoying science. I have nothing against science, or liking it even, I just have absolutely no interest in it, I was no good at it during school and found it terribly boring. I know it is important for the military though, and it has already come in handy in several of our missions.

"I've heard a lot about the shadowing program and it's just another part of the military that drew me in." *Now we are getting somewhere.* "I know that if I want to use something I love to do, the military is the place for me, especially since you offer the best practical lessons out of any of the other job options." It is true, since we do a lot for the cause we earn the most funding for supplies and training, right up there with the hospitals. Others throw you in and it's either sink or swim, so you better learn how to swim fast, or you may end up begging for work elsewhere.

"Our programs are pretty outstanding, you've come to the right place if you're interested in an opportunity to expand your knowledge and explore multiple career paths, even with the military. Is there anything else you would like to tell me about yourself? How about your hobbies and your aspirations?" He certainly is a tough nut to crack, I feel like I'm doing everything I can to pull answers out of him.

"Um, well, hobbies…I don't know that they're too different from what I enjoyed about school. I really enjoy everything involving chemistry, so at home I put that into cooking and baking. Chemistry is all about making concoctions and it's the same way in the kitchen with food. I recently created my own cheesecake recipe that is to die for!" *Oh good, finally someone that can cook other than Lee. I'm sure he'll appreciate the help.* The rest of us can cook, sure, but it's mostly buttered noodles. Our last few cooks couldn't *actually* cook; they just lied on their resumes to get a spot with us. The last time someone other than Lee tried cooking something outside of the box it was so bad that the lot of us ended up with food poisoning and were out of commission for two days.

"That's great! We can always use a soldier that can cook on the side, we get a lot of takeout around here." I glance at the empty pizza box sitting on top of the trash. "Last question, what are your aspirations?" This is the longest pause he's taken yet, and I don't think this one is for him to calculate how to answer but figuring out what his answer is.

"I think I just want to make my family proud of me for being me, for doing my own thing. I think everyone expects me to be the man my father is, and there's nothing wrong with him, but I also want to be able to be my own person." *Wow, that says a lot.* "I want to be able to be a good soldier, but still not lose sight of the things that make me, me. So many people become so hyper focused on their Graduation results that they forget to live their lives and that there are more parts to them than what the Graduation evaluators say they are." *Wow.* He's not wrong, so often we forget to still live our lives past our jobs. Myself for example, I've stopped making time for reading because I spend so much time at work and then resting for work. He is going to be a great influence on all of us, maybe we'll all start to find some kind of work life balance.

"Theo, you would make a great addition to our military, and we would love to have you join us. How does that sound? Are you interested?" His eyes light up like a child seeing an assortment of sweets, like I have just given him the best gift he could ever receive. He takes several deep breaths, giving me too much time to think about how strongly I came off.

"Yes, of course!" He kind of yells at me and then flushes after doing so, realizing how eager he's come across. His eagerness doesn't put me off, I'm excited to have a recruit so excited to join us.

"Great!" I stand to shake his hand, "We look forward to having you join the military. You can come by Monday to start your sign up process and then placement will begin. I think you could make a great addition to our weapons division, but we will go about actually placing you once you've started training, so we can see exactly where your strengths lie." I take a breath, "Just keep in mind that some people may not end up on the Alpha team, but we work to find everyone the place where they fit best." He's still smiling, a goofy smile, ear to ear as he gives me a nod of understanding. His enthusiasm about joining us confirms my decision about asking him to come here. Even after telling him that he may not be on my team directly he keeps a positive attitude. "Bye, Theo." He smiles once more, giving me a small wave and turns to leave. As he heads out the front door I turn to my brother to see him looking at me, rolling his eyes as always. He hates being wrong, and this was his biggest mistake in a while.

"Do you have anything that you would like to say to me?" My arms are crossed, not forgetting how rude he has been about my pick.

"Nope!" The same mocking smile he always gives, planted on his face. This is the biggest issue of working with your brother. The condescending, mocking attitude is only used with his little sister.

"Ugh! You know, you could acknowledge, FOR ONCE, that I do a great job here."

"I can't. Your head will get too big." There it is, the same stupid half smile that he's had since we were little. He flashes it at me before turning to walk away from our conversation. I reach my arm out and smack him across the back of the head with all of the force that I can muster up. He snaps back around, still smirking. *Prick.*

"Could you at least just tell me how you're feeling about Theo?" I'm doing the best I can to resist smacking him again, maybe this time would wipe the stupid grin off of his face.

"I think he's going to be great for us, doesn't hurt that he's got a powerful family too. That could mean even more for our team, if his grandfather and father come along and give us some boosts." He shrugs.

"Okay, but besides his lineage?" I wave my hands at him, inviting him to say more.

"I think he's a good kid, he's going to be able to do great things for us." *Seriously, that's it?* His tone comes across as though he's trying to hold excitement back, but also irritation that he didn't find Theo himself.

"And?" I can't believe I'm having to prompt him for this.

"You were right." He mumbles under his breath as he dips into the bathroom to escape the conversation.

Next week is going to be great. I'm really excited to see all that Theo brings to the table. The rest of the people coming for interviews are people that my brother had chosen or walk-ins, so I decide let him handle the rest of the interviews, with the instructions to bring me in if needed, so that I can spend the rest of my week training in the armory and coming up with different training plans that I think might be able to test the recruits and their all around abilities. The rest of the week goes by quickly. Including Theo, we will have eight recruits coming back for placement. Unfortunately, the weekend goes by just as quickly as the week did.

CHAPTER FIVE
THE RECRUITS

I wake up feeling a bit jittery from a combination of excitement and nerves. It feels like Graduation was just yesterday. *How has it already been a week?* Today is the day all of our recruits come together with our existing team to see who is going to be a good fit with us and who will go on to do other types of jobs for the military or be on other teams where they may fit better. Some people may end up with our Beta, Omega, or Reserves teams while others may end up with our other essential departments like administration or food service. Every area in this building holds its own significance. This year is unique, because we are replacing so many of our previous teammates due to our recent betrayal, it's going to be a rebuilding year.

When I arrive at Headquarters it's clear that everyone else feels the same way. It has been roughly a week since I interviewed Theo, but I'm still very excited to see him again, and I am confident that he is going to be one of the ones to join our team. As we all stand around waiting for everyone else to arrive, he walks in with confidence about him, but not in a way that could be considered arrogant or cocky. The way he's carrying himself today makes me even happier about my decision and him being here. I'm not the only one to notice him, the other recruits around me are looking at him and then one another, as if all agreeing that he is their main competition. My fellow teammates meet me with smiles and even a wink accompanied by a shoulder to the arm. I didn't get the chance to, but it is clear that Hudson must have told them everything before today. There are eight recruits here today, the same number of people that we invited from the interviews, meaning no walk-ins, which I am surprised by.

As I look around at the recruits I notice what looks like a pair of siblings, maybe even twins. It could be interesting to have another set of siblings on the team. Hudson draws me from my thoughts. My brother, like always, is chomping at the bit to get things moving, his voice booms "Good morning, everyone!"

Some muffled *good mornings* reply, but the loudest come from our existing teammates hollering different greetings and laughing with each other. We spend almost every day together training and even most of our time outside of training is spent together too. Even though we spend so much time together we are always excited to see each other, we've become one big family.

I step forward to speak before Hudson can get going, "We thought that it would probably be best to start today off by explaining a little more about what today is all about and how things will progress throughout the week. After that we will go ahead and introduce the rest of the team, and then get things started." I'm not looking forward to doing all of the talking today, but if I let Hudson do it the day might take an entire year with all of his sidetracking. I take a second to crack each knuckle on my fingers before continuing on.

"Let me start by welcoming you all here on behalf of our team. We are all very excited to have you here and look forward to choosing which of you will make the best fit for our team." I let out some air before continuing on. I hate that I'll have to crush some people's hopes and dreams today. "As for those that we don't invite to join the Alpha team, you will still be an important member of our military either on another team or in some other form. Our military is extremely important, especially now. The East is making headway, but all of the divisions are feeling more pushback from The South than ever before. It is our duty as members of The East to continue to push forward and reunite the divisions." Even though these people only showed up in the hopes of making it onto our team, they fake any excitement when it comes to the possibility of being assigned any role in the military, that isn't as a soldier. I hate telling people that they didn't make it on our team, because no one takes it well. We've experienced reactions from sobbing to throwing things across the room, it's never a fun time.

"My name is Major General Margot Briar. I am our team's lead strategist in addition to working to ensure that the team is fitting together like a beautifully complex puzzle. If you ever have any questions or concerns, please feel free to come to me with any of them." I don't love introducing myself because there aren't really words to describe what I do here, I mean honestly I do everything in my power to keep things moving, but it sounds full of myself to say that. My specialty very quickly became leading our team. I was able to bring people together and find where they best fit within our team. It was Theo's grandfather that noticed this and suggested that I become a leader of the team, along with my brother due to his work with weapons. Hudson took on the physical side of combat, while I took on the mental side of it, drawing up battle plans and coming up with strategies. We'd both found our niche.

"Now, I would like to introduce everyone to the rest of the team. First, we have Colonel Lee Braxton. Lee is our head medic and in charge of the health of everyone here. He will now go over what his role entails and the training that goes into becoming one of our medics."

In typical Lee fashion he takes a step forward and gives a grand bow, pretending to remove a top hat while bowing. Lee, like Hudson, is quite tall. Hudson is the tallest on our team, followed by Bentley, then Lee; all of them over six feet and towering over me. Lee's hair always has a bit of frizz to it, with so many tight curls on top of his head. Indoors it looks black, like Hudson's, but when the sun hits it, it looks like the most beautiful caramel color. "Good to meet y'all. Being a medic isn't just blood and guts; your mental health is part of your health too. I will not only be a part of your physical training, but the mental as well. During your time here your physical and mental health will be monitored." A couple of the recruits snicker at this, not taking it seriously. "It is important for us to monitor everyone's health during training and while we're out there in the thick of it. History has taught us that the mental health of our soldiers has often been overlooked; if they weren't dying on the battlefield they were dying when they got home." At this everyone's gaze drops. When The Great Divide first began the war took a toll on everyone, people were forced to fight people that they had once thought to be friends, even their own families, simply because their opinions differed. When they got back from battle no one took into account what having to fight or kill someone could do to a person. Even though they'd dealt with war and soldiers before, the suicide rates rose and caused additional deaths as a direct result of the war.

"Next, we have Colonel Bentley Adler. Bentley oversees all things transportation. Now, this is more than a job for him, it's a lifestyle. Just, don't get in the car with him unless you're looking to get where you're going in record and barrier breaking time." Everyone releases a nervous chuckle. I'm not sure if they think I'm trying to be funny, or if they're now truly worried about riding with Bentley, which they should be.

Bentley steps forward with an awkward wave. Bentley looks intimidating, in part due to his stature. Not only is he one of the tallest people in the room, but he's also one of the strongest. His tattoos peek out from under his sleeves, depicting different parts of cars. His hair is long enough to run through his fingers, which he frequently does especially when he's stressed or talking. He begins to open his mouth, *well there's no stopping him now, I might as well let him go.* "Afternoon ladies and germs! Name's Bentley, like the antique car, my dad's a car guy too, so what more can you expect? With the name of a car, it only seems fitting that I love cars and anything you can drive. Good luck, 'cause this next week is going to be brutal." He shoots me a smile and backs off. He knows I can't stand it when any of them try to intimidate the newbies. "My department is in charge of making sure we have the abilities to get where we're going. If something breaks down, it's our job to fix it, even if it's in the middle of the battlefield. We're also responsible for coordinating how we get from place to place in the most efficient, and if needed stealthy, manner."

"Thanks, Bentley. Next up we have Lieutenant Colonel Emma Leigh Maddox. Emma Leigh is the head of our technology department. Emma Leigh, do you mind giving a quick introduction?" Emma Leigh hates public speaking; she'd much rather stick to her computer and inventions. She gives me a small nod and steps forward, but barely. Her hair barely reaches the sweater that she often keeps wrapped around herself. Emma Leigh is small, reminding me of my sister, small yet mighty. Though quiet, she speaks loud and proudly whenever she is telling us about her inventions and findings. Her sound level reaches new heights when someone she loves is in question, she goes from a tiny church mouse to a mighty mouse in the blink of an eye. But now, in this moment, her words are barely making it to us-she talks so low and toward her own chest.

She mumbles, her words mashing together, "Hullo, my name is Emma Leigh, and I take care of all of our technology, which helps all of the other departments as well." Emma Leigh quickly steps back and looks away from me so that I don't try and make her talk anymore. Her lack of an introduction, compared to the guys, brings about confused looks from those that are here and don't know her. I take this as my cue to add a little more.

I clear my throat to cut the tension and take a step forward; Emma Leigh gives me a look of thanks for saving her from further public speaking. "Thank you, Emma Leigh. I'd like to go into a little more detail about our technology department. Obviously, Emma Leigh is our department head; our technology department handles everything from the simple side of things including our personal technology, like phones, to larger scaled things like weapons and breaking into enemy systems." At this, everyone's ears perk up, new recruits always enjoy hearing about how they can be involved in the war. Most graduates don't want to be recruited by the military because they think it might be fun, no it's because they're passionate about what The East stands for in the war, and they want to join us in that fight in the most direct way possible. You don't put your life at risk for a cause you don't believe in.

"Last but not least-" I can't even finish my sentence without Hudson butting in.

"Definitely not least, and I appreciate you for recognizing that." *Here we go*...typical Hudson acting like my big brother even in our professional environment, this will forever irritate me. I didn't get to where I am without a lot of hard work, I earned it. Him treating me like his little sister in front of other military members, especially men, that are supposed to respect me doesn't help anything. I make a mental note to discuss this with him the next time he comes over for dinner. I know he can see the irritation in my face, but he continues on as though he's done nothing wrong. He struggles to admit he's wrong.

"Good morning, recruits! As you should already know my name is Major General Hudson Briar. I came here straight out of Graduation where I was recruited for my impressive physical scores. I oversee weaponry, which includes working together with Lee to make your body a weapon as well. Thanks to the two of us you are about to get into the best shape of your life in a very short amount of time, that is *if* you are selected to join our ranks." The recruits shudder and look around nervously at this, Hudson's smile grows. "Your physical fitness goes hand in hand with our weapons department. You must be able to handle the power of your weapon, especially if that weapon is your own body." The tension in the room could be cut with a knife. I had already mentioned to them that they may not stay with the Alpha team, but of course Hudson has to bring it up again. He enjoys watching people squirm ever since the betrayal. This is the damage that it has done to him, I suffered in my own way and also changed as a result.

Hudson begins again, taking advantage of their discomfort, "Now, you may or may not know that we are only looking to fill a few spots on our team this year. Of course, I wish we weren't having to fill any spots, but thanks to traitorous scum we are left in this position." No one has shifted since Hudson began speaking, all looking too afraid to draw any attention to themselves. I take this time to look around at the new faces, to see if they are showing any kind of reaction to this, if they've heard the rumors and what they think about it. Studying those around me is a key part of my role. I am one to talk for hours on end, but I also understand when it's time to be quiet and listen to what's going on around you. You learn a lot when people don't think you're paying them any piece of mind. I've only been fooled once, and that was because I allowed them to get too close. I had trusted the traitors and couldn't fathom them ever having done what they did, especially to those I was supposed to care about.

"Last year our team lost not one, but three people. Ryan, along with his two lackeys, thought that they were better than the lot of us, better than our division. That The South has the right idea when it comes to how this country should be, once reunited. I will tell you now, that if another member of our team falls to their ways that their fate will be worse off than living in The District. You will wish that you were six feet under." I shuffle forward while clearing my throat. I know that my brother still holds a lot of guilt and resentment for what happened and that if unchecked he can end up in the deep dark really fast, and he seems like he's about to make that plunge.

"Major General Briar makes some excellent points. Treason is not something that is tolerated here, and if you have any doubts about our cause, it would be best for all involved that you leave now." Everyone remains still, I silently hope that's a good sign.

"Now, we are replacing three members with three placements in mind, but we may consider a reorganization or cross training if we spot someone that we really want on our team in some shape or form. Ideally, we'd like one person to end up in our tactics department. We're looking for someone that is going to help with devising plans and helping to build this team up, bridging the divide between the existing members and our new ones." I already know that I want Theo for this role, but I promised Hudson that I would go into today with an open mind in case there was someone else here that might make a better fit on our team.

"The other positions are not as defined, these people will need to be adaptable, but still need some specific skills. The two people that were in these positions before were able to assist not only in our technology department, but also in transportation. Sometimes these two departments work hand in hand, so it's important that we find two people that can float between the two departments when needed. Of course, additional skills are a plus. We wish you all good luck and look forward to, hopefully, all of you joining the military of The East." I take a moment to crack my knuckles once more. "With that, unless there are any questions we will begin some basic trials to determine where everyone's skills lie and whether or not you will make a good fit on our team or if we think you will be better suited elsewhere."

I had felt the need to repeat myself about potentially not making the team, hoping it will soften the blow for those who don't make it. We have eight recruits here today and will only be taking three of them on the Alpha team, it is important they don't get their hopes up too high or have false expectations. Everyone is still standing around, Theo beaming at me, the rest standing there with expressions of nothingness, lost deep in thought about their futures. Clearly Theo already knows where his future is headed, and it is with me. Me and my team.

"Alright, since there are no questions, we'll go ahead and get this day started."

"Finally…" I turn towards the recruits to determine who had made the remark, I can't tell right off since I haven't spoken with anyone but Theo during the interview, but I have a sneaking suspicion that it was the stocky man standing next to the shifty looking girl; it was clear from the moment that they walked in that they knew each other, just from how close they were standing.

"If you have better places to be, feel free to leave, the door is open, don't let it hit you on the way out." I cannot stand a rude person and definitely not one among us after all we've been through recently. We've had enough drama to last us a lifetime. Everyone looks around, no one pointing out who the perpetrator was. That's fine, I'll know soon enough. Today is going to be jam packed with skills trials and observations, so that by the end of the day everyone will have a placement and know where they stand.

Everyone quickly breaks off from the large group, each of our existing teammates going to their respective offices, well not real offices, rather their workspaces. Bentley has his garage, Emma Leigh her computer lab, Lee his laboratory and gym that he and Hudson share, Hudson and I share a room that most resembles an actual office. Our sides of the office are separated by a couch. My side of the office is full of prints and plans and its very own virtual reality headset setup, similar to the one that is used at Graduation. We often use this to test any plans that we create to see how they will fare in action.

Since my position is one that requires someone to be able to lead in all roles, I spend my time wandering and listening to those around me. I need to figure out who is not only skilled enough but has the personality type to be among us. The first recruit I notice is at Hudson's firing range, the tall stocky guy I had suspected of the back sass and being friends with the other recruit. He's making a scene and doesn't seem to think that it will have any effect on his results today.

He's yelling at another recruit, "You're doing it wrong, you're supposed to hold it like this!" He snatches a gun right out of one of the other recruit's hands, Hudson's face is one of complete shock and I step in before he has the chance to. The second I step forward the snatched gun is fired into the air, accidentally by this arrogant recruit. *Thank God it wasn't aimed in anyone's direction, and the ceiling is padded to absorb stray bullets.*

"You! What exactly do you think you're doing!? Stand front, what's your name?" The grin across his face is one that I would love the chance to wipe off. He is handsome enough with perfectly quaffed hair and teeth that look so perfect they almost look fake, I'm sure he is used to flashing a grin and getting his way, not here, not in my house.

He has the audacity to extend his hand out to shake mine in introduction. "My name is Wesley Fowler. Pleased to meet you." *Seriously?!* The audacity.

"I find it telling that you think that me asking for your name in this instance is a good thing. What makes you think that you have any right to tell anyone else here what to do?" I'm almost talking faster than I can think, "Furthermore, why would you ever think that it was appropriate to snatch a *loaded weapon* out of someone's hands?! Especially from a potential teammate during tryouts!"

Nothing is getting through to him; he is looking straight through me with a look of someone who thinks they are untouchable. I notice Bentley stepping forward, he has just seen the entire interaction and is boiling just like Hudson.

"Recruit Fowler has been causing issues since the moment he got here, thinking that he's in charge and attempting to tell the other recruits what they can and can't do and how to do it." Bentley is confirming what I already knew. I knew he was bad news from the very start of today. My father, who loves his garden, has always said to me 'One rotting fruit can encourage unwanted creatures to come and taint the rest of the harvest.' We heard this a lot growing up as a caution about who we surround ourselves with. Fowler is a rotting fruit, and it is time to get rid of him.

I step within inches of Wesley's face, "Mr. Fowler I'm going to go ahead and save us all some time and place you now. You clearly will not make a good fit on the Alpha team, for now I'm going to go ahead and send you down to our laundry department and see if you can learn how to follow directions. There are always opportunities to move from department to department, but if you want to be a part of this military that is where you'll be starting." I barely finish speaking before he kicks a nearby trashcan and glares at the girl that I suspect that I knew before coming in here. Another fruit poisoned by the rotting one, I'll have to get rid of her carefully. At his first act of aggression Hudson, Lee, and Bentley all moved forward in a protective manner. The three of them went to school together from the beginning and have always been around to protect me, nothing changed when we all started working together five years ago, just an even closer bond. It is Bentley who beats them all to the punch though, verging on literal.

"Fowler! Out! Now! You've been given your order, head straight to the basement for laundry duty. If you don't like it, see your way out and try explaining to the next employer why your Graduation placement didn't work out." Bentley's entire body is tense, clearly from restraining himself from getting physical with Wesley.

With one final dirty look at us and a look of longing at the girl he came in with he heads towards the stairs to the basement. Laundry calls us a few minutes later to confirm that he has arrived and to get the real story from us, since he had been placed with them midway through our placement day, mid-day placement isn't typical. The day continues on alright until the girl Fowler came in with starts to show her true colors. Everywhere I go I notice her not far behind me, seeming as though she is watching me and listening to everything I am doing. I don't trust her, and if I can't trust her that means that she can't be with us. I am doing my best to wait it out to see if my feelings change, but then I notice her whispering near the stairwell, and see that it is Fowler hiding in the stairwell, who shouldn't be anywhere near us anyways. I quickly beeline towards her.

"You! What's your name?" She quickly steps forward, letting the cracked stairwell door shut completely. Emma Leigh, of all people, is right at my side when she hears my voice, with a grin like a cat that just caught a mouse. She is up to something.

"My name is Victoria Friedman…ma'am." It's clear she's trying to get herself out of the hole that she has just dug for herself. Acting as though she respects me.

"Would you like to explain to me exactly what you were just doing?" She quickly starts running her fingers through her hair, like it might buy her enough time to come up with an answer, but nothing is going to save her from what is coming. Emma Leigh steps up and cuts me off before I can even get my first word out.

"Ms. Friedman here was just on her way out, Major General. Unbeknownst to her I've been working on my latest bugs and have overheard the toxicity that she's been spreading around since the moment she arrived with that other recruit." Emma Leigh is grinning in an almost sinister way, although I don't think it's due to catching Victoria for being sneaky, but because her newest invention was successful. "She's been going around planting seeds in other recruit's heads, trying to convince them that they don't want to be on our team. It seems like it was her plan to eliminate the competition and give herself a better chance. I think I can speak for all of us when I say we don't want a slithering snake anywhere near us." I'm always so thankful for Emma Leigh and her gadgets and now is no exception.

"Well, Friedman, I think that Maddox has brought up every point we needed to hear to make this decision. You can go ahead right out that door you've been whispering through and find yourself down in the basement with your friend, but instead of taking the right to laundry hang a left and head to our uniform department where you will help make and alter uniforms as needed." *If looks could kill.* The piercing glare that she shoots mine and Emma Leigh's direction is one that I don't think I'll ever forget. She says nothing as she gives me this look and walks, with confidence, out the door. I do not look forward to having to deal with her in the future.

The rest of the day, luckily, goes on without any more drama. We are finishing our day with six recruits left and still have to cut half of the field before allowing anyone to leave for the day. Unfortunately for us all six of the recruits that we have left are all great candidates, it's so much easier when they're awful like Friedman and Fowler. Everyone is gathering together, anxiously awaiting their fate. The entire team is a part of the decision on who will be on our team. It takes us all of ten minutes to decide who belongs where, as we have been having side conversations with each other all day. Best not to keep the recruits waiting, it is cruel. I decide to break the tension

"Thank you all for coming out today, putting your best foot forward, and dealing with the drama in a professional manner. You have all impressed us today and made this decision very difficult. While we can only take three of you onto our team, we feel that the other three of you would make great additions to our Beta team, who is working on rebuilding as well, and deserve a spot with them. There will be times when we will work together, and we all look forward to it." Everyone seems to relax when they hear this, no one wants to be sent to laundry. They came here to be soldiers, no matter what team they ended up being placed on.

"The following recruits will be joining our Beta team: Roy Smith, Kathrin Grey, and Terry Le. The remaining recruits will be joining us on our Alpha team: Theodore Flynn, Felix Perez, and Auriella Perez."

CHAPTER SIX
CONVERSATIONS

I almost can't believe that we were actually able to fill all of our spots and still have three great candidates to add to the Beta team. The Beta team recently had several people leave to pursue other positions, so they'll have a lot of chances to prove themselves there. Roy, Kathrin, and Terry all proved themselves today and I wish that we had had room for a bigger team to bring them on too. I know they're going to be great with our Beta team though, and we'll still get to work with them in some training exercises and bigger missions, which is exciting. I can't help but feel smug about my single recruit being one of the three to make it onto our Alpha team, I will never let Hudson live this down, and I have a feeling most of the senior members on the team won't either.

I'm excited to work with Theo and to mold him into the incredible leader that I know he's capable of being. As for Felix and Auriella, I've found out that not only are they siblings, but twins. I've decided they'll start with Emma Leigh and Bentley due to their extensive knowledge of all things technology. They are full of excitement to be here, and I think they might actually be the ones to pull Emma Leigh the rest of the way out of her shell. Sure, we're all close, but she still stays to herself a lot of the time-with her thoughts and her gadgets. Especially as of late, she's been even more quiet than usual.

This time last year I would have never imagined that a year later we would be in this position. Ryan, Kris, and Lena had been with us for years, we are all so close in age that we were friends in school, even before joining the military together in our respective Graduation years. Ryan graduated with Hudson, Lee, and Bentley, while Kris and Lena graduated with myself and Emma Leigh. They became family and the scar that they left on everyone's hearts when they betrayed us is one that is deep and one that I don't think will ever fully heal. They are all people that we grew up with, they have made so many memories painful for us. I often find myself filtering my thoughts, because the majority of memories that I have involve at least one of them. I can't continue living in the past though, we have a new team now, eventually they will become new members to our family. Hopefully they will be what we need to move onward, the pain will stay with us as a reminder of what we've been through, but we can't let it continue to control us. If they aren't already, one day the traitor trio will be sorry that they chose to cross us, to cross The East.

No time will be wasted on moving onward either, training will start tomorrow and that's when the real fun is going to begin.

Tonight, though we get to let our hair down just a little bit, before everything takes off and we have no time for ourselves. Unfortunately, this includes my new book I've recently started. It's a real pity because I've just gotten to the good part in the romantic adventure that I need to escape this hectic world I call home. At least I'll have time during my lunch breaks to read, that's if people actually leave me alone.

Tonight, we will be meeting at Bentley's parent's house for our annual pre-training dinner. The past few years it's just been a couple of friends getting together, like we had during our childhood. This year we will be using tonight as a chance to get to know Felix, Auriella, and Theo. Bentley's mom is one of the best cooks I've ever met, her food is sure to put everyone in a good mood. Dad even tried recruiting her as a chef for several years, but teaching is her first passion.

Of course I'm the first person to arrive at Bentley's house, not even Bentley is here. His family lives in one of the large cookie cutter designer homes that became popular a little over two hundred years ago. It's gorgeous but most people can't afford them. A lot of these styles have become abandoned. Fortunately, I noticed that there were no other cars here before walking to the door. Maybe I can take advantage of these few minutes for myself to catch up on my book. I barely make it five pages before I see headlights turning into the Adler's driveway, at least I got a little reading in I guess. I luck out because it's Lee, and I know he'll avoid going in and having to talk to Bentley's parents alone. *But of course, he's getting out to bother me. Why, just why?*

Before I get the chance to finish the page I'm reading, Lee is opening my passenger door and getting in, uninvited.

"Hellllooooooooo Margooottttt!" *Why me?* I want to shove him out and lock the doors.

"Hi, Lee. Can I help you?" I look over at him to find him adjusting his curls in the mirror.

"You looked bored, so I thought I'd join you while we wait." *He could not be more wrong.*

"Lee, how many times do I have to tell you that reading isn't boring and that it makes me happy?"

"You say this, but the face you get when reading just looks like you're totally out of it and not on the same planet." He mocks my zoned-out face, but for extra effect he allows his tongue to hang out of his mouth.

"Well, that's the point of reading, isn't it? To go on an adventure that you'd never be able to go on in your normal life? To be transported to another place, another life, to escape this one."

The blank stare on his face confirms my suspicion that he's never truly *read* a book, he may have read the words on the pages but never allowed himself to fall into them and swim in a sea of words.

"Um, I guess, if you say so?"

Before I can reply I jump, accidentally beeping the horn, at my dumb brother banging on the window, which sends Lee into a fit of laughter that would have been contagious had he not been laughing at me. I shoot Lee a look that prompts him to get out of the car immediately before I unleash my irritation on him. I don't like being scared, I'm a jumpy person. Always have been and now even more so with the tension rising between The South and everyone else. As I get out of the car I notice that everyone else arrived as I was lost in book world with Lee, everyone is standing back and have just seen Lee getting out of my car with me *and* Hudson scaring me. Bentley looks like he's lost on how he's to feel, whether he should be laughing with Hudson or being empathetic towards me. Then he gives a dirty look in Lee's direction as he gets out of my car, looking away quickly, probably thinking no one noticed. *How strange.* I don't have time to think of it right now though, right now I need to deliver payback; I snap the door open as hard as I can smacking Hudson in the leg causing him to hop around yelling obscenities at me. I am not to be scared, he knows this.

"Seriously? Why would you hit me with your door? We have training starting tomorrow, I need to be ready!"

"You deserve it, don't mess with me. That goes for everyone here!" I point around at them all, hoping the new recruits don't think Hudson's behavior is acceptable.

Bentley is the only one who moves, draping his arm over my shoulders and leading me forward. This is normal for Bentley;

he is always clapping someone on the shoulder and walking with them to avoid team conflict. Although it is usually Hudson or I being walked away by him. I can hear footsteps moving behind us after we've gotten a car length away.

"You can't let him get to you and make you react like that, especially in front of the new recruits."

"Whose side are you on, Bentley?" My tone is harsh as I shrug myself out from under his arm, I just want a moment alone to not be bothered by anyone. He tries to grab my hand, but I pull away and head back to my car as though I've forgotten something, I realize during my walk that I've actually forgotten my purse in the car. That'll make me look less dramatic when I come back inside at least. As I make my way back up I figure I'll find Bentley waiting for me, but it's Hudson. Bentley and Lee probably sent him.

"I'm sorry." He says, staring down at his shoes with his hands in his pockets.

"For?"

"Seriously? We're doing this? Why can't you just accept?"

"If you really mean it, you'll know what it is you're apologizing for." He stares at me, with the same look that he's given me since childhood, the look that because he's older I should just listen to him and agree with whatever he says. Even his pathetic attempt at an apology.

With a final roll of his eyes, he finally looks up at me from his shoes, "Fine, I'm sorry for scaring you and doing it in front of everyone."

"Thank you." I learned a few years ago not to say *it's alright* to people when they apologize to you, because what they did isn't alright and them apologizing doesn't make it so. However, you can thank the person for apologizing and recognizing how they made you feel.

We head inside acting as though nothing had happened. We quickly take our seats, Mrs. Adler already set the table with seats for each of us and put a whole buffet on the table for us to serve ourselves, family style. We are a family after all. Just as quickly as she sat the food on the table it's gone. Mrs. Adler always cooks the most mouth-watering meals, so good that you don't have time to talk to one another because you are too busy stuffing your face. Tonight is no different, between the gooey mac n' cheese and fall off the bone ribs we're all happily getting our fill. That's okay, the talking and getting to know each other will come afterwards, for now it could wait. As we finish our meals Theo is quick to get up and begin helping with dishes, I offer to start packing up the food. Mrs. Adler made extra food and laid out containers with each of our names on it, so that we could take food home with us.

Once I'm finished packing everyone's doggie bags, I grab the trash to take it out as the others work on cleaning the table and the kitchen. At this moment I'm proud of the decisions we made that brought this group of people together on our new team. As I make my way to the bin at the far corner of the garage off the side of their house I can hear footsteps behind me, I drop the bag and turn around ready to fight. *Sigh. Of course, Bentley has followed me out here.* I grab the bag of trash, turn around, and continue my trip to the bin, allowing Bentley to follow me, but not giving him the satisfaction of starting a conversation.

I throw the trash in the bin and turn around just to smack into Bentley, "Can I help you?"

"I feel like you're mad at me." He refuses to make eye contact as he kicks around a rock.

"I'm not mad, but I'm not happy either. I'm the same rank as Hudson, yet everyone *always* finds time to laugh at me. It's not enjoyable and I'm over it. I don't want to be called out of my name for standing up for myself, but I feel like it might be my only option at this point. I can't continue being a bug, allowing everyone to step on me constantly. Look what happened the last time, we ended up with not only one, but three traitors, and I'm probably partially to blame." Bentley's look says it all, I can tell he truly cares for me, maybe that's why it hurts me more when I feel like he doesn't have my back. Maybe earlier wasn't him not having my back, but him trying to help me. Ryan's betrayal has really taken its toll on me, more than I realized. I can feel the tears building up, threatening to spill over, I look down to avoid Bentley seeing even one tear.

Suddenly, I'm enveloped in Bentley's embrace, his warmth instantly making it easier to breathe. He towers over me, so I can hear every beat of his heart, it steadies my breathing. But try as hard as I might, I can't resist returning the hug, I need this. I make the mistake of looking up at Bentley, he's staring down at me with a look that I can't put a finger on, and I swear I hear him whisper *"beautiful"*. As he tucks a loose strand of my hair behind my ear, I can't keep the tears back anymore, but it feels good to let them all out. Bentley allows me to cry as he stands there holding me, for a brief moment I feel him press his lips to the top of my head.

It's dark out and Bentley's family lives in a part of the division without streetlights, so I'm pretty confident we won't have prying eyes on us, since the motion activated light has long since turned off. I finish my cry and look up at Bentley who wipes the remaining solitary tear from my face with his thumb. I stand on tiptoes to place a light kiss on his cheek, "Thank you, Bentley." I quickly flush and turn to head inside, I could have sworn I saw Bentley turn slightly red himself. I can't believe I just did that. All of the emotions and my recent book must have gotten to me. My walk inside is a lot like the one to the bin, where I can hear Bentley's footsteps just a few paces behind mine.

What have I done?

"Hey! Where have you two been?" Of course, Hudson needed to make it obvious that the two of us have been missing, together. Then to top it off he has to do it in front of everyone as we enter the game room of the Adler's home. Some are sitting on the couch and others on the floor around the television, holding controllers, paying us no mind. They probably wouldn't have noticed either if Hudson hadn't opened his big mouth. Before I get a chance to respond to Hudson, Bentley is there *finally* protecting me.

"We were taking the trash out and got to talking about training. Specifically, about how out of shape you are." Bentley pokes Hudson right in his stomach, and I can't stop myself from busting out laughing, it feels good to laugh after crying my eyes out. At this point everyone is laughing along with us. This is the ice breaker I needed, and to escape the conversation about why Bentley and I had been gone all this time together. I'm not even sure at this point how long we had been out there.

I step forward towards the middle of the room, "Alright everyone, I think it's time that we all try to get to know each other, especially our newest recruits." Everyone looks around nervously, most of all Emma Leigh, I don't want to push her too far today. "Since the existing teammates already introduced themselves during placements, why don't we start out with our newest recruits. Theo, do you mind starting us off? Maybe tell us a little about your background, your strengths, what you like to do in your free time?" I didn't think this through. "Stuff like that, I don't know. Just introduce yourself." My brain is all over the place. As I look down nervously, Bentley gives me a quick wink, letting me know I'm okay, one corner of my mouth turning upwards. I take a seat on the floor close to Bentley's feet, but not too close to prompt Hudson to say anything. I don't know what's gotten into me, Bentley is just a teammate, one of my brother's best friends at that.

"Uh, alright...uh my name is Theo, Theodore, Flynn. My great grandfather, my grandfather, and my father have all been in the military, so I guess it was the natural course for me to follow.

My great great grandfather was actually in the military when the great divide began, I think it's what drove my great grandfather, grandfather, and father to join the military themselves." He looks around nervously making sure no one is upset at him for bringing up his lineage. "He fought when everything began and they found it their mission to finish it for him, unfortunately they stopped going into battles before the end. Now I'm here hoping that I can see the end of it, and that my son or daughter won't end up having to fight in this war. I care about people deeply, so you're all in for it now that you're a part of my family." He takes a few deep breaths, "Uh, I don't really do too much outside of work, or school when I was there, but I guess if I had to pick something it would be playing video games-specifically fighting style ones." *I wonder why he didn't mention cooking or baking.* Theo takes a bow and looks around for applause, Bentley and Lee are quick to the punch; cheering, clapping, and whooping for Theo. The smile on Theo's face, priceless. This is my family. Theo is going to fit in just fine.

I look to Auriella, "Thanks, Theo. Auriella, would you mind going next?" We lock eyes for a moment, and she quickly jumps to her feet.

"Sure thing! Name's Auriella, I am here because it means that I can work on inventions while trying to make a dent in this war that has consumed us all. As far as things to do for fun, I enjoy spending my free time at the pool hall shooting pool and–"

"And hustling people." *If looks could kill.* Auriella throws daggers at her brother with her eyes for calling her out in front of the team, she says so much without even opening her mouth.

"It's not my fault that idiot men, like yourself, think that I'm no good simply because I have boobs. If they want to play for money without ever seeing me play, and then they lose all their money when I wipe the floor with them, that's on them." Everyone starts laughing hysterically.

"She's got a good point you know, girl power!" Emma Leigh laughs through her words, she and Auriella are going to get along, I think, even though they're quite opposites. Everyone underestimates Emma Leigh because she is so quiet, and she really enjoys using that to her advantage, much like Auriella.

"Alright, Felix, that means you're up!" After hearing his sister's introduction, I'm excited to hear his.

"My name is Felix Perez, the hustler over there is my twin, but as you all can see I am the one who got all the looks." A pillow whizzes past me and hits Felix square in the face. At this point the entire room is laughing uncontrollably. Of course, the leader and trainer in me can't help but recognize this as a potential strength for Auriella, provided we match her with the perfect weapon to hone in on these skills she has. Felix isn't enjoying this as much as the rest of us, his face says it all. I suddenly feel bad, because it was me earlier being embarrassed by my sibling. I feel compelled to speak up for him.

"Auriella, mind saving that for training?" She looks at me and gives me the biggest grin, I know she'll take what I've said literally, training is going to be…interesting. "Felix, please continue."

Felix stands there for a moment rubbing his eye, it seems like the corner of the pillow made direct contact, poking him right in the eye. "Uh, yeah sure. Where was I? Right, I'm the better-looking twin and clearly the more levelheaded one." He flashes his sister a sinister smile. *They are going to be a handful.* "I've always had an interest in how things work and repurposing them into something more useful for me. Most recently I took apart an alarm clock and turned it into a mechanism that can jump start any vehicle without having its key."

Bentley almost can't stay in his seat, "Wait, seriously?!" Felix has Bentley's full attention now.

"Yeah, I kept losing my key, so it was out of necessity." Bentley starts laughing hysterically.

"Well then, I'm going to need you to bring it with you to training, because this is the kind of thing that will be incredibly helpful during this war." Bentley looks to me, "Imagine being able to use any vehicle when out on the battlefield, enemy included. This could be a total game changer." Felix is grinning from ear to ear, redemption after being clobbered with a pillow by his sister.

"Alright, I'll make sure I bring it with me. I'll teach you how to use it and maybe you and Emma Leigh can help me tweak the design with your knowledge of cars and hers of technology."

I stand as Felix is finishing up. "This. This is exactly why we do this. A great example of understanding each other and our strengths. I really do feel great about this team; we are going to be a force to be reckoned with." Everyone is smiling and high fiving one another; tonight, may have started out rough, but I could not be happier with where it ended. I feel conflicted about my feelings surrounding the Bentley situation, but I don't have time to worry about that at the moment.

As the night comes to an end everyone collects their to-go boxes from Mrs. Adler, she's even included a little cupcake in each bag, made from scratch of course. I notice that Bentley doesn't grab one, he must be staying the night with his parents tonight. Everyone walks outside together and to my surprise everyone is shaking hands and hugging goodbye. Bentley pulls me in for a tight hug, which isn't unusual for us. He faintly whispers in my ear so no one else around us can hear, I almost can't hear him myself. "Text me when you get home, tonight was nice."

I can hear the smile in his voice. I can see Hudson approaching and quickly whisper back, "I had a great time too, and I will." I can't stop myself from smiling, even though I know whatever it is that's going on here is wrong and a horrible idea. I say goodbye to my brother and quickly hop in the car; I can feel how flush my face is and I don't need Hudson putting two and two together that I am flush after Bentley released me from a hug. Bentley and I hugging isn't out of the ordinary, but the redness in my face definitely is. Sure, I've always found Bentley attractive, but I've never thought twice about it past a silly childhood crush. Like seeing an expensive item, you know you can't afford, knowing the closest you'll get to having it is just looking at it.

My drive home is quiet. I have the radio on, but I can't even hear what song is playing. I continue to replay the night's events involving Bentley over and over again in my head. I am so lost in thought that next thing I know I'm pulling into my parking spot. I notice Hudson pull in right around the same time, which is kind of nice; at least I'll have someone to walk up with, since it's after ten. Hudson catches up to me rather quickly, with a smirk on his face. We make it to the elevator before he starts a conversation with me.

"So, did you have a good night?"

"Yeah, I am really happy with the decisions we made for our team. I'm glad that I got Theo to join us. I think that Auriella and Felix are going to be great additions too."

"Yeah, me too." He's very quick to move on, "So, uh, you and Bentley? What's going on with you two? You were both acting super strange." He's refusing to look at me, how strange.

How to answer without being caught in a lie?

I answer quickly so as to not raise any suspicions, "We just got caught up in talking about things from the past, you know, the traitors; I kind of just dumped all of the emotions I was feeling on Bentley." I mean, we did talk about that briefly, so not a total lie. Plus, Hudson hates talking about it, so I know that he won't make me discuss the conversation any further.

We quickly make it to my apartment and Hudson uses this as his way out of the conversation. "Alright. Well guess it's time to call it a night, give Jethro a pat for me. Goodnight, Margot."

"Goodnight, Hudson."

He waits until I'm inside my apartment before he walks away, I can hear his door opening and closing a few moments later. I give Jethro some love and let him out onto the makeshift grass pad I have for him on the balcony. Once he's back in we both head to our bedroom and snuggle up in bed together. My queen-sized bed is barely enough room for the two of us. I place my book down on my nightstand with the intention of reading it tonight to unwind before bed and send a quick text off to Bentley.

Made it home…Hudson caught up to me and walked me to my door. Thanks again for being there for me tonight, means a lot :)

It's like he is holding his phone, waiting for my message. My phone almost immediately buzzes with a reply.

Bentley Adler
I'm glad that you were able to let some of what you've been holding onto out. It was nice to be able to be there for you :)

Bentley really does have a sweet side to him, one that's not often seen due to the nature of our work. Being in a field that involves working mostly with men means he's not often sensitive, typically keeping a hard exterior, not until tonight with me.

Thanks again! Dinner was great...we need to do it again sometime.

It was nice hanging out, not at work. Ever since the betrayal we've spent so much time working we haven't been able to hang out much as a team outside of work. I wish there was more time for it. Especially getting one on one time with Bentley. Just like that, like he is reading my mind another text comes through.

Bentley Adler
If you're down, we could do dinner again...but maybe just the two of us this time?

Within seconds, another message.

Bentley Adler
I'm sorry if that's weird or overstepping. You can just ignore that lol.

Is he thick? Does he not remember everything that happened tonight?

Don't be stupid, Bentley. I'd really enjoy that :)

Bentley Adler
I didn't want to assume anything!

Well, I'd love to have dinner with you. Just let me know when...we can talk more tomorrow. Jethro is snoring, I better be off to bed too...we all need our rest for training to start tomorrow. Thanks again, Bentley, goodnight :)

<u>Bentley Adler</u>
Can't wait! Goodnight Margot :)

Tonight, sleep comes easily, and I drift off thanks to Bentley Adler, of all people.

CHAPTER SEVEN
TRAINING BEGINS

As I mindlessly rub Jethro's ears I replay everything that happened last night in my mind. I'm still trying to figure out how I got from being pissed off with Hudson and then Bentley, to being held by Bentley and feeling like that was where I belonged. I can't even begin to process all of this. First, I have to get through training, after that I can start dealing with and processing the whole Bentley thing. I know that everything with Ryan has hurt the way that I process these kinds of feelings, but this feels a lot different than everything that happened with Ryan. I'm still unsure where these feelings have come from, it's like a switch has been flipped. I'm pulled quickly from my thoughts as Jethro pulls away from me and jumps off of my bed to paw at the bedroom door.

"Okay okay, I'm sorry bud. Time to get moving."

I quickly grab my sweats to pull over my shorts, grab my phone and head to grab a glass of water to drink while sitting out on the patio with Jethro. I spent too much time in bed thinking, so I don't have the time to walk Jethro this morning. This will have to do, *sorry Jethro.* As Jethro does his morning stretching and business I glance over my phone. I feel stupid that I smile when I see that there's a text from Bentley.

Bentley Adler
Good morning! Happy first day of training! Let's plan dinner- not in front of the others...you know how they can be. They'll be fools about everything. ESPECIALLY Hudson lol.

Ha! The fact that he even thinks I would say something to anyone, especially Hudson, is hilarious. I know that everyone we're friends with and work with would never let anything like this go. Best to hold off on saying anything to any of them until there's actually something to say to them. I don't even know what this is. Friends who want to date? *Date?* Wow. I need to get moving...I'm allowing my mind to wander way too much. I'm getting ahead of myself; this isn't that serious. I guess I owe Bentley a quick text since he was on it first thing this morning.

Morning :) Running late, thanks to you lol. Obviously I wouldn't dare to say anything to anyone...bunch of drama queens and gossips. See you there!

I hit send and look at the time, realizing that unless I magically poof to Headquarters that I'm not making it in time. *Thanks, Bentley.* I rush inside with Jethro in tow and quickly change, brush my teeth, put on a smidge of mascara and get going.

As I'm about to push the button to call the elevator I realize that I've forgotten my book and have to run back to grab it. Poor Jethro gets excited when I come back in, I toss him a treat and head out the door again. At this point I'm late and it is what it is, at least I'll have my book to keep me company during breaks.

<u>Bentley Adler</u>
Running late? Because of me? Interesting lol. Look forward to hearing about this later. See ya soon!

At this point I don't even bother sending a reply, chances are he's already there and he usually leaves his phone lying around. We don't need his phone lying around and someone looking at it and seeing my name popping up; especially if his messages show on the screen and not just who it's from. I guess this is probably something that I will have to mention to him the next time that we talk. This secret could be fun, but it would definitely be hard work keeping it quiet. I don't even know what secret this is yet. I keep getting ahead of myself. I might just be taking his kindness out of proportion.

Somehow I manage to make it to Headquarters in record time, so I'm not as late as I could have been. As I walk in I can see that everyone is gathered together in a morning huddle. Bentley shoots me a quick grin before Hudson decides to lay into me.

"So nice of you to join us today, Major General Briar." The grin on his face is like a child who just got away with saying something cheeky in front of the entire family on Christmas morning. If he wants to start the day out with sass I guess I'm going to have to give it right back to him, two can play this game.

"Why thank you, Major General Briar. I just thought my back could use a little break from having to carry your weight on this team all the time."

Thankfully it's not just Bentley who bursts out laughing, but Lee too. Hudson glares in their direction to make it stop, but they continue to laugh a little longer. They've known us the longest and have always found joy in the banter between Hudson and I, it's like their own personal television show. Hudson is now looking furious, but I really don't care. I'm in a great mood and no one is going to bring me down today, not even Mr. Grumpy Pants.

"If you're ready then, do you think we can start on today's agenda, Major General? Or would you prefer I call you 'Princess' since you seem to do whatever you please?" His look is pointed.

"Princess would be wonderful, Hudson. Thank you." I have to bite my tongue, to avoid laughing at myself.

Bentley and Lee both can't contain their laughter anymore, try as they might. Lee's even gone to the length of biting down on the collar of his hoodie. Hudson is clearly pissed with me, but he'll get over it. Today is going to be a great first day of training for our new recruits, I have every bit of the day planned out for us all. I already have the full agenda printed and ready to go. Without looking back for Hudson's response I quickly pop into my office to drop my things off and grab the itinerary for the day. When I come back out to the group I quickly hand out the itineraries to each person. Once everyone has one, I turn to face everyone and address them. Hudson won't make eye contact with me yet.

"Today, everyone's schedule will be the same. Going forward everyone will be responsible for their own schedule unless there's a specific team activity planned. You'll have the flexibility to make the most of your day however you see fit. This morning is all about getting through the mandatory paperwork type things, hopefully we'll have all of that finished by lunch, and then we'll move onto the actual training." I double check my notes.

"Our first order of business is getting everyone registered in our systems. If you look on the back of your schedule you will see that I have also attached a map of the facility. We will be seeing the majority of it today, but that's a good reference for you to have for the first few weeks while you're still learning your way around. There are a lot of twists and turns to this building. Obviously this is the ground level where we do the majority of our training, recruiting, and team meetings." I hold up my map so that everyone can see and start pointing, "The Beta and Omega teams also have their areas on this floor, Beta is to the right and Omega is to the left of us. Now that you're on the team you'll use our entrance, while the civilians use a separate entrance forcing them to go through security before entering. We do share the facilities on the floors above and below us, but this section we're in is specifically for our training. No one is to go into anyone else's designated area unless it's by invitation or an emergency. Now, we will head to the third floor where they handle everything that has to do with the paperwork. Everyone, follow me to the stairs, no need for the elevator today, consider this our warmup." I put my map under my arm and turn towards the stairs.

We all make our way to the stairs and walk in an oddly grouped fashion to the third floor, *Human Resources*. Before we walk through the door to their floor I turn to address my team,

"Alright, everyone, here's our first stop. New recruits will be assigned identification numbers, fill out the required paperwork, have fingerprints taken, and have their picture taken for their identification badges that will be used to access the building and other high security areas. As for returning team members, we will be updating our information in the systems, including our fingerprints, and taking new photos today." As the words come out of my mouth I realize that I forgot I had to get my picture retaken today. Maybe I can sweet talk the person working today into letting me make mine up tomorrow, since I'm feeling less than presentable.

Everyone makes their way through the door into the waiting room. Hudson is already making his way to the front desk to get us checked in. I kind of think he's only taking the initiative here as an excuse to talk to the cute girl at the front desk. There are several different teams, in addition to the other day-to-day roles in our building, so we have to make appointments to make sure that

Human Resources will be able to see us. Between laundry, janitorial, administration, and every other department in between there's easily over one hundred fifty people in this building at any given time. Our Reserves team has our largest number of employees, but the majority of them work second jobs and aren't in the building most days.

"Alright, everyone, go ahead and chill out until your name is called." Hudson is fast to get us checked in, but he has friends in every department so it's not surprising. Everyone is always willing to do favors for Hudson Briar. I roll my eyes thinking about how he even used his charm as a child to get what he wanted from everyone, including our parents. I go ahead and grab the only seat available, next to Bentley, convenient. I smile as small as possible, so no one notices it and make my way to sit beside Bentley.

"So, late? Care to explain why?" Figures he'd open with that one. I roll my eyes in an exaggerated fashion before giving him any kind of response, in a hushed tone.

"Yes, I stayed up too late texting someone and then let them invade my thoughts again this morning. On top of that I was so lost in thought that I forgot today was picture day and didn't get fixed up for it." As I say this I look around and can see that everyone else has made sure to look their best for their pictures. Even Emma Leigh, who always keeps her hair tied back to keep it out of her way while working, had made sure to leave her hair down today and style it in a fashion that will read well on her identification badge. Her beautiful ringlet curls, in shades or brown with streaks of red, styled in a way to frame her face. As I refocus and look back to Bentley he's giving me a small smile. I probably shouldn't have said what I said, but it's too late now.

"Well, I think that sounds like a good use of your time, and you should *definitely* do it more often. Although maybe not the running late part, Hudson was a grumpy old man this morning about it." He laughs at himself, "As for getting fixed up, I'm not sure why you would need to do anything different; you look nice." It's like he forgot that we are surrounded by our entire team and the moment those words left his mouth he snaps back to reality. He quickly looks around to see if anyone heard what he just said. We both sigh a small sigh of relief and smile at one another, glad that no one heard us. We spend the rest of our time waiting in silence to avoid any other mishaps. I take this as an opportunity to read my book. I am quickly engulfed in the story, finding myself jealous of the main character whose only worry is the man that she's falling in love with and finding the perfect dress for the ball they're attending. What a dream to have worries so small and trivial. What a thought; to only have to worry about whatever is going on between Bentley and I and not a war that's been going on for decades and seems to be reaching its' climax.

"Margot? Margot?" Bentley is shaking my arm trying to bring me from my thoughts.

"Hmm?" I look up and see that a Human Resources representative waiting, not so patiently in front of me, who knows how many times she said my name before Bentley had to pull me out of the rabbit hole. "Oh, I'm so sorry, I just got a little distracted with my book. Is it my turn?" I feel like her glare could turn me to stone.

"Yes, follow me please, we're running on a tight schedule today." *Yupp, definitely pissed her off.* She might be my only chance to request a makeup photo day. I guess I'll wait to be sure she's the one who'll be handling my ID update and then plead my case. I follow her down a hallway to a room where I am to update my picture, fingerprints, and the rest of my information. Every year when the new recruits come in we use it as an opportunity to update everyone's information. Recently, as we have become more involved in combat we've implemented annual fingerprint updates as well. We came to the realization that the amount of trauma some people put their hands through was changing fingerprints to a point where they were unrecognizable, which doesn't help when certain technology runs fingerprints to allow us to use it. Folks on the team like Emma Leigh and Bentley especially were having this issue due to the number of burns and deep cuts they end up with. As I sit down to fill out my paperwork the girl who led me in here doesn't leave, guess she's the one handling my new photo.

I take my chance, "Um, excuse me? Would it be possible that I schedule another day to have my picture taken, but get everything else taken care of today?" She looks up slowly from her paperwork. *Could she look any more serious?* Her hair perfectly straightened, her eyeliner whipped into the most perfect cat eye, not a wrinkle on her blouse.

"No. Your appointment is today, if you needed to reschedule you should have called in advance." There's no empathy in her response. *My my, isn't she pleasant?*

"Alright, thank you." No sense in arguing with this woman. She might have snakes for hair and actually turn me into stone. I'm hoping that at least the new recruits got someone a little more friendly. Honestly, she's the worst interaction I've ever had here, she's nothing like the girl I had last year, bubbly and wanting to gossip the whole time. I got my picture taken, I'm not happy about it, but I guess it could have been worse. When I walk back out to the lobby everyone else is standing around, waiting for me. We make our way below ground, so that we can make our way to where the laundry and alteration rooms are. Luckily this facility was built with several floors underground as well, housing many essential departments.

Everyone is issued a standard sized uniform; it is then tailored to fit perfectly for each person. We are also given an array of training gear, sweats, shirts, etcetera. We go into the alterations department where there are bags of uniforms waiting for each of us with our names on them. Even returning members get new items due to the stress we put them through throughout the year.

"Alright everyone, please come forward to claim your bag. This will have your formal uniform, field uniform, training gear, and some loungewear. Today you will try on your formal and field uniforms to have any necessary alterations made, once alterations are made, you'll also have several extra field uniforms custom made. The training and lounge attire are both standard size issued, so those will be in whatever size you told us you preferred. Your formal attire is only to be worn to official meetings or events with high level officials. Occasionally there will be a formal to celebrate our recent achievements, for those you can choose if you'd like to wear your issued formal attire or something of your choosing." It's been a while since we've had a ceremony, we're probably due for one soon. "Your field uniform is only to be worn on official missions, whereas training gear is to be worn for training, it can also be substituted for your lounge wear."

As I speak I look around and notice everyone is already going through their bags. Pulling out various t-shirts, sweatshirts, sweatpants, leggings, long sleeves, everything comfy enough to train in and maybe pass out in after. Everything is either gray, white, or purple. When The East formed their division they chose the color purple for their primary color to use, by combining the blue and red from pre Great Divide United States. They kept the white and brought in the gray to remind those from before that there is more to an argument than two sides, that we have to find the gray zone sometimes. I take my bag and make my way towards the tailor, the quicker I get this done the quicker I can have a few moments to myself. *Crap. I forgot she was here.* With everything being a bit chaotic this morning I completely forgot that we had sent Victoria down to work with the alterations team. I was hoping that they would have assigned her to work on sewing in the back, so I wouldn't have to see her today. Although my luck means that

I will have to face her today, and of course she is the one altering my outfits. I decide that I will play nice with her and get through this as quickly as possible.

This is possibly the most awkward interaction that I've ever had. The entire time she's working on my fitting she doesn't say a thing. She simply wanders around me in silence putting pins in places that need adjustments. When she's finished she takes a step back to look at her work and then looks at me and mumbles, "You're finished, leave everything in a pile on the chair. It'll be ready in about a week, and you'll get an email when it's ready to be picked up." She walks away without another look or word. The more I think about the interaction the more I think that maybe she is hiding something or being sneaky and that's why she chose not to talk or look at me, unless absolutely necessary. I'm overthinking this, I shake off the feeling and move on, I can't focus on something that is probably all in my head.

I quickly change back into my clothes from this morning, and head back up to my office. Hudson is capable of making sure that everyone makes it back upstairs to finish out our day of training. I find my book on my desk and settle onto the couch in my office and start reading, getting lost in a romance that I wish could be something for me, but no, I have a war to focus on. I hear my door creaking open and look up, expecting to see Hudson here to yell at me for wandering off, luckily it's Bentley. He makes his way across the room and plops down on the opposite end of the couch from me, moving my feet onto his lap. A smile creeps across my face, I've always been a romantic, and reading this book is definitely putting me in a chocolates and flowers kind of mood. *Stupid war*. Apparently, his lips touching my skin one time opened Pandora's box.

I look to him, I can feel the grin on my face growing, "All finished with your fittings? Where's the rest of the team?"

"I went in right after you, I thought I could get out quickly and sneak up here to hang out with you a little bit before the rest of the crew finishes. Hudson said he's going to wait for everyone else and then have them head up together."

"Good, I need a little time away from Hudson today, you can tell that he's feeling some kind of way about having a new team. Maybe you should tell him you want to take me to dinner, make him focus on something else." My whole face feels hot as I turn red and begin laughing. Hudson would lose it if he could read my thoughts about Bentley. Bentley throws a pillow at me, but he's smiling.

"Yeah, why don't I do that? Then you can watch me be torn limb from limb and then have to go eat dinner all by your–" We both sit up straight and scoot even further to opposite ends of the couch; footsteps are approaching, it sounds like enough to be the entire team. Sure enough, moments later, the rest of the team is entering our area. I place my book on my desk and exchange it for my tablet to get all of the notes and information for the rest of the day. I happen to glance at the time and realize that it's already noon, might as well break everyone for lunch.

I quickly move to greet them, "Hi everyone! I hope y'all had a good morning and learned a little more about the layout of our facility. Next stop is the cafeteria!" The team looks excited at the mention of food, "Now, you don't have to buy food from there or even eat your food there, but it's open from 7am to 7pm, so you can always stop by for a full meal or even just a little snack. Oftentimes we either eat in there together or all eat in the cafeteria together. Of course, there's no harm if you want to eat alone, that's fine too."

We all decide to eat together in the cafeteria up on floor four, even though most of us brought our lunches today. Lunch is pretty uneventful, Hudson keeps to himself for the majority of it, only chiming in to the conversations when it is absolutely necessary. Bentley and I share a couple glances out of concern for Hudson, Lee notices as well and joins in in our concerned looks to one another. I take this as an opportunity to send the both of them, and Emma Leigh, a message suggesting that we head out tonight to get Hudson out of his head. The originals only, no need to include the new recruits this time. Emma Leigh quickly responds that she already has plans, but to go ahead without her and fill her in later. Something is up with her too, but probably nothing more than normal, it isn't unusual for her to keep to herself and only interact with others on her terms. I shouldn't be surprised that she's declined the offer to hang out, but I'm still a little disappointed. We agree on dinner and a few games of pool once training is complete and we each have a chance to go home, shower and change. I'm grateful for Bentley's suggestion on this because it means that I can try to look presentable, since I didn't get the chance this morning.

We finished eating and headed back to our floor for training. It's very convenient for us, being on the main level, it means that all of our facilities can be together, including Bentley's garage with access to the street. All of the original members break off to their own departments: Hudson to the armory, Lee to our medical area which he pairs with our gym because he works on all aspects of health, Bentley to the garage, Emma Leigh to technology, and myself into my office. I notice that Theo, Auriella, and Felix are still with me. "Uh, why don't y'all go ahead and explore the different areas. Maybe go to something that interests you or on the opposite end of the spectrum, something that you know nothing about. I'm going to go ahead and stay here for a bit to make sure that all of your paperwork from this morning has been processed correctly, and then I'll make my rounds to make sure everyone's getting along okay."

Everyone quickly breaks away; Theo makes his way immediately towards Hudson, Auriella towards Lee, and Felix towards Emma Leigh. I thought Bentley had said that Auriella had shown an interest in technology, but maybe she wants to separate herself from her brother, something I can understand completely. I take the next couple of hours going through paperwork and making sure that everything is in order and that everyone's photographs and fingerprints have been uploaded to the system. I'm confident that everything looks good and give myself some time to walk around and check in on how everyone's doing. To my surprise Theo is thriving at the physical activities, Hudson is working with him on hand-to-hand combat while Bentley watches. Hudson always says that your hands are your greatest weapon, following your brain.

Hudson notices me standing at the door watching and walks over to me, having Bentley step in to continue sparring. "He didn't show it during Graduation, but the kid is strong and he knows how to use weapons. I guess it's from his family background. He's probably been shooting since he was able to hold a gun."

I give him the smuggest smile I can muster up, "Hmmm how interesting, I was right. I told you! He's going to be something great for us!" Without him missing a beat Theo knocks Bentley down and leaves him with a bloody nose. Hudson and I rush over to make sure Bentley is okay, when we get there Theo is apologizing profusely.

"I'm so sorry, Bentley! I lost my footing and didn't mean to actually catch you in the face." Theo is actually on his knees apologizing to Bentley, who is now sitting up, head tilted back, trying to stop the blood.

Lee comes rushing into the gym and takes in the scene, "Bentley, did you seriously let the new kid bloody you up on his first day?" Lee's office is next door with windows looking in. He must have seen the whole thing and is laughing hysterically with his first aid kit in hand, getting out the gauze for Bentley to put under his nose. "Well, good news it isn't broken, bad news is that laundry is going to be pissed that you brought back bloodied laundry on the first day." We all laugh as Bentley stalks off. I wait a reasonable amount of time and follow off after him. I find him in my office using my mirror to get himself cleaned up.

"Hey, are you alright? Can I help?" He turns around and mostly looks normal, a bit swollen and bruised but at least the blood is gone.

"I'm all good, thanks for checking though…even if it was after you laughed at my near-death experience." He shoots me a wink, and we both laugh.

"Well, why don't you head home now so you can finish cleaning up and I'll see you at dinner?"

"Sounds good to me. Oh, don't ride with your brother, let's go get ice cream after, just the two of us."

"Okay! Works for me." I'm smiling ear to ear, and I don't care that he can see how excited I am. I'm being a bit reckless, but it is what it is. Bentley heads out and Theo spends the rest of the day apologizing. Hudson is hesitant to agree about dinner tonight, but finally gives in. Bentley's bloody face seems to seal the deal though and guilt Hudson into going, probably wanting to talk smack about Theo and make fun of Bentley at the same time for letting the new recruit beat him up. The day quickly dies down, and everyone heads out for the evening.

CHAPTER EIGHT
CHANGING TIDES

Again, I find myself taking way too much time thinking about the events that have already occurred and have left myself with basically no time to prepare for the evening. With no one to pull me from my daydreams I easily get sucked into them. Any minute now Hudson is going to show up and ask me to ride with him to dinner. I'm going to have to come up with a reason not to ride with him, so that I can spend some time with Bentley afterwards. Everything about this is dangerous: anyone on the team finding out about us, either of us being distracted when we should be focusing on the war, or a bad ending that could possibly destroy the team or myself...again.

I shake off the feeling. I have never let myself enjoy life, always worrying about work and our division. Even when I was involved with Ryan, although brief, I kept my happiness to myself barely even letting him in and even that wasn't enough. He somehow still got in close enough to cause me lasting damage. It's a lot more difficult for someone to tear you down if they're working from the outside. Ryan somehow had, and I'm still mad at myself for it. I had learned this in other relationships, even the platonic ones can completely wreck you. You're better off not letting anyone in if you can avoid it. Even giving someone an inch they can make a mile wide hole in your heart. Something about Bentley feels different, anyways it's just ice cream though, nothing serious.

As I put on the final touches to my hair and makeup, I find myself struggling to choose what to wear tonight. I want to appear casual but also want to look nice for ice cream afterwards. I don't typically dress up for a night out with the guys, and I don't need anyone to be suspicious. I'm dancing on a dangerous line. I start haphazardly ripping things out of my closet and throwing them on my bed, poor Jethro being covered in clothing. I grab a plain top and a plain dress and hold them up to Jethro as though he might actually help in making the decision.

"Alright Jethro, we have an important decision to make here. Which should I go with tonight?" Jethro looks from me to the clothes and back to me before putting his head down and attempting to ignore me so that he can go back to sleep.

"Thanks for the help, bud, I really appreciate it." I end up throwing on the shirt with a sweater overtop, jeans, and a pair of fuzzy slip ons. October means that it is warm enough to go out without a coat, but you need layers for when it gets chilly in the evenings. I should probably bring a sweatshirt along too, just in case Bentley and I end up being out a little later. It's a weird sensation the thought of being out with a guy on my team, not worrying about the war. Not to mention a guy I've known for most of my life and never had more than a schoolgirl crush feeling towards until now. I know this opportunity of having free time won't last long though.

Everyday we're hearing more and more reports about what is happening in The South. The fire in their belly is growing and soon enough they're going to be ready to burst, and on the other side of that hell fire will be The East and my team leading the cause here prepared to take them down. I used to be terrified as a child about what was going to happen to me when The South finally attempted something and then as I grew I became angry. Angry, mostly that I'd allowed the thought of them to consume so much of my time. Once I completed Graduation and started in the military, I developed the mindset that it's better to be proactive rather than reactive. I can't change how others act, only how I react to them. I couldn't allow myself to spend my days sitting around waiting for the inevitable. I started to force myself to spend my free time doing things that make me happy, even though that is a very small amount of time. But, I make sure that my time at work is head down, nose to the grind, trying to figure out exactly what my team and I are going to do and how we're going to finish this war.

Tonight will be a night to enjoy free time. I quickly grab my bag to empty it of the day's contents and put in anything I might need for the night. *Huh?* My book isn't in here; I must have left it on my desk. It's okay though, because hopefully tonight is a late night and I won't have free time when I get home before heading to bed. I make my way to the door and Jethro looks up at me, only so that I will feel bad for him and toss him a treat before leaving. Hudson is in the elevator, like he has been waiting for me.

"Hey sis, want to ride together tonight?" *Crap. I haven't figured out how I'm going to get out of this yet...*

"Uh, actually I'm going to drive myself, I've been having some lady issues today," I grab my stomach pretending as though I have the worst cramps of my life. This'll make him stop questioning things immediately. "I want to make sure I have a way out if I start to get really bad. Plus, I'll probably have to stop for tamp–" His face, it's almost too much for me not to start laughing out loud about, completely blowing my cover.

"Nope! No, no thank you. I don't need to hear anymore."

At this point I can't help but laugh, "Hudson, you've literally seen everything terrible that a battlefield holds and this is what bothers you?" His face is ridiculous, I mean seriously, this man has seen horrific scenes during battles, and this is what freaks him out and where he draws the line? Amazing.

"That's different Margot, this is TMI and not my business. Let's hurry up before we're late." I've been so busy laughing at my brother's reaction that I don't realize we are already at our cars, conveniently parked next to one another. We get in and Hudson takes off, trying to escape any further conversation with me, I guess. My eyes might roll into the back of my head due to his dramatics. The restaurant that we chose isn't that far from our apartment. Lee and Bentley are probably already there since Bentley was visiting his family before, he had some time to spare after leaving Headquarters early. Lee had stayed late at training discussing different technological creations with Auriella for taking care of soldiers in the field to improve their chances and allow them to keep fighting a battle even while injured. I have a feeling that that's not the only reason he stayed late with her, but that's none of my business, and it's only day one. Besides, I have my own romantic life to worry about.

When we pull up to the restaurant Bentley and Lee are already waiting outside beside Lee's car, they're both smiling, but poor Bentley is wearing a bruised face from Theo's hit. The guys dressed pretty casual for our night out. Bentley is in a hoodie that he frequently wears, and all I can think about is curling into him. It's funny, if someone had asked me a couple of weeks ago, before Graduation, if I had any feelings towards Bentley Adler I would have laughed. He's always been one of my brother's best friends that I got to hang around with too, and I'd never thought anything differently, maybe when I was younger, but any thoughts were put out of my head because he was my brother's friend and off limits. But thanks to my idiot brother being a jerk and our time out by the trash bin, of all places, it feels like everything is changing. I'm not mad about it, just cautious and hoping that nothing goes south with it. I need to stop overthinking. I wish my brain would shut up for even five seconds.

I get out and walk towards the others, Hudson is walking right behind me, so I have to play it cool. I give each of them a side arm hug, Bentley giving me an extra tight squeeze, and we all head inside. There aren't many restaurants in The East, but there are enough that people can enjoy going to them and they aren't constantly packed to the gills with people. My dad owns one of them, which is our usual go-to place, but we decide to go to another in hopes of getting Hudson to open up. We are seated towards the back which sends mixed emotions through all of us. It's nice because it's a little more private and we can speak freely; the downside though is that we're unable to see the entrance and be able to be on guard about anyone coming or going. It's sad how much being on the verge of war can change you, having to constantly be vigilant and on guard because anywhere at any time someone can attack you or those around you. We can't even fully enjoy a night out without overthinking it. We're barely seated before the chatter about the last week starts, from graduation, to interviews, to training.

Lee is the first to start in on Bentley, "I still can't believe you let the new kid bloody you up on the first day!" He's loud enough for our waiter to hear, he and Hudson can't help themselves and are already in a fit of laughter. At least Hudson isn't brooding, though I wish it wasn't at Bentley's expense. I sit quietly, eyeing Bentley. I hope he knows that I would defend him if that were an option, but right now it's just not and he's smart enough to know that. But, what I can do is change the subject.

I interrupt their laughter, "So aside from Theo, what are y'all thinking about the other two, Felix and Auriella?" I give Lee a side eye glance, "Lee, I noticed that Auriella spent a decent amount of time with you today, how'd that work out for you?" Lee makes a face at me like I'm trying to insinuate that something is going on between the two of them, I honestly meant it in a purely professional manner.

"She's doing well, I think. She seems to have a pretty thorough understanding of biology and has some impressive ideas about how we could use technology to make our healthcare here better and more efficient." He's mindlessly wrapping and unwrapping his paper straw wrapper around his finger, "She has a lot of interest on how to go about healing soldiers in the midst of battle. We have so much technology at our fingertips, there's no reason that we should be having casualties from minor injuries. It ends now with Auriella's ideas in combination with my knowledge of the human body."

Lee has seen death up close on countless occasions due to his position. I've seen people injured or even killed on the battlefield, but Lee has the task of holding people's hands as they cross over; to keep them calm and remind them that they aren't alone. He always acts like it's not something that bothers him, but how could it not? We're all human and have emotions, Lee is the one reminding us of this all the time. He's always saying that your mind can be broken like a leg, and both are important to heal.

Hopefully Auriella can bring him some kind of hope for this situation and keep an eye on his mental health at the same time.

Before I can respond, Hudson replies, "What kind of ideas does she have so far? Do you think she could be useful in the weapons department too?"

"Honestly, I think she could be great in any department if she's able to use her knowledge about technology, but I've noticed that Felix has more of an understanding about weapons, so he might be your guy. Theo too, but I don't think he has much of an understanding of technology, but he could work with them to help you figure out some fresh ideas." He gives a sideways glance to Bentley, "I mean, he certainly has the understanding of using his fist as a weapon." Lee's smirking gives him up, I know where this is going to end up. At this point the guys are laughing, Bentley included, so I force myself to laugh along with them so as to not look suspicious. I'm glad Bentley seems to be handling all of this well. Our food arrives, leaving the table quiet for a bit, as we all stuff our faces from the huge bowls of pasta in front of us, trying to regain our energy, after a long first day with the newbies. Unfortunately, dinner takes longer than expected, so pool is now out of the question. Once our food is cleared we have a few minutes to chat with one another before calling it a night.

Lee has a serious look on his face as he pushes his drink away from him and begins to speak. "Listen guys, I didn't want to bring this up before dinner because I didn't want to ruin the mood of the evening, but I heard some rumblings that spies are being sent into The East from The South to plan a new attack from a different angle." I begin cracking my knuckles and look at Bentley who's running his fingers through his hair. We all knew this was going to happen eventually, but actually hearing about it is stressful. "Now, I don't know how true these rumblings are, and they could just be rumors, but I swear I saw Kris roaming nearby Headquarters, this evening as we were packing up. Wesley was talking to this guy, whether or not it was Kris, I can't be one hundred percent certain." Everyone's bodies tense up at the mention of Kris' name. Kris is one of the three traitors that left us most recently, he followed Ryan, surely this would never be something he'd come up with on his own. It made the betrayal sting even more because he was one of us too, and one of our friends. We all took it personally when he left along with the other two, but we all also know how skilled he and the other traitors are, making it even more dangerous that they are no longer on our side.

Hudson straightens up, "We all know that Kris isn't stupid enough to try and enter The East after abandoning all of us. If he is here he isn't one to work alone and isn't going to make it long here without being caught or someone coming along to help him."

I chime in, "We need to make sure that we just keep our guards up, like we always do, and remain vigilant. Anything goes in war, and that includes espionage and traitorous behavior. These people are no longer our friends as they once were; they're our enemies and should be treated as such." I look at Bentley who's still running his fingers through his hair. He was close with Kris, so hearing his name understandably has him stressed.

We all agree that this should be the approach and head out for the evening. Lee was right that bringing up Kris, even though they're hopefully just rumors, would ruin the evening for all of us. At this point I'm hoping that it hasn't been ruined to the point that Bentley decides he would just rather go home than continue hanging out. But of course, I'm not that lucky, between getting punched by Theo and now hearing about Kris I can already tell by his expression as we walk to my car. Hudson and Lee didn't wait to pull away after Bentley ran back inside claiming he had forgotten his wallet. I sit in my car and wait for them to pull off before I get out of my car to stand in front of it right as Bentley is making his way out. Bentley makes his way over to me and takes my hand. *Welp, here it comes.*

"Listen, I think we should probably just call it a night. Tonight was a lot to think about and I'm still pretty sore thanks to *your* recruit. Rain check?" Of course. Of course, those traitors are continuing to ruin things even after being gone over a year. Could I just have one thing for myself?

"No, uh, yeah…that's fine. Rain check, for sure." I barely finish my sentence before the wind is being knocked out of me as Bentley pulls me in for a hug. He towers over me and nuzzles himself into my hair. I can tell that he is actually upset that we're not going to be able to hang out this evening. I'm relieved because as a damaged person, I was starting to think he was having second thoughts on being alone with me. He gently traces my spine before unfolding from me. He pulls back and gives me a look, a look of all that this evening might have been, a first kiss even. It's okay, we have time. *I hope.*

"I'm going back to the apartments tonight, so I'll make sure you get up to your room, before I head to mine. The rumors that Lee was talking about have gotten me in my head a little bit." He runs his hands through his hair once more.

"Thank you, I appreciate it. It has me feeling a bit on edge too." As teammates we have always had each other's backs, but this feels different. This felt like it was coming from a place of him wanting to protect me more than a teammate wants to protect another teammate. This doesn't feel like it's coming from a place of obligation, but desire.

We drive back to our apartment building and are able to find parking spots next to each other and head up to our floor together. Being on the same team means that we are all housed on the same floor, we have other people on our floor from other departments, but housing always does its best to make sure that teams are close to each other, even if their rooms aren't side by side. Even Felix, Auriella, and Theo already have apartments on our floor; they took over the ones that had belonged to the traitors. We make small talk the entire elevator ride, but once the doors open we both stop talking and walk towards my door in silence, because we have to walk past Lee's room. We stay apart from each other just in case anyone walks out of their room, teammates or not, someone would say something if they saw us too close. We can't allow rumors to start up because our teammates would hear them sooner than later.

We arrive at my door, I open the door and turn back, Bentley envelopes me once again. Planting a small kiss on the top of my head and quickly releasing me, "Goodnight, Margot."

I'm blushing and playing all that this night could have been in the back of my mind, "Goodnight Bentley."

I stand on my tiptoes to lightly kiss his cheek. I turn, without looking back; I go in and shut my door, listening to Bentley's feet as they slowly walk away, replaced with the sound of Jethro's big paws bounding towards me. I feel bad, but it's too late for me to be out there walking alone, so a balcony trip it is. I grab a glass of water, and we make our way to the balcony. I sit down and can't help but check my phone to see if I have anything from Bentley. Nothing. I guess I should make sure he got to his apartment alright.

Hey, I know you just left, but I wanted to make sure that you'd gotten back to your apartment alright. Had fun tonight, looking forward to that rain check :)

Again, it's like he was waiting to receive my message, or he was thinking about messaging me himself. Just as quickly as I sent the message I got a response.

Bentley Adler
Lol. I made it back alright, just settling in and heading to bed with an ice pack. Rain check will take place sooner than

later. I promise. Something better than ice cream too for making you wait. Goodnight Margot see you bright and early.

Sounds like a plan to me! Goodnight, Bentley.

Morning comes much too quickly, my alarm is blaring, and I refuse to hit my snooze button. Jethro deserves a walk this morning, since I let him down yesterday. I head to the front door, leaving Jethro in bed, and grab his leash. The moment my hand is on it, he's running out of our room to me, so that he can get out to some real grass. Our walk is like any other, but I keep getting the feeling that I'm being watched. I'm constantly whipping my head around to make sure that someone isn't following behind me. Jethro being with me puts me at ease at least, no one is going to mess with me when he is walking beside me. Jethro doesn't really care for strangers approaching us on walks, so if someone was to come near me I'm sure he would defend me.

We head back to our apartment, without incident, where I get ready and head out the door, choosing to leave Jethro behind today. Bentley is there waiting on the elevator, which makes my heart skip a beat. He's smiling too as he holds the door for me to catch it before it starts heading down.

"Good morning, Margot, glad to see you're running on time this morning." He's smiling, as I nudge him, but he's right and I know everyone is going to call me out once I get to Headquarters anyways.

When we arrive at Headquarters everyone is already there for the day, but something seems off. I'm still getting a feeling like I'm being watched, and Emma Leigh seems especially flustered. In fact, everyone seems like they're chaotically running around. I look at Bentley and we both head for Emma Leigh to find out what's going on with her this morning. Her face is flush and she's typing faster than I've ever seen her type before, she's shaking too; I notice this now that I'm standing over her desk.

I place my hand on her shoulder to pull her from her work, "Em, what's going on? You seem upset, is everything okay?" She looks up at me slowly, allowing herself to finish whatever she had been typing while giving herself a moment to collect herself. It is unlike Emma Leigh to show any emotion other than nervousness with public speaking. Otherwise, she is a pretty reserved person, putting on a mask, never allowing people to see how she's feeling. I can see that she's still shaking even though she's taking several deep breaths trying to calm herself.

"Something is going on with all of our tech. this morning, especially our surveillance equipment. The cameras keep going in and out. It seems like they're being tampered with; every time that I get into the system to try and reboot it or diagnose it, I'm kicked out.

Auriella walks over, at least bringing some brightness with her. She must have spent the majority of her night customizing her training uniform, her standard issue shoelaces have already been swapped out for some bright yellow ones, and she has some cutesy bows pinned onto her uniform to match. Unfortunately, her face doesn't match the warm sunshiny feel that her outfit gives me.

I go to address her, but Emma Leigh beats me to the punch, "Any luck, Auriella?"

Auriella looks down with a look of defeat, "Nope, can't get through whatever blocker was put up. Doesn't seem like any technology that we use here. It's similar to ours but definitely has tweaks that are like knockoffs of our system." Emma Leigh's face drops, and she looks from Auriella to me.

"Margot, I think we may have had some kind of hack, but I can't be certain until I do some additional research."

I begin to feel anxious and hope that cracking my knuckles will ease some of it, "Alright, Emma Leigh, just take a second to breathe, and let me know the second you have something. I'm going to head to my office and see if any other departments or teams are having any kind of issues with their technology. Could just be a system wide issue." I say this as though I have any knowledge of our systems, I'm really just hoping that it's nothing serious.

She gives me a look as though she knows that it's something a lot more serious than what I'm alluding to but goes along with it as to not freak herself out anymore, or anyone else. I head to my office, with Bentley behind me, but he gets hung up checking in with Hudson and Lee who happen to be standing outside of mine and Hudson's office leaving me to enter my office alone.

I instantly head straight to my desk and start looking around to make sure that everything's in order. I immediately realize that my book is not on my desk where it should be, since I forgot it here last night. I head over to the couch and check there to see if maybe I had left it there, even though I vividly remember leaving it on my desk yesterday after talking with Bentley. As I walk towards the couch I notice that my book is on Hudson's desk. *Maybe the cleaning crew moved it last night?* Although, that seems like an odd thing for them to have done. I pick up my book and as I do, a note falls out onto the floor. I audibly gasp, but not quite loud enough for the guys to hear me, even though they're standing right outside my door. I slowly bend to pick up the note unsure of who it's from, hoping it's a romantic gesture from Bentley. As I begin to read I realize very quickly that I'm wrong. So very wrong.

Surprise, Margot. Guess who? Did you miss me? You messed up by not coming with us. Now it's time to pay. You and your meathead of a brother made it worse for yourselves pissing off a recruit and sending him to laundry, giving us the in we needed. You've dug your own grave, now it's time to lie in it.

See you soon, bird.

My hand begins shaking so violently that I drop the note to the ground as a scream out of pure fear and frustration escapes my body. My breathing becomes heavy as my legs carry me out of the room without me registering it until I get right outside of my office door and slam into Bentley who's running towards my scream along with Hudson and Lee directly behind him, and the rest of the team not far behind them. I let Bentley hold me close, not caring who is near us, everything is racing through my mind so quickly that it takes me quite some time to realize that Bentley is trying to talk to me to figure out what has just happened. I can barely hear him over my thoughts and rugged breath.

CHAPTER NINE
BREATHLESS

I hear a faint voice. "Margot, say something, please." I hear Bentley's voice, and I feel like I'm coming out of a fog. I am unsure how long he's been trying to pull me out of my own head. My mind is racing. I know exactly who this note is from. It's unsettling that he touched my book, that he was in my office, that he is somehow in The East…that he left a note for me and me alone. Far less important, this note means that everything will likely come out about Ryan and me. I need to find a way to discuss this with Bentley alone, before mentioning it to the entire team. I finally feel like I have enough composure to talk.

"There was a note. In my book. From Ryan…" My words are breathy. I peek around Bentley, still clutching to him. The looks on everyone's faces are those of horror, but Hudson's face is one that sends shivers down my spine. The amount of rage I can see flowing through him is more than I have ever seen in my life, and I have been on the battlefield with him. At this instant he pushes me and Bentley aside, almost running to get to the note on the floor. I turn my body, remaining in Bentley's arms feeling I might collapse on my own, to watch my brother. Bentley doesn't seem to mind; he tightens his grip on me. I can see him reading the note to himself over and over again becoming more enraged. He slams the note down on his desk and looks over at me, at this Bentley relaxes his grip on me, though still holding on.

"How do you know this is from Ryan? Couldn't this be from any of the traitors?" I can feel everyone's eyes watching me, waiting for a response, especially Bentley's burning a hole through the back of my skull.

"No, Ryan used to call me bird because I was so small, this note is from him."

I can tell that Hudson is mustering up every ounce of strength he has to stop himself from shredding the note in a blind rage. He knows that we're going to need it as evidence and destroying it won't help us in the long run. I finally feel strong enough to leave Bentley's arms, squeezing his hands as I walk away and make my way over to my brother. I cautiously place my hand on his arm to bring him back to us, if any of the guys tried this they'd likely be swung at.

"Hudson, we need to figure out how he got here and that starts with finding out exactly where Wesley is. While we're at it we should probably try to locate Victoria too, since she seemed to be chummy with Wesley during placement." Emma Leigh, Bentley, and Lee had made their way into my office, leaving the new recruits outside while I am bringing Hudson back to level ground. This is personal for the five of us and the new recruits seem to understand that and are giving us space while still remaining close by. I feel a hand loop into mine…I jump a little, because my guard is already up and I think that it's Bentley risking things in front of everyone. I'm hoping everyone assumes we embraced each other so long due to circumstance and he being the first one I literally ran into. This is too bold though.

I realize this hand is too soft though to be that of a mechanic, I look down at the hand and up at the person and see that Emma Leigh is standing next to me, offering comfort. I smile at Emma Leigh, and she returns it. She has never been the type of person to want any kind of physical contact. Even a high five is asking too much of Emma Leigh, most days. I appreciate this small gesture from her; it truly means a lot to me. Although just as quickly as she grabbed my hand she lets go and is walking away.

When she gets to my door, she turns back and yells to us, "I'm going to work on figuring out how they hacked our systems, you guys work on finding the other idiots. Felix, Auriella, I could really use your help on this one." They quickly follow behind her, looking enthusiastic about being able to help her and the team.

Emma Leigh never takes charge, not in a way that's recognizable at least. She usually wanders off quietly and does things on her own. It is out of character for her to announce that she is doing something and to take charge, ordering others around. Thanks to Emma Leigh's encouragement I feel a push to start getting things done as well. Hudson is still too enraged to do anything of the sort.

"Alright everyone, we have to get moving. I know we're all upset, angry, and feeling a lot of different things right now, but none of that is going to help us find out what's going on and hopefully put a stop to it." I take a breath as I can already feel myself talking at a rapid-fire pace, "Here's the plan: Hudson, you and Bentley are going to go track down Wesley and bring him back here. Lee and Theo, you two are going to go track down Victoria and bring her back here. Emma Leigh, Felix, and Auriella are currently working on getting the security and other systems back up and running and investigating what exactly happened with them." My heart feels like it may beat out of my chest, "I'm going to work on letting other departments know that they need to remain on high alert for the rest of the day, in and out of the office. Keep all of this hushed up and only give the minimum amount of information that is necessary. Nothing about the note and nothing about specific names, just that we've heard of a potential threat. We definitely don't need word getting out and we don't need to send everyone into a panic."

Immediately everyone jumps into action, and I start making calls to each department and team, rather than sending out anything in writing to avoid any more hacks, while waiting for the others to get back. Hudson and Bentley make it back first, they went to the laundry department and were told that Wesley hadn't come in today; that he stayed late last night, after everyone else had left, based on his timecard punches. Clearly he wanted to make sure he got paid for his traitor behavior; I shake my head in disgust. Lee and Theo come back shortly after with Victoria in handcuffs, they walk her past Hudson and I as we stare her down, both wearing matching looks of disgust and anger. She's quickly whisked away to the holding cells, which are conveniently located on our floor, in the furthest corner, with completely soundproof walls. Our interrogation rooms are there as well and built with the same soundproofing. Theo and Lee make their way back to my office to find out their next assignment. Bentley and Hudson are in the office with me, none of us exactly sure what needs to be done and feeling a bit damaged from a stupid piece of paper.

"Guys!! Get over here now!!" Emma Leigh is standing at her desk shouting at us with a booming voice I've never heard her use before. Emma Leigh doesn't have a typical office; she has a huge area that is all glass walls that are covered in notes she's written in wipe off marker. She has so many computers that she often rolls around from computer to computer on her chair. It is always a good laugh to look over and see her whizzing to another station on her chair. I begin to laugh but quickly remember that now is not the time. The guys and I jog over to Emma Leigh who is flanked by Felix and Auriella. Once we make it to her she wastes no time to start debriefing us.

"Alright, we found out what the issues are with our systems." Auriella spins her chair back around to her computer, typing furiously on her computer while Emma Leigh begins to explain everything to us. "The systems were definitely hacked into. The most concerning part about the hack is that the part of the system that was broken into in order to complete the hack is only known by two people, myself and Kris. He helped me to create this system, so he would be the perfect person to break into it, knowing its innermost workings." I feel like I'm going to be sick, everything starts to spin around me, and I can feel my body shaking. If they've broken in both digitally and physically I have a guess on what they're going to do with this information.

Bentley must notice me shaking because he places his hand on my shoulder as he addresses Emma Leigh, "Alright, so we need to go back to a system that he doesn't know or create something new. Until then we should probably go off the grid and not use any of our technology for storage, planning, or communicating." Bentley removes his hand from my shoulder not wanting to leave it there too long and I instantly feel vulnerable again. "We also need to determine if they entered our systems from a remote location or if this is something that they did in house. Felix, can you pull the surveillance tapes and see if you can spot anything or anyone suspicious?" Felix nods to Bentley and starts typing quickly on his computer, almost in sync with Auriella and Emma Leigh.

I wander back to my office, numb, in a zombie fashion, followed by Bentley; Lee, Theo, and Hudson are nowhere to be seen, I can only assume that they're headed to the holding cells to talk to Victoria. Although I know not much talking will actually be happening. No, they will be interrogating her and using whatever means necessary to get her to tell the truth. The technology that Lee has modified in the last couple of years now allows us to hook up wires to a person's head and heart, externally, to be able to determine if they're lying. Lee took a basic lie detector machine and revamped it to be more accurate and allow you to ask an array of questions, rather than sticking to a singular topic.

I take a seat on the couch and Bentley shuts the door, moving swiftly and crossing the room to sit next to me on the sofa. He quickly pulls me into his arms on the couch; hearing the steady sound of his heart gives me something to focus on, it begins to calm me. I can feel myself drifting off, exhausted as my adrenaline starts to fade. I don't know how much time passes when I finally wake up on the couch. I have a pillow under my head and a blanket covering me, Bentley is gone, and the office door is still shut. I am completely alone in my office. I start to panic and throw the blanket off of me, running to the door when I happen to glance at the clock, it's lunch time. I spot everyone, which eases my panic. They are all together, sitting at a table where we would typically have meetings, eating pizza out of the box and discussing something. As I approach, Theo makes room for me on the bench by scooting closer to Bentley. Asking Theo to slide in the opposite direction would be too suspicious, so I take my seat and send a smile in Bentley's direction. I hope he knows how much I appreciate all that he's done for me today.

Hudson is currently talking and barely acknowledges the fact that I've sat down and am listening to him as well. "Here's what we know so far, the traitors have definitely returned from The South, but in what capacity is still unknown." Hudson's face is still tense with anger, I don't think it's relaxed since this morning, "We know they've hacked our system and at least had one person working on the inside, whose whereabouts are currently unknown. Based on an analysis of the note, the handwriting seems to be Ryan's, and the ink seems to be fresh, he definitely wrote this, it's not something that was scanned and printed. So either he mailed it to Wesley to leave in Margot's book, or it was hand delivered either by himself or someone else." I get chills thinking of someone touching my things.

Hudson continues, "The next few days are going to be critical. Everyone needs to be on high alert. We have known for quite some time that this war was coming, but we were never sure how soon it was going to get here. We are going to continue doing research and digging, but for now let's take a little time to regroup. Does anyone have any questions?" Everyone shakes their heads, I'm sure the questions that are going around our minds at the moment are ones that Hudson doesn't have the answers to, not now at least.

Everyone breaks away, back to whatever they had been doing before lunch started. I grab my unfinished slice of pizza and head back to my office. I put my pizza down on my desk and realize that both my book and the note are still sitting on Hudson's desk. I quickly open my supply cabinet and grab out two plastic zipper bags and a pair of rubber gloves. I place the book and note each in their own separate bags, to prevent any further contamination, I know at least myself and Hudson have already touched it. We need to preserve as much evidence as possible, especially since whoever did this will be charged with treason. If it was actually Kris, Ryan, or Lena who planted it then it only adds to their outstanding treason case from when they left us originally. I start to read the note over and over again. The things that stand out the most to me are that Ryan has a wish for both Hudson and I to be dead, that he called me out individually by his pet name for me on top of putting it in my book, and that he mentioned us not coming along with him when he left. He had never personally invited us to go with him, not me at least, but I think that Hudson would have told me had Ryan ever mentioned it to him.

There's a light tap on my door followed by it creaking open, Theo is peaking in. Innocent Theo, not yet tainted by the battlefield or by traitorous acts that will make a person question everything that happens and every person in their life.

"Is it alright if I come in? I wanted to check in on you to see how you're holding up." This is exactly why I chose him, he's brilliant, but also possesses so much empathy. The original members are too wrapped up in today, with all the work needing done along with the emotional toll it's taking on all of us. It makes it difficult for them to take a step back and check in on me, which is understandable, I haven't checked in on any of them either. Bentley had made an effort, but that's different.

"Yeah, that's fine. Thanks Theo, I'm doing alright, obviously still shaken by everything that's happened today."

Theo looks to my desk, I see him eyeballing the slice of pizza I took with me from the table, that I've barely touched.

"Margot, have you eaten anything today? Other than the bite of pizza that's missing?"

This takes me by surprise, and I really have to think about this. While it's barely after lunch time this day feels like it's taken an entire month, and I am struggling to remember any minor details from this morning. Now that I really think about it I know I didn't end up eating anything this morning, I wanted to be on time and had planned to eat a morning snack before lunch. Before everything went sideways.

"You know what Theo, I don't think I have." Suddenly I can feel how hungry I am.

"Well that settles that, we're going to head up to the cafeteria and grab something to eat, I'm still hungry anyways." I've barely spent two days with Theo so far, interview day and yesterday. One of the things I've noticed about him first is that the kid is always eating. Though he doesn't look like it he's probably one of the stronger people on the team. He could probably beat most people in an eating contest or a wrestling match. I chuckle to myself about the idea.

"Alright, we can head up, just let me lock this stuff up in my desk. I don't want it contaminated or lost." I pause thinking of someone coming into my office, "Or stolen for that matter."

Theo and I make our way up to the cafeteria. The building is full, but it feels empty due to the majority of departments keeping to themselves today thanks to the intrusion. The normally busy halls are completely empty. When we arrive at the cafeteria it's no different. The only people, other than ourselves, that are in the cafeteria are those that are working the food lines. Even the food workers are limited, many were probably sent home due to the forecasted slow afternoon. We make our way through the line where I grab a sandwich along with some freshly made french fries, Theo gets a burger and fries along with a milkshake. He might be onto something here, I order a milkshake as well, hoping it will improve my mood. We pay for our meals and make our way to the table furthest from the food lines and any prying ears. We each sit at opposite corners of the table across from each other, but facing the door just in case anyone decides they want to attack us while we're trying to eat. Fortunately, there's only one way in and out of the cafeteria, so there's only one door to monitor. Theo inhales his food, and I haven't even made it halfway through my fries by the time he finishes eating. Probably, in part, because I'm taking the time to dip each fry into my milkshake.

He uses this as his chance to control the conversation, "So, Margot. Honestly, how are you holding up? I know today has been a lot for you and with everyone being so busy working on solving this that you haven't had a moment to talk to anyone and get everything off your chest." He sneaks the next bit in, "Unless you and Bentley spoke before he snuck out of your office." *Crap. Theo had noticed that Bentley and I were alone together.* Theo smirks at me as though he can read my mind and see the slight trace of anxiety on my face that I'm trying to conceal from him.

"What are you talking about?" I'm doing my best to control my face.

"Come on, Margot, you know I'm not stupid. I'm probably the most vigilant on the team, you should have known that I would notice the relationship the two of you have." Welp. He knows something, but hopefully not everything. I don't fully trust him yet, but I guess I need to start somewhere and telling him the bare minimum that everyone else already knows won't hurt.

"It's funny, because that's exactly why I chose you for this team, so I definitely should have known better. Bentley and I are just very close with each other, we've known each other for a long time. He's a great friend of mine. We didn't get a chance to talk though because I passed out the moment I sat on that couch."

He looks like he believes me, and why shouldn't he? I told him the truth, even though I left out some of the more intimate details. Not *technically* lying.

"Told you I know these things." Theo laughs a little. "So, do you want to talk to me about this morning, since this table should be a little more difficult for you to fall asleep on." He grins so wide that I'm pretty sure I can see every tooth in his mouth. He truly has a kind face, one of someone who genuinely cares about what is going on in your life. Maybe this is why I've decided to pour out my soul to him.

"I guess the biggest thing about this morning that I'm dealing with at the moment is the flood of emotions that are coming back. I don't think I ever truly dealt with them leaving us in such a horribly abrupt way. You never expect your teammates to be traitors, and definitely not ones that you've been friends with for as long as you can remember." I try to distract myself from crying by focusing on the sound of my fingernails tapping on my milkshake glass, "Ryan and I had become especially close, but I somewhat wonder if that was just in an attempt to gain some extra intelligence to use against me and the rest of our team. Now looking at the big picture, maybe it was all a ploy to get more information to use against The East." I sigh.

"Every day I live with the constant reminders of what happened and find myself questioning whether or not I could have prevented it. Were there signs that I missed? Surely, I should have noticed that my friends were acting fishy and that they were all up to something right under our noses." Theo is listening to me intently with his chin propped up on his hands, "Hindsight is twenty-twenty of course, certain things I remember now were obvious attempts to gain power and would lead to them leaving us. After Emma Leigh mentioned the program, she created with Kris it all came flooding to me. Kris enjoyed technology but was never one to come up with new ideas. Him bringing forth a new idea was odd, but no one wanted to stop his progress. Kris was never one to take the initiative and preferred to just follow Emma Leigh's lead, helping when instructed to do so and always following someone's lead." I fake a yawn, hoping that it'll either stop or disguise the tears that I can feel surfacing.

"Kris had been having a lot of private conversations with Ryan before he brought this idea to Emma Leigh and the rest of the team. Emma Leigh has always been hungry for new ideas and was more than enthusiastic when Kris brought this new security software idea to her, they got right to work. She and Kris had always been close, they enjoyed keeping to themselves. They made good company for one another because no communication was really required."

Theo is staring at me, not in a creepy kind of way, but in a way that shows me he is hanging on to my every word. Drinking in every detail like someone who had been in a desert for months. I appreciate this, because sometimes you need someone to listen, without judgment or asking anything, just listening to let you get it all off of your heart.

I continue, "This new system was going to be one that we would be able to control remotely and access the information at Headquarters even if we were away at a battle. It would allow us to communicate with those in the office, pull battle plans, and even personnel files. These types of things are especially important when someone has been injured or killed in the line of duty. It was supposed to decrease the time that it took us to contact their emergency contact." I place my head in my hand, rubbing my temple with irritation, "Looking back I can understand why Ryan would have wanted Kris to develop this kind of technology. Once they left The East it would give them an easy way to get back into our systems. All Kris had to do was hack a system that he had helped to create. He knows all of the security features and how to go about getting around them from the outside. They made the perfect plan." Theo looks almost sad. Maybe he can tell how horrible I feel about the situation.

"I should have known that something was going on the moment Kris decided that he wanted to stop being a follower and finally decided that he was going to contribute something new to our team and how we operate. No, instead I was actually impressed that Kris had gone the extra mile and was thinking that he was almost ready for some kind of promotion. I'm an idiot." I slam my fist on the table. Mad at them for doing this to us, mad at myself for letting them get away with it and allowing them to continue to make me feel so pathetic and helpless.

"Hey, hey, don't talk about yourself like that. You're supposed to be able to trust your teammates. It's a fundamental part that makes a cohesive team. If you can't trust them then what is the point of being on a team together?" He's right, but still, so much could have been prevented if I had just opened my eyes a little wider to what's going on.

"You're right, it's just tough. Sometimes I allow my emotions to get the best of me."

"Don't apologize for having emotions, Margot, you are human after all." Theo gently pats my hand that's resting on the table.

"I know, I wish that none of this had ever happened. It was painful enough when it happened the first time, and now it feels like it's happening all over again. I can't help but reimagine these events over and over again in my head. Every memory I have that involves them has now been tainted by them betraying us. Even simple things like dinners that they were at, I think of them and immediately feel rage in me. To be clear, I never knew they were going to leave, it was never mentioned to me, and I was never asked to join them. They were members of the Alpha team, but also our friends from even before the military. None of us ever expected that they were working, for God only knows how long, on betraying The East and joining The South. None of us saw it coming and it makes us question everything and everyone." I add that last bit, so Theo doesn't think poorly of me. I can't believe I just dumped all of that on him.

"Margot, this is what they want. They want you to feel weak and let your emotions overrun you. You need to be logical here. You're allowed to feel your emotions, but at the same time you need to keep your head about you and use all of this as motivation to catch those scumbags and get them out of your present and future once and for all." He sighs, "The past is the past and you can't go back and change it, but today and everyday forward is yours to make."

The dam breaks and I burst into tears. It's been a long time since I've been able to have an outside perspective on the entire situation, one that's not biased or so filled with hatred towards the trio that they don't fully listen to what I'm saying. The only person that's come close recently is Bentley, but even he has history with them, so I know it's not his favorite subject. It's not something I would even want to burden him with. Theo gets up and gives me a hug, while I remain seated. Not a hug like the ones the Bentley has been giving me where I feel completely enveloped and at home, but a hug where you can release your emotions and the person hugging you is a sponge to absorb it all and help you move forward. The hug of a true friend, nothing more and nothing less. This hug with Theo is distinctly different than those I share with Bentley. I realize at this moment that maybe my feelings for Bentley, I've been trying to squash down, might actually be real.

Theo releases me quickly; I get up and clear our trays before we make our way back to our team's area. When we enter the room it seems as though not much has changed. Felix, Auriella, and Emma Leigh are still typing away at their computers, stopping every so often to analyze whatever is on their screens. Bentley, Lee, and Hudson are all in the weapons room looking like they are preparing everything to go into battle at any moment, Theo heads off in their direction. I'm sure that Bentley has already fueled up all of the vehicles and is prepared to leave at a moment's notice. Theo makes his way towards them. I can see Jethro in my office, meaning that Hudson went to get him and probably called my parents on the way to let them know that if we had to leave quickly that they could meet us here to take Jethro home so that they could watch him.

I watch as Jethro sniffs at Hudson's desk and around his side of the office intensely. Something is up, and Jethro's interest in that area gives me an idea.

CHAPTER TEN
CALM BEFORE THE STORM

Jethro isn't trained in searching, but that dog knows when something doesn't smell right or when someone with a scent that he doesn't fully recognize has been in his space. I know that he's been around the traitors in the past and he met all of the recruits, including Wesley and Victoria during interviews, but if he's not around the smell often enough he doesn't usually remember it and acts suspicious. Hudson, Lee, Bentley, and Emma Leigh have spent enough time around him that their scents wouldn't be foreign to him. If Jethro can sniff out their scent that they left behind, what other clues were left behind? What else have we missed? Everyone's currently in their workspaces, this is my chance to tell them about my thoughts on everything from this morning. My chat with Theo really seems to have helped things, my mind is finally clear enough to see everything with a new perspective.

I call out on the video intercom, "Hey, can everyone listen up for a few minutes? I think I have some ideas on what may have happened and how to figure out exactly who was where and maybe even when." Everyone has their attention on me; Theo has even given me a thumbs up of encouragement. I smile at my new friend.

"Jethro seems to be really interested in Hudson's desk, where the book and note were left, like he's picking up on an unfamiliar scent. I think I need to comb through the note, book, and our office again to see if there are any more clues as to what happened here." Everyone is laser focused on me, "Emma Leigh, I need you to delegate and have one person focus on pulling any viable security footage that we have since we left last night until the first person arrived this morning from our team, the other two people need to continue working on tracing the hacker and seeing if we can determine how that happened. We can regroup in an hour, if anyone finds anything before then we'll come together sooner. Theo, why don't you come with me and help me sort through things?" Bentley gives him a sideways glance as he leaves the armory to head over to me.

Everyone goes back to what they were up to as Theo quickly makes his way into my office where Jethro comes bounding at me, like this is a reward, him being here. He stops short before knocking me down, just so he can stand on his hind legs with his front paws on my chest, allowing me to mindlessly rub his ears without bending over. Poor thing, I wish that I could explain to him everything that's going on, but then again it must be bliss to be unknowing of the troubles that are going on in our world. I force myself to snap back to reality and the task at hand. I stop petting Jethro so that he'll get down and go curl up in his bed.

"Alright, Theo, first things first let's go ahead and see if there's anything we were missing from the note- a hidden message, something."

"Do you know what page it was on, could that have any significance? Also, how would whoever put it there know that that was your book and why was it left on Hudson's desk?" Theo is examining the book through the plastic bag like he's waiting for a clue to fall out.

"I was wondering the same thing. I know for a fact that I left my book on my desk last night before leaving. So, whoever placed the note either wasn't careful, or was deliberate in placing it on Hudson's desk as a message to both of us. Either way, it could tell us something about our mystery messenger." *But the note was addressed to me.*

After that our conversation abruptly stops as we begin to quietly comb through the office, carefully removing things and placing them back exactly where we found them. *Oh my gosh! How could I be so stupid?*

"Wait! Stop! Theo, put that down for just a moment." I yell so loud that not only do I startle Theo I also startle Jethro who had been snoring in his bed. "We need to be wearing gloves while doing this, in case any evidence or DNA was left behind." *How could I be so careless?* We each grab a pair of gloves and continue searching. Theo is now holding things up for me to look at to determine whether or not they're suspicious, since he hasn't had the chance to learn Headquarters yet, let alone my office. Each time he holds something up I shake my head at him, nothing else has been touched...but wait. Hudson's watch, the face has been smashed. I wonder if this was Hudson's doing or a sign from the messenger that his time's up too. It doesn't make sense that Hudson would have broken it, he barely wears it because it was a gift from our Pop Pop; it had been his when he was in the military. I know if he'd broken it he would have told me. I grab my phone and quickly dial Hudson's number, since he's likely still picking through weapons with Bentley and Lee, to confirm my suspicions. Theo is still staring at me, waiting for a head nod or shake. I ignore him because I won't know until I've spoken with Hudson.

"Hello?" He sounds apprehensive.

I'm nervous to ask, "Hey, Hudson. Pop Pop's watch, did you break the face on it?"

"Did I do *what*!? What are you talking about Margot, it's not broken!" I can tell that he's running at this point, because his words have become staccato with each of his strides. Within moments Hudson is in the room with Theo, Jethro, and I. Staggering behind him are Bentley and Lee who look completely lost and only followed Hudson because he took off running. "Let me see it!" Hudson is holding out his hand, demanding I hand him the watch.

"Alright, Hudson, it's your turn to take a breath. I can show it to you, but you can't touch it unless you put gloves on. We're treating this area now like a crime scene while we search for clues." Hudson quickly puts on gloves to examine the watch. He's in disbelief, I feel like I just crushed my brother's heart. I wasn't the one who broke his watch, but I presented it to him which feels just as bad. "Hudson, I think this is a sign from the same person that left the note. Either they know how important that watch is to you and they want to crush your spirits, or they are sending the message to the both of us that time's up."

Hudson still isn't speaking. I can see his rage levels rising. Whoever did this to him isn't going to survive once he gets to them. Theo attempts to gently take the watch back from Hudson, who then steps back and pulls the watch tight to his chest, not even allowing Theo to look at it. Our grandfather meant the world to us. He's been gone for years now, but there's not a day that goes by that I don't think of him. I like to think that he would be proud of all we've accomplished during our time in the military. I wish he'd been able to see how far we've made it. I know Hudson is hurting too.

"Theo, it's probably best if you give Hudson a minute, we can put the watch back once he's done with it. He's wearing gloves, so it's no harm." I know my brother, and even though Theo is one of us, he'll still rip him to shreds out of convenience.

"Sorry, something just came to me. We're handling everything with gloves now, but maybe the messenger wasn't. We could scan the watch, the office, your book, and the notes for fingerprints and see if we can recover any that don't belong to any of us." I can see the gears turning in his head. "Everyone who has ever worked here gets fingerprinted and those stay in the system, so if it was Wesley or one of The Trio then we'd know immediately after running the fingerprints that are all over the evidence. Shouldn't take that long to get answers either."

I can't believe that we didn't think of this sooner, especially since Theo and I agreed to start wearing gloves. This had to have been an inside job, or at least one that involved at least one insider, and this is going to be the quickest way to figure it out. We have so much technology at our hands, and we've barely used any of it! I ball my hands into fists at my sides, frustrated with myself and the amount of time that we've wasted. Checking for fingerprints would take a matter of minutes using Emma Leigh's technology. She created a device a couple years back that scans any surface and can determine if there are fingerprints there and then she can choose which databases to search and it will tell her if there are any matches; the military personnel database, criminal records, things like that. It's genius.

"Theo! That's it!" I hit the button on the intercom, "Emma Leigh, could you come here please?" Emma Leigh must notice the sense of urgency in my voice because the next thing I know she's sprinting down the hall followed closely by Felix and Auriella. "Emma Leigh, we need to scan this whole office for fingerprints, especially my book, the note, and Hudson's watch."

Emma Leigh rolls her eyes at me, I know she's irritated that I made her run all the way here and now she's going to have to go back to get her scanner and then turn back to scan the office. Emma Leigh hates running, she always gets great physical scores and participates in physical training when she has to, but she will do anything she can to get out of it.

Emma Leigh starts trudging back to her desk and stops mid stride, "Felix, be a doll and go grab the scanner off my desk please." I can't help but laugh. Just what Emma Leigh needed, someone to do all her running around for her. We're in trouble, Felix and Auriella even more so, Emma Leigh might be the one to abuse her power when it comes to these newbies. Felix makes a mad dash back to Emma Leigh's desk and comes running back with the scanner, he walks into the office and Emma Leigh immediately sticks her hand out for the scanner. The look of defeat streaks across Felix's face. The poor guy actually thought that Emma Leigh was going to allow him to do the fun part, no way. Instead, he's left standing there to watch, huffing and puffing, trying to catch his breath.

Emma Leigh begins scanning the office, starting with the door, but unfortunately we've been in and out so much today all of the prints are smeared, and she can't get any clear readings. She turns to me, "Alright, where's the note? I think that might be the first thing to give us a hit." I hold out the note and Emma Leigh begins scanning it, the scanner is pinging so quickly that it's hard to count how many hits it's getting. I don't want to get too excited, but the note may actually lead us somewhere.

Once it stops going off, she looks at me, "Alright, lucky for us we've already got several hits, which means it's working. Let's see, hits for...Hudson, Margot, Bentley, Theo, and AHA! Ryan's prints are definitely on this note! Looks like his prints are the only ones on there, aside from our team, so I'm going to say that either he was here and placed the note himself, or whoever placed the note wore gloves." Emma Leigh hands the note back over to me to place it back in the evidence bag.

"Next, the watch, Hudson, if you don't mind could you please hold it out for me to scan?" Hudson reluctantly holds out the watch and Emma Leigh begins scanning. More pinging than last time. She tries, but fails, to hide the excitement in her voice, "Alright, again several hits: Hudson, Margot, Theo, and Lena! Alright, two of the three, so they must have chosen to divide and conquer." Hudson quickly pulls his hands back, wrapping them protectively around the watch.

Emma Leigh looks to me once more, "Last, could I scan the book please?" I grab the book and unwrap it from the evidence bag. This time the scanner barely pings. "Just your prints and Ryan's on the book, Margot. This makes me think he was definitely the one who planted the note, this was personal for him." Emma Leigh's face lights up, she's had an idea. Off she goes, actually running across our building towards her station. Everyone is running after her, because Emma Leigh running means something urgent.

"I should have thought about this sooner! My computer! I wonder if whoever hacked into the system did it from inside our office, rather than remotely. We haven't started looking through the interior footage yet, just the exterior, assuming that no one would be so bold as to actually enter Headquarters. We were thinking they used Wi-Fi access from just outside. If they were already here it would make sense that they took the easy approach and actually used our gear, rather than plugging their own stuff in." Again, Emma Leigh is scanning away, this time at her keyboard, the scanner going off so rapidly that it's difficult to determine how many individual pings there are. "I knew it! Kris' prints are all over my computer! He's the only one who knows how to get through my system. He must have hacked in and made it, so everything crashed today, I'm betting he got into our camera systems too. Wesley's prints are actually here as well, so he must have helped him with this project." The scanner records all findings, down to when, where, and what was scanned. Immediately Emma Leigh goes back to typing away on her computer, she must have another idea. I can see a slight trace of sadness in her eyes.

"I'm going to try and see if I can pinpoint the keystrokes that Kris used and get to the bottom of this hacking. I also wonder if I can pull the cameras and see if anything was left or if they erased all of that evidence." As Emma Leigh starts researching, we all stand over her shoulder waiting patiently to see what she finds.

Emma Leigh is muttering to herself as she quickly clicks and types away. "Alright, I think I've figured it out. Wesley must have been the one handling the cameras, he tried to delete all of the footage from before they got to our office and disabled them until they were done. He's definitely not a tech genius like Kris or myself though, because I was able to recover all of the footage that they didn't want us to see."

Emma Leigh begins projecting the camera footage from her computer onto the big screen in the middle of our headquarters. At the beginning of the footage, you can see one figure in a black sweatsuit, hood pulled tightly around their face letting three other figures, dressed the same, into the building through the dumb waiter that goes into the laundry room. This must be Wesley who is letting The Trio in. You can see them sneaking into Headquarters, two entering my office while the other two get to work, straight away, on the computers. They start to become too comfortable though, as they're making their way out they decide to take off their hoods, one even taking his sweatshirt all the way off, overly confident in their ability to not be caught on camera.

There they are, looking just as they did the last time I saw them, yet so different. They're not the same people I would have died for a year ago. Each with their own recognizable features, that could easily be picked out in a lineup even if they weren't your friends and teammates turned traitors. Even looking at them from behind they're easily recognized. Ryan with his earrings and tattoos, each one something related to his time in the military; the most recognizable being the large realistic gun going down the back of his arm, from shoulder to elbow. Kris with his recognizable gray mini mohawk with purple tips; his hair went gray the second he turned twenty and he's been dying the tips a different color every week ever since. Odd, though, that he'd ever choose purple again after the betrayal, feels like he's rubbing it in our noses. Then there is Lena, her hair so red that if you gave her a quick glance you might think that her whole head was engulfed in flames. Wesley is pretty plain compared to the others, but his stature is stocky and towers over the rest of them, even though Kris and Ryan are both pretty tall themselves. In the frames that Emma Leigh has found them in so far we can only see the backs of them, but we're all positive that it's them.

I look over and notice that not only is Hudson fuming, but Bentley, Lee and Emma Leigh as well. Emma Leigh looks like she's holding back tears of rage. Somehow, I've managed to remain calm even seeing these people on the screen violating us yet again. Lee and Hudson are talking back and forth, sharing their anger, with insults directed towards the people on the screen. Bentley is standing next to me, I elbow him and tilt my head to the front door that leads to the street, hoping he'll catch my drift and follow me outside for a walk. We could both use the fresh air. I make my way out the door and walk away from the windows to wait in hopes that Bentley will have followed me outside. Within moments I hear Bentley's footsteps behind me, racing to catch up. He takes no time to reach me, looping his arm through mine and we begin walking towards the local park that surrounds a lake.

This morning's events have me second guessing everything that I'm doing with Bentley. Is it wise for me to allow myself to get so close to him and risk ruining our team and our friendship? Even the friendship between him and my brother? I am so in my head that I don't realize that Bentley stopped walking. I look back at him to see he's taken a seat on a bench next to the lake. He pats the spot next to him, inviting me to sit with him. I slow my pace walking back to him to steady my breathing and calm my heart. I'm overly excited to be out here, just the two of us. I distract my brain by taking in the scene of the lake. Aside from the deer I saw near my apartment, the lake is the only other place I've seen a wild animal lately outside of the occasional squirrel. I notice two ducks paddling around without a care in the world, hopefully another good sign. The rapid building of homes and other buildings from before caused so many animals to lose their homes, and a lot unfortunately died or left the area before being able to find new ones. I hope they're coming back; it would be nice to live somewhere where we share our surroundings with the other creatures. Bentley brings me back to reality, giving me a warm smile that makes me forget my worries. I take a seat next to him.

The moment I'm seated he dives into the conversation, "How are you feeling, Margot? I know it's been a rough morning for you." Theo asked me how I felt earlier, but this is different, coming from a different place, of deeper care.

"I guess I'm doing as well as expected. Today has been draining, I feel like I'm not only dealing with the emotions from today, but it's bringing everything that I felt from them leaving us originally back to the surface." I'm staring at my hands, but I can feel Bentley's eyes piercing me.

"Yeah, I understand that, I think we're all kind of feeling the same way. I think you and Hudson got it the worst though." He pauses as though considering what he's going to say next and whether or not he should, "Why do you think Ryan singled you out with the letter, and the nickname? I've never heard him, or anyone for that matter, ever call you *bird* before." Great, he noticed, even after the day I've had this ranks highest on my stress meter. Ryan not only came back and messed up my day, but this little stunt could mess up my future as well. I can't lie to Bentley like I had to Theo though, I respect him too much and care about him a great deal. Ryan calling me bird is one of the things that really drove the knife in today, like he wanted this secret to be exposed. He wants to throw doubt into the team that I've kept this secret from them. He wants them not to trust me anymore, especially my brother. Continuing the lie now after all of this won't do me any good.

Time to rip off the bandage, "I'm not really sure what to say…at one point there was something between Ryan and I." Bentley looks crushed, I quickly add, "It wasn't anything serious, so we decided to keep our dating a secret from everyone else. I thought that I might be interested at first in it being more, but he didn't treat me very nicely towards the end. I was so excited to

146

finally be noticed by someone that I missed all of the red flags. I thought that it would be better for the group if I just played along with it even when he started treating me like garbage." I sigh, "When he started calling me *bird* I got nervous because things were escalating and I didn't want to be on the ride anymore, it was getting rough. Even when he'd kiss me, it became forced, an obligation, something I didn't care for. Maybe in the beginning I did, but the further into it we got the less I wanted any of it." I shudder remembering the night he forced his body on mine. I pushed him off of me, I can vividly remember the look of disgust he gave me when I refused to give him what he wanted. The feeling of his hands wrenching my thighs apart telling me that he could take it right now if he wanted and there was nothing I could do to stop him. I feel bile rise in my throat at the thought and thank God that he walked away that night without another attempt ever after that. "I had no idea of his intentions to leave and take the others with him, nor would I have ever considered going with him. Never in a million years, this is where I'm meant to be."

I can tell that Bentley has gone down the rabbit hole and is thinking over all I've just said. He's staring down at his hands, anxiously playing a game of thumb war with himself. While I stare a hole through him, waiting for some kind of response, wishing I could read his mind, because the silence is killing me.

"I see." Another long pause of Bentley searching for what to say, "Is that what this is to you? Some kind of obligation?" His voice is angry and full of hurt, I try to reach out and touch his hand, but he recoils like someone who touched something foul at the bottom of a sink full of dishes, before I can even touch him. I can feel the emotions welling up inside me. It is now or never. I don't give up, I force him to hold my hand, he doesn't try to pull away this time, but he's not holding my hand back either. If I was to let go his hand would fall away, limp.

"Bentley, this is nothing like that. Nothing at all, and I hope you don't think that. Now that I look back on it, it almost feels like Ryan was trying to get me under his control to get more information before leaving. I was nothing but a pawn to him. A sad, trapped, pawn." Bentley still won't look at me and it's killing me. I didn't mean for this to hurt him, but I had to be honest. I turn towards Bentley, releasing his hand to hold his face in both of my hands to turn it towards me. I look him in the eyes, so that he can see my sincerity. I have to break through his hurt and anger. "Bentley, I've enjoyed this little bit of time with you so much and I hope that you'll continue wanting to be around me in a way that's more than teammates." Bentley says nothing. His hands are now over top of mine, which are still on either side of his face.

The way Bentley looks at me causes my breath to hitch, I gasp, my breath suddenly gone, is this what it means when someone says that something *took their breath away*? That's exactly how I feel at this moment. Bentley shocks me, moving his face towards mine and gently kisses me, kissing away the sadness that I've been feeling all day. I don't hide my eagerness to kiss him back, turning what started as Bentley's gentle kiss into one full of hunger. I know that this isn't supposed to be happening, it shouldn't happen. But why would something that's not supposed to happen feel like finding the last piece to a puzzle, that you thought was lost or stolen by someone trying to get at you. When Bentley pulls away I can feel how bright my face has become, the blush on my cheeks warming me on this cool autumn day. Bentley is beaming at me; I can tell he believes me. That night when Ryan kissed me, meant nothing. But this, this is something that means everything that I will remember and take with me.

Bentley stands and takes my hand so that I'm standing with him and pulls me into an embrace, we only hug this time, and that's okay with me. I'm not sure how long we've been standing like this, while it feels like forever it still doesn't feel like long enough when he releases me. We say nothing as we loop arms and walk back to Headquarters, unsure how long we've been gone.

Bentley finally breaks the silence during our walk back, "Thanks for trusting me with your story about Ryan. I know it's hard for us to talk about anything involving him or the others, but I'm glad to be on the same page with you. It's not right what he did to you, and I promise you that I will never allow something like that to happen to you ever again." When he wants to be sweet, he can really pour on the sugar. I can feel his sincerity though, even his words feel like a security blanket.

"Thanks, Bentley. I hope that this means we're still on for ice cream soon."

"I wouldn't miss it for the world." I don't think my smile can get any bigger.

As we get closer to Headquarters, we see Emma Leigh bursting out of the front door waving papers around above her head. Bentley and I keep our arms looped so as to not cause any suspicion; it's not unusual for me to link arms with whoever I'm walking with, and Em knows this. Me pulling away would only cause alarm and suspicion, two things we're trying to avoid. Emma Leigh doesn't give our looped arms a second look.

"You guys gotta see this! I found out more information on the break-in. Those little weasels." The tone in Emma Leigh's voice conveys how angry she still is, but at the same time I can tell how proud of herself she is for having found out some additional information. We follow her inside; she's almost bouncing as she walks back to her station. Emma Leigh has always been kind of shy and reserved for as long as I've known her, but occasionally she lets us have a glimpse into how she's really feeling. The second that The Trio betrayed us it was like she recoiled back into her shell and didn't want to make the same mistake again, not even showing slight emotions. Maybe she is like me and fears that allowing even a little out might result in the floodgates bursting wide open. Maybe she's choosing to block out anymore potential hurt, I don't blame her.

I can relate to Emma Leigh on this level. Ryan has made me feel the same way. I had finally opened my heart to someone and then began to realize that his motives weren't pure. It's made this last year increasingly difficult. I might have started to realize how I was feeling towards Bentley, and picking up his hints sooner, had it not been for Ryan completely breaking me. I might even have allowed myself to acknowledge the way that I'm feeling towards him by now. Kris and Lena hurt me too, but in different ways. Together they forced me to build my walls up higher.

As I watch Emma Leigh now surrounded by our teammates, old and new, I can kind of see a part of her coming back that's been missing for a long time. Everyone is surrounding the conference table as she starts laying out the papers that she had been waving around outside to get our attention. These must be her findings, and it must be something big for her to have printed them out rather than projecting them on a screen. We will have to remember to destroy these after the meeting, so that no one else has access to them.

As we approach the table I can't believe what I'm seeing on these papers that she has laid out for us. This must have taken everything she knows to find, especially if Kris was involved in trying to hide it from us. Hudson's face is contorted, and his fists are balled up at his sides, I can't say I blame him, I feel the same. As I move closer to my brother, detaching myself from Bentley, I can see the bit that's making him fill with rage.

CHAPTER ELEVEN
CAUGHT RED HANDED

I n front of us lay printouts from the camera footage, now very clearly showing the four faces that have betrayed us, some for a second time. We all already knew that it was them just from seeing the backs of them, but this confirms it. Next to those are more sheets of paper with different coding on it, but that's all I can make out. Technology has never been my strong suit, but I have watched Emma Leigh so many times that I know on a surface level that this is something to do with coding. I pick one up, pretending like I'm interested in it. Fooling myself that maybe if I stare at these mashed up characters long enough I'll be able to understand it. Emma Leigh knows I have no idea what I'm looking at, and I know it's for my benefit when she starts explaining everything that's laid out before us. She must be extremely proud of what she's found, because for someone who hates public speaking her voice sounds strong.

"Now that everyone is here, allow me to explain all of the papers on the table in front of you." Emma Leigh collects the pictures and holds them up for everyone to look at, "Obviously these are the faces of the people who have violated us and our space. They are enemy number one. Burn these images into your brain." I peek over at my brother; Hudson can't even look at their pictures; I don't blame him. Emma Leigh is quickly, yet carefully, shuffling through her papers.

She holds up another set, "This next group of papers is all of the keystrokes that they used to get into our system. It's clear that this is Kris' style of hacking, we also have the camera footage that I was able to recover to show us that he was the main hacker as well. I can tell now that he did hack in, not only with the intention of messing up our system, but also for stealing information."

I can't believe what I'm hearing. They stole our information. Who knows what they are planning on doing with it. *SLAM*! I jump, along with everyone else. I quickly realize the sound was Hudson punching the table with his full weight behind it, his hand already turning an angry purple color. Our tables are metal and in the fight between him and the table, the table won. Everyone averts Hudson's glares, not wanting to be his next target after he lost to the table. Emma Leigh continues on, pretending as though nothing happened.

"I'm still working on exactly which files they viewed, but I can tell for sure just by looking at the surface that they got into emails, browsing history, and some basic attack plans. Our highest-level security plans with actual dates and exact details are stored elsewhere with more secure levels of encryption, so they weren't able to get to them." *Thank God.* While it's not as bad as it could be, they have an idea of our strategy and they will be able to train their soldiers against it. Unfortunately for them though, they just lit an incredible fire under Hudson and I'm sure that he'll be using this anger to make new plans and run all of us through the most intense training of our lives. Plan creation is typically reserved for me, but Hudson and I work together on this quite often since he has a better understanding of our fighting techniques. I understand the human aspect of it best and apply his knowledge of combat to it. At this point everyone is frantically discussing what all of this means. I need to get this under control before everyone is too far gone.

I climb onto a chair, everyone so lost in their panic that they don't notice, "Hey! Everyone, listen up!" Everyone stops talking and quickly brings their attention to me. As their leader it's my job to be their lighthouse in the storm. "I know today has rattled us all, some of us more than others due to history. Now is the time to come together and work toward the future, as a team. We've spent the day reacting to what they've done to us. Now, it is time for us to be proactive, so that we have the upper hand." Everyone is holding on to my every word like a life raft trying to get them through the rest of this day. I begin cracking my knuckles, even my neck because I feel so overwhelmed. "We start now by setting traps in case anyone else tries to come back tonight. Em I need you, Auriella, and Felix to start going over everything with our camera systems. Why don't we lay some hidden cameras as well that aren't attached to the main system. Let's make sure that even if they mess with our system again we'll still get alerts and footage if anyone decides to break-in tonight. Everyone else, let's get to work on different weapons and traps."

The moment I finish speaking everyone quickly disburses. Emma Leigh, Felix, and Auriella head to their computers to start working on the security systems. The rest of us look like we're rigging up a crazy boobytrap system that could be used in a real-life board game...we could call it rat trap when it comes to these sneaking traitors. We lay out an assortment of traps designed to catch the spies, rather than harm them. Although if Hudson had his way they would be designed only to harm. It's hard to get a handle on him when all he wants to do is inflict pain on those who hurt him.

As he fiddles with his knives he turns to me, "I don't understand why we can't make the trap take off one of their limbs, it'll stop them. *Plus,* if Emma Leigh's security system is working we'll get the alert and we'll probably get to them in time to get them to hospital to save their lives. But, if not, well, not our problem." He shrugs his shoulders, "Play stupid games, win stupid prizes. Don't break into a military headquarters, it's that simple." Bentley and Lee are looking around at me uncomfortably because they know that Hudson is serious, hoping that I might reign him in. Theo keeps a straight face, he knows his place as a newcomer and isn't trying to ruffle any feathers, which leaves me to reign Hudson in.

"Hudson, I get that you're upset, but we can't go around hurting people unless it's truly warranted. It's better to catch them and be able to ask them questions or use them as bait." Hudson stalks off, clearly not happy with my response. Lee follows off after him and Theo busies himself by laying some additional traps that require more technological components than Hudson knows how to use. It's impressive how much he can do, that he didn't show at Graduation.

I start to wander to my office and can feel Bentley close behind me. I pass my office and head into the hall hoping that Bentley will follow me. We're nearing the end of the day, finally, but I'm not looking forward to tonight and what tomorrow may bring. I can no longer hear Bentley's footsteps. *Guess he's gone off elsewhere.*

"Hey, Margot." I jump. "What's your plan for tonight?" Bentley needs to wear a bell; I have no idea how he caught up to me so quickly and quietly.

"What do you mean?" *Is this him asking me out? Kind of poor timing.*

"You had someone threaten you today, someone who knows you personally and chose to single you out from the rest of the team. Obviously going home alone isn't going to be a good option, someone should stay with you tonight." His voice is almost demanding.

"Moving a little quick there aren't you Bentley? Already inviting yourself over for a sleepover." We both laugh. *Gosh I needed that laugh.*

"You know that's not what I meant. I do worry about you though and I don't think that you should be spending the night alone."

"I won't be alone, I have Jethro." He would take someone down for me if he had to.

"I know, but I still think someone should stay the night with you tonight. As much as I would like that person to be me, on your couch of course, I think your brother might catch on. I think he needs to stay with you tonight as an extra layer of protection."

I take a moment to consider what Bentley's said. Ideally it would be nice to have him stay over and continue our conversation from earlier. He's the only thing that has made me feel safe today, even though I've an entire team of soldiers surrounding me, including Jethro, and a gun on my hip. If Bentley can't be there for me, I guess Hudson will have to do.

"Fine, I will ask Hudson to stay with me tonight, only since you don't want to stay with me." I give him a nudge and a smile to make sure he picks up on my sarcasm.

"As long as you're safe, I'm happy. Please keep me updated as the night goes on though." Bentley places a light kiss on my forehead and heads back into our area. I wait a few moments to head back in myself, so no one thinks anything of it.

Everyone is winding down for the day. I am proud of the team that we have, going through what we've gone through today and coming out on top confirms that the team that we've put together is one that's going to prevail against the traitors, and everyone else that we're fighting in this war. The breaking point is coming. We've had minor battles at our borders before with The South, but I can feel it in my bones, the big one is coming. A war bigger than The Great Divide. Each of us are going to have to fight for our lives and our way of life, and that fight began this morning. The approaching war has been like a small flame lingering, we all knew it was there and that it could turn into something so much more, but we all decided to watch it from afar, hoping that it would eventually go out. This morning The South went and poured gasoline all over that little flame and now The East is engulfed, and we have to do everything we can to extinguish the fire and hold those responsible for turning it into a full blown inferno.

As I look around I look for the hidden cameras that Emma Leigh has placed, I can't find a single one, even though I'm actively looking for them. Hopefully this means that someone, not looking for them, won't see them either. The rest of the team laid out several decoy traps that were obvious to whoever may be creeping around to distract them and lead them into the actual traps. There are many rope traps set to grab the person by their foot and hang them upside down, nets and cages to trap people in, and even holes for them to fall into; using the removable flooring in the garage and the other floor panels that we can remove to use as storage. If they are bold enough to come back tonight we will catch them for sure.

Everyone gathers to admire the work that we've done here today, everyone looks proud of themselves. But Hudson still looks off, disturbed. Hopefully I can talk to him tonight and try to help him get out of this funk. I get that he's upset, and why it's hurting him so much, I'm right there with him. Even so, he can't spend his time moping around though and taking things out on our team, that's not what a good leader does, our team deserves and needs better. I decide that it's time to release the team for the day, since we're all standing close enough to each other.

I raise my voice, "Could I have everyone's attention, please? It's been a long day, and I think it's time we call it quits and head out a little early. I really appreciate how hard everyone worked today. It was far from easy, but we stuck it out and made sure that we got the job done. Please go home and rest tonight, but keep your phones on and near you in case something happens overnight, and we need to rush back here. We have to be prepared for anything, while also making sure that we're rested so that we can handle anything that may happen." I quickly add in, "Hudson, you'll be staying with me tonight, since I seem to have a target on my back." Hudson just looks at me, emotionless, obviously he didn't expect this to be a part of his night. *Too bad.* Bentley gives me a small wink, clearly happy that I took what he said about not staying alone tonight seriously.

Theo, Auriella, Emma Leigh, and Felix quickly grab their things to head out, anxious to put this day behind them. I can't agree with them more, what a day. I grab my book from evidence, thanks to the technology we have available to us, all of the evidence needed from it has been documented so I can have it back. I head to the front door with Jethro to wait for Hudson. He's walking slowly toward the front doors with Lee and Bentley flanking him. The others had made a mad dash for the door the moment their things were packed up. We all head out the front door together and lock up, making our way to our cars.

"Alright, Margot, I guess we'll all follow you home, just in case." Hudson sounds irritated while saying this, he must have had something planned tonight, since it seems like having to stay with me has ruined his plans. I give him a small nod and get in my car, we all make the short drive home without any event, thankfully.

Once we're home we all park near each other and walk in tight ranks inside our building, making our way to the elevator where we pile in with others that have also just gotten off work for the day. Hudson and Lee stay towards the front with Jethro while Bentley and I end up wedged in the back of the elevator. His hand finds the small of my back, accompanied by his protective stance, he's on edge, I can feel the tension through his fingers that are making small circles on my back. I smile, not making any attempt to look in his direction, because the last thing we need to do is bring attention to ourselves. I take several deep breaths, savoring Bentley's touch. Time feels frozen as we slowly make our way up to our floor, the doors opening on each floor to allow a person or two to exit. All I want to do is lean into Bentley and rest for a while.

The doors open once more, finally on our floor, and we all move to make our way out. We decided to clear all of our apartments together, to make sure that no one had done anything to tamper with them, the other half of our team was given the instructions to do the same. Lucky for us, no one has. While clearing Hudson's apartment we grab him a small overnight bag, which he packs in an irritated fashion, balling things up and aggressively throwing them in. Hudson and I drop Bentley and Lee at their places and then head back to mine to settle in for the night. Jethro seems thrilled that we're having a guest tonight. The moment Hudson sits down on the couch Jethro promptly makes himself comfortable with his head in Hudson's lap. The rest of him is sprawled across the couch and between the two of them there is no room left for me.

I head off to my bedroom to change into my pajamas, I grab my chair from there and drag it out to the living room, making a scene to show the both of them that I'm irritated. Neither of them budge. I sit down with a huff and look at my brother who is rubbing Jethro's ears while staring at a spot on my wall. He is so deep in thought I second guess whether or not to say anything to him, since it might spook him. I give him a few more moments in his thoughts before gently interrupting them.

"Hudson?" My voice is so quiet that I barely hear myself.

He looks up at me, snapping back into reality, trying to ground himself from the trip he just took back from his thoughts. Undoubtedly deep in a rabbit hole that he created for himself, "What?" His voice is almost vacant.

"Whatcha thinkin' about? You seem pretty involved in whatever it is." I pet the blanket on my lap to avoid eye contact with Hudson.

"I keep replaying everything that's happened today, and I can't believe that we've ended up here, especially considering that this time a year ago we would have been hanging out with them. Now they're enemy number one to The East. I can't believe it." He takes a moment, taking several deep breaths. "Ryan was my best friend, we grew up together, and now this. I keep wondering if there is something that I could have done to prevent all of this. I replay every interaction that I had with each one of them, trying to pick out anything that they said that may lead me to something. Maybe something that they said that showed they weren't going to be staying around much longer. I just wish I had been able to stop them before we got to where we are." Luckily Jethro is on his lap because I can hear the rage in his voice building.

"I know Hudson, believe me, I get it probably better than most." At this he looks up to me as if he wants to ask me to go into more detail but avoids the conversation for now.

He makes the attempt to change the subject, which I gladly accept. Of course, his concern is now food. "So, do you have something that we can whip up for dinner, or do we need to order something?" I make my way to the kitchen to take inventory and see what we can make quicker than trying to have something delivered. It is getting late anyway, and the day has exhausted me. As I search I find a frozen pizza and hold it up for Hudson to see, without saying anything. He shrugs, "That works."

I preheat the oven as Hudson heads off to take a shower. I quickly reclaim my seat back on the couch next to Jethro. It is my turn to get lost in my thoughts with Jethro. The moment I begin down the rabbit hole the oven beeps reminding me to put the pizza in. I put the pizza in the oven, set a timer, grab my book, and settle back on the couch. Hoping to use the next twenty minutes to catch up on my book. I can't bring myself to read it though. Ryan has ruined this book for me, I feel dirty just touching it. I chuck the book aside and decide to order a new copy, hopefully the entire book hasn't been ruined for me, but just this copy.

I've accomplished nothing and Hudson is already making his way out of the bathroom, now in his pajamas as well and the oven timer is going off. I make my way to the kitchen to plate our food; we opt to eat outside on the patio the fresh air will be good for us. We take our seats and begin to dig in; all the while Jethro is sitting at Hudson's side drooling. Jethro's head quickly jerks away from the pizza, he's noticed something in the field straight out from my patio. Both Hudson and I rise, Hudson has his weapon in his hand, he usually doesn't carry it while at home, but today must have really gotten to him for him to be pulling a gun at dinner, that was holstered under his pajamas. Neither of us are able to locate whatever it was that caused Jethro's alarm, then out of nowhere a deer runs from the field, being chased by another deer. We sit down and burst into laughter. A welcome relief.

It seems like just yesterday the three of us were sitting out here together and spotted the first deer. I can't believe that it's already been almost two weeks since Graduation. Our team has already come so far and overcome so much. Time is only going to make us stronger. I feel like the increasing deer are a sign of what's to come, a rebirth. I refuse to allow The South and The Trio to put any more fear into me than they already have. No, I'm going to use this as the push I need to keep moving forward.

This time it's Hudson pulling me out of my own head. "Margot, I need to ask you something."

Oh boy. He must have seen Bentley and I, or maybe Emma Leigh said something to him about seeing us sneaking back together. "Uh, okay, shoot."

Hudson sits up straight in his chair, *this is serious*. "Earlier before going off to make dinner you mentioned that you thought you probably knew what I was feeling better than anyone else. What did you mean by that?"

I get up from my chair, grabbing both of our empty plates, "Hudson, why don't we go inside to talk, you never know if someone is listening." He gives me a suspicious look, but doesn't question me, as we both head inside. Hudson and Jethro, once again, make themselves comfortable on the couch while I go to put the dishes away. When I come back and take my seat Hudson stares at me, waiting for me to start the conversation. Making sure I don't avoid his question.

"Um, I'm not really sure where to begin, so I guess I'll dive right in. But you have to promise me you'll let me finish without interruption." The suspicious look on Hudson's face only grows, but he gives me a nod of agreement. We'll see if he can keep his promise.

"Well, this all started in the winter before they left us. Ryan and I kind of began hanging out with each other a lot one on one. I guess most people would kind of consider it dating, but towards the end the whole thing was very one sided on Ryan's side. He started trying to control me. He was always putting me down and trying to convince me that he was the only one there for me." I can tell that Hudson wants to lose it on me for keeping this secret, but he's keeping his word to allow me to tell my story without interruption. "I quickly realized that I wasn't as interested as I thought I was, especially due to his tactics, but he wouldn't take no for an answer. He started calling me '*bird*' and trying harder than ever to get on my good side." I look at my hands and begin snapping at the hair tie on my wrist, too embarrassed to look up. "I was doing my best to let him down easily because I thought it would be best for the team, but I think that no matter how I did it he was still going to be pissed. Looking back on it, I think he was just trying to get as close as possible to me to gain as much information as he could before leaving.

He was sweet to me for the most part, always sneaking me breakfast or bringing flowers and dinner to my apartment, until he wasn't. Even though I knew he was manipulating me, I enjoyed the attention for a while. No one had ever paid me any mind like that before, but he became more aggressive, and he finally pushed me to a point of no return, and I cut off our ties completely. I'm sorry that I didn't tell you, but he was your best friend, and I didn't want anything to come in between your friendship." I feel the heat on my face, the tears are coming, "I'm sorry."

Hudson is looking at me clearly lost for words. I should have been honest with him to begin with, but this is exactly what I was afraid of happening.

"Ryan. Of all people, Ryan? The guy may have been my best friend, but even I knew he was a tool. He was always looking for ways to use people for his advantage, even if it hurt them in the long run. I really just wish that you had said something to me and that you hadn't left me in the dark up until now."

"I know, and I'm sorry. I didn't do it for any reason other than to avoid any kind of awkwardness or fighting." Hudson can barely look at me, busying himself by petting Jethro.

"Margot it's worse off now that you didn't tell me while it had been happening. Did *anyone* know?"

"We had agreed to keep it quiet, but I'm sure he ended up telling Kris." It's a good thing Hudson doesn't want to make eye contact. I don't think I would be able to handle seeing the hurt on his face that I'm hearing in his voice.

"Alright, just curious. Please don't keep stuff from me anymore, and maybe not date my friends or our teammates." I smile at him, now is not the time to tell him how I've been feeling about Bentley. We have more important things to worry about.

"Same goes for you, Hudson." I check the time on my phone. "Huds, it's late, probably best we try and get some sleep now in case our night gets interrupted."

Hudson agrees and quickly pulls the couch out turning it into a bed, I bring over some extra sheets and help him to make it up. He climbs in and of course Jethro joins him, guess I'm sleeping alone tonight. I make my way to my room and hop into bed, grabbing my phone to check it before bed. I notice that I have a couple of unread messages, both from Bentley. I was so involved in talking to Hudson that I hadn't bothered looking at my phone.

Bentley Adler
Everything okay over there?

Bentley Adler
I'm sure you're fine- but just check in with me when you get a moment please.

It's sweet that he worries about me.

Hey, Bentley, sorry for the late response. Hudson and I spent some time talking about the day's events, along with past ones. I told him about Ryan, he isn't thrilled, but he also wasn't as mad as I had guessed he would be.

Ding *The* speed of his response leads me to believe that he's been anxiously awaiting my response.

Bentley Adler
Well that's good. He probably handled it better than me. I'm sorry for getting upset about that earlier. I care about you a lot and don't want whatever this is tainted by traitorous scum like him.

It's so interesting, seeing this side of Bentley I've never seen before.

I care about you too, Bentley. Don't worry about things between us changing. If anything...today changed it for the better. Thank you for being there for me today. I really don't know how I would have made it through without you by my side.

Bentley Adler
Of course Margot. Now get some rest. We have our work cut out for us going forward.

Goodnight, Bentley.

Bentley Adler
Goodnight Margot. Call me if anything happens. I'll be by in the morning with Lee to pick you guys up.

I smile thinking about seeing him first thing. Bentley is different from Ryan in so many ways. Ryan always made me feel pressured to feel a certain way and do certain things, with Bentley things are easy. This is good, because with the approaching war I don't have time for distractions. The moment I shut my eyes I fall into a deep sleep, a much-needed rest after the day I've had.

CHAPTER TWELVE
COWARDS

Ugh what time is it? I grab my phone to check the time, hoping I still have time to sleep. *Crap!* Late again. I rush to brush my teeth and get dressed before rushing out of my bedroom to get Hudson and Jethro, we all must have overslept. As I enter the living room the couch bed is empty, no sign of either of them anywhere.

"Jethro!? Hudson!?" Nothing. I am answered by silence. Why would they leave me here alone? Did they even leave on their own accord? How did I not wake up to them leaving? Panic is setting in. I open every closet door and check on the balcony before realizing they're gone. I check my phone again for a message or a missed call from Hudson. Nothing. I check the fridge for a note stuck to it with a magnet, like mom always did growing up, still nothing. I grab my bag and keys and rush out of my apartment. I make my way to Lee's apartment and then Bentley's, banging on their doors, nothing again and again. I can feel the panic tightening in my chest. Something is very wrong here.

I take the stairs, not wanting to be trapped in the elevator with someone and having no way out. I can't take any chances; the worst possibilities are filling my mind. My brother, my dog, my friends- all gone, without a trace. Either they were taken or they were lured out. Their cars are gone, the only place that they would all be together is Headquarters. I get in the car and make my way there, blowing through the single red light. Nothing matters other than the safety of my family.

I arrive and see everyone's cars parked in their usual spots, but something is wrong. Jethro is locked in Hudson's car. It's fall, so the car is cool enough with the windows cracked, but I know that Hudson would never dare leave Jethro in the car unless absolutely necessary. Jethro is more than welcome in Headquarters, him being out here by himself while everyone else is inside doesn't make any sense. More panic floods my brain.

I get out of my car, gun in hand. I check on Jethro before making my way towards the front door. When I can finally see through the window, all I can see is the pure chaos that has happened here. There was a battle, and my brother must have left me home to ensure my safety, but why bring Jethro? This is the kind of brother he is, willing to do anything to protect myself or Eloise. I press my face against the front door, so I can get a clear picture. I can't believe my eyes.

Blood. Everywhere.

171

Bodies. Everywhere.

Broken bodies that have been defeated in battle.

I push the door open and rush inside. I run past Theo's body that's tangled with Auriella's. They must have been killed trying to fight together against whoever had ambushed them. I don't stop. I can see Hudson's body in a pool of blood, I rush to him, staring at him the entire way. *Wham!* I slip onto the floor with a smack. I look back at my feet to see what I've tripped over as I lay in something warm and sticky...Bentley's blood. I turn around and begin shaking him, hoping that it will bring life back into his body.

"Bentley! Bentley! I need you to wake up!" Panic flows through my plea. He's gone. With tears hot on my cheeks, I rush to my brother next, praying that he's okay.

"Hudson! Please, please don't leave me." I'm too late, his body is destroyed. He died trying to protect me, and I was too late to save him or even thank him. I hear a creak, like someone shifting on the floor. I whip my head around hoping to see one of my teammates alive. Then I see him, the disgusting coward, standing there looking over what's happened as though he's proud of his work, with the bodies of Emma Leigh, Felix, and Lee at his feet. I'm locked on to him so intensely that I don't notice myself rising as he's moving closer to me, walking slowly.

"Hi, bird. Glad you could join my little party." He spreads his arms as though presenting the scene to me. His smile is like a cat who just caught a mouse, so smug and so proud. There used to be a time that I actually enjoyed that smile, now all I want to do is punch him square in it.

"You coward! How dare you!" My feet begin charging toward him before I can think of the consequences, only thinking about wrapping my fingers around his throat. I barely make it a couple of steps before I'm grabbed from behind, someone holding me back from taking my revenge.

Then it hits me like a tsunami of emotions. Strangled sounds escape me as I scream incoherently all while sobbing and cursing at those who did this to those that I love, all while trying to release myself from the grasp of whoever has stopped me. Dying to get my hands on Ryan.

"No! No! No!"

I can feel myself being shaken, "Margot! Margot, what's wrong? Margot wake up! You're alright!" I slowly open my eyes to find Hudson sitting on my bed, shaking me awake, with Jethro by his side. I start sobbing hysterically as Hudson pulls me in closer, into a hug. It was all just a dream...a nightmare.

It takes me several minutes to regain some kind of composure. Hudson is patient with me, allowing me to work myself out of this panic attack that this nightmare has spun me into. I finally feel calm enough to look up at Hudson, who is staring at me with his eyes full of concern. I look towards the window, the sun has barely risen. Realistically there is still time to sleep before I need to start preparing for the day, but there's no chance that's going to happen.

"Margot? Are you alright? Do you want to talk about it?" There's nothing to say, I shrug my shoulders at him. Sure, I've had nightmares surrounding this war, but never anything like this. Nothing that has ever felt so real and rocked me to my core like this.

"I'm sorry for waking you up Hudson, I'm okay though, just a nightmare." I can't look at him without seeing his mangled, dead body. I choose to look at my hands and crack my knuckles to avoid his gaze.

"Do you want to talk about it?" He looks worried as he waits for my answer.

"No, I don't remember it really." *A lie.* "I think I'll stay up, why don't you try and go back to sleep? I might try and take Jethro for a walk, I'll see if Lee or Bentley are up and want to join us, if they're not we will just keep to the balcony."

"You sure you don't want me to go with you, since I'm up?" I can see how tired he is, but I know he'd come along anyways, just for me. Even though we run a military together, I'm still his little sister and on occasion it's nice that he still treats me as such.

"No, Hudson, it's okay, go ahead and go back to sleep. If I end up leaving I'll leave you a note." Hudson gives me one last squeeze before heading back to the couch. I grab my phone to see if either of the guys are awake. I decide it's easiest to send them a message in a group, that way if Hudson asks Lee can confirm I asked them both.

Hey guys...either of you up? Hudson is going to sleep a bit longer and I'd like to take Jethro out for a quick walk but need someone to have my back.

All too quickly Lee responds, Bentley didn't even have a chance.

Lee Braxton
Good morning! I can be at your door in five minutes. Be ready!

I wait as long as possible before making my way to the door with Jethro leashed up for his walk. I was really hoping that Bentley was going to respond, but Lee is always up at the crack of dawn, I should have known better. I open the door and there's Lee standing there looking as chipper as ever, he's probably already showered and eaten breakfast, meanwhile I'm still in my pajamas and haven't even thought about touching my hair. It is what it is, I had a rough night, and it's just Lee.

Maybe this is a mistake, Lee is way too awake for this early in the morning, even his greeting makes me want to slam the door and go back to bed, "Goooood morning!!" I quickly shut the door, so that Lee's shouting doesn't wake Hudson.

"Too early, Lee. I'm going to need you to take it down about five notches." Lee heads off to the stairs and Jethro happily trots along behind him, while I'm practically being dragged by Jethro; how tired I am is finally hitting me.

Once we get outside we start to make our way around the walking path that goes through the little field across from my balcony. For the majority of the walk we walk in silence, aside from the occasional comment about something that Jethro does. On our way back to the front door Lee decides to try and start an actual conversation. I almost got through this walk in silence, I wish I had, because I don't really feel like talking right now.

"Margot, can I ask you something?" *Ugh.*

"Depends, what's up?"

"I was just wondering after everything that happened yesterday, what the plan is? Clearly this is personal for all of us, but I feel like you and Hudson were definitely called out specifically during the whole thing." Lee has no shame in asking the difficult questions and being direct about it. This is why he's in charge of our health. He doesn't put up with the excuses we try giving him or sugarcoat anything. But, he has a point, and this is something that I've already thought about. Probably exactly why I had that nightmare last night.

"I really don't know, Lee. I guess that's something that we'll all go over today. The next step is coming up with a plan to take them down. First, we need to figure out if they're working independently or if this is something that they did on behalf of The South. I know that Ryan rose up in the ranks pretty quickly there."

Thankfully the rest of what I say gets us inside and to the stairs, Lee knows the conversation is over the second that we start heading towards our apartments. Lee drops Jethro and I off at my apartment. The smell of food hits me when I open the door, Hudson is already working on making some eggs for breakfast. Jethro quickly makes his way to sit next to Hudson at the stove, patiently waiting for some eggs to be tossed his way. We must have been walking longer than I realized, because now I only have about half an hour before it's time to head out. I run into my room to start freshening up for the day, when my phone buzzes. A message from Bentley, separate from what I'd sent to him and Lee this morning.

Bentley Adler
Hey I'm sorry about this morning. I would have gone with you and Jethro but I overslept and didn't hear my phone going off. Did it go okay?

I quickly tap out a response. I can't be late.

No worries! Everything went fine- we spent most of it in silence thankfully. Even when we did talk it was just about planning for what we're going to do about the traitor trio.

Bentley Adler
Oh good. Well I'm going to rush to get ready. Lee and I will be over soon to collect you and Hudson...and Jethro?

I feel like a small child that's been left with a babysitter.

Of course Jethro is coming! See ya soon :)

The rest of the morning goes on without an event, which I consider a good morning. Lee and Bentley come by to collect us and the four of us make a caravan and drive to Headquarters. Emma Leigh had decided to meet up with the other team members, so that our caravan didn't get too large and we all weren't together on the drive, making us an easier target on our way in. When we park at Headquarters everything looks normal from the outside, but I still hold my breath as we walk towards the doors.

As we walk in I cautiously look around, nothing seems to have been touched, *thank God.* I don't think my heart could handle my nightmare becoming a reality. We all take a few moments to walk around, checking all of the traps to see if any had been set off or tampered with. Everything looks to be intact. Once we've finished up, Auriella, Emma Leigh, Theo, and Felix come in. Today Auriella has changed her laces and her hair bow to match how all of us are feeling, red with anger. *How many different sets of laces and bows does this girl have?*

Emma Leigh doesn't even look at any of us before making her way to her station to start checking the computers, making sure nothing happened remotely. Emma Leigh has never been a people person, but it has always been worse in the mornings. I rush to grab her a cup of coffee to help perk her up. She gives me a small smile when I hand it to her. I wait for her to take a few sips before she gives me her update.

"Fortunately, nothing has been tampered with overnight. I don't see that anyone has messed with our footage, and there's no one coming or going last night that would cause us any alarm." She leans in closely to her monitor, "Wait a second!" She begins rewinding and prints something out.

"What is it Em!?" I *hate* when she does this. She will start something aloud and then get in her head and not finish her thoughts to the rest of us. My yelling has alerted everyone else; they rush to join me in standing around Emma Leigh and her computer.

"Oh right, sorry. Look who decided to show up to work this morning." Right there clear as day we can all see Wesley, that little weasel, walking right into the building this morning and heading to the laundry department like he didn't betray The East yesterday. Before I can give any orders everyone is running towards the stairs to head to laundry. Luckily Victoria's been in lock up all night, so she wouldn't have been able to tip him off. We've got him now. We all make our way to the door, and I rush to get in front to stop everyone.

"Guys, we need a plan, we can't just storm in there. There's only one way in and out, so I think it's best if some of us wait out here for a moment in case something happens, and we need backup. Auriella, how about you head in first and distract him?" I shoot her a wink. Auriella is gorgeous and the men here are always stopping to stare at her. It feels wrong resorting to objectifying someone as part of a tactic, but sometimes it's the sweetest trap that catches the most rodents. We quickly make our way down to the laundry room, all of us wait outside the door as Auriella walks in immediately engaging Wesley. I wish we had thought to stop and put our communicators in our ears, but it's too late for that, we'll just have to make do. From where I'm standing I can *just* see Auriella twirling her hair around her finger while pointing around at the piles of laundry, she must have told him that she was looking for something. While he's got his back turned I use this as my chance to sneak in, instructing the others to stay behind. I hide myself behind a tall stack of laundry before he turns back around, finally able to hear their conversation.

He looks at her like he's sorry to disappoint her. "Sorry, I don't see your uniform anywhere, Auriella."

"Are you sure Wesley? I'm sure I dropped it off two nights ago, were you here?" I've never heard her speak in such a soft, sweet tone like this before, she's really laying the sweet on thick with Wesley.

"I was here, even had to stay late that night, but I can't seem to find it anywhere."

This is my chance. I step out from behind the pile of laundry I am hiding behind. "That must be because you were too busy that night being traitorous scum and helping known traitors to actually do your jo-" And just like that, for the third time in twenty-four hours I've had the breath stolen from my lungs. Mid-sentence Wesley threw himself at me to get past me and out of the laundry room, knocking me into a large basket of laundry with wheels and clipping my face with his elbow. As I scramble to get up I see Bentley storming into the room, right as Wesley is about to get to the door, followed by the rest of the team. Bentley delivers one swift punch to Wesley's jaw; Wesley cocks his fist to swing back at Bentley. Before Bentley can react, Theo comes out of nowhere and tackles Wesley to the ground, quickly flipping him over and placing him in handcuffs. As Theo and Bentley lift him to his feet, my face and head are throbbing as I make my way over to him and stand inches from his face,

"Wesley Fowler, you are under arrest for treason against The East, and we can go ahead and add assault to that charge." I look at Bentley and Theo. "Take him out of here, guys."

Bentley gives me a look, silently asking me if I'm okay. I give him a silent nod to reassure him before he and Theo march Wesley toward the cells, where he will be detained away from Victoria, and anyone else for that matter. Solitary confinement for the little weasel. We can't risk him making friends or making plans. There aren't many people that are kept in our small jail, but the people that are here are people that are currently being questioned for crimes that pose a direct threat to The East. Once we're finished questioning these people they are sent off to the larger prison, closer to our border, to be held until they can be tried and, possibly, punished for their crimes pending the outcome of their trials.

Wesley is currently the most dangerous and we will be keeping him even after we get him to break and give us information that we need about the break-in. We'll need to use him to figure out what The Trio is up to and what their next moves are. We might even be able to use him as some kind of bait, but I doubt that someone as fresh as he is will be enough of an asset that they would risk being caught to break him out of here. We all make our way back to our area to finish our morning's rounds and check the rest of the systems that we didn't get to before Emma Leigh found that Wesley had decided to show his face.

I just need a moment to sit down and put my feet up, this day has already sucked all of the energy out of me, from the moment that I opened my eyes. I plop onto my couch and try to relax, scrolling on my phone, for a few minutes to distract my brain. Of course it's not something that I can do, the second I start to feel my brain relaxing Hudson comes into our office and plops himself onto the couch next to me.

"So, Theo." Ha! I know exactly where this is going.

"So...*Theo*?" I can't help but lead him into this conversation. I hide my smile, only allowing one corner of my mouth to rise, though I'm sure Hudson can hear the satisfaction in my voice.

"That was a pretty impressive tackle today. I don't think we truly know who he is yet. He didn't show us any of this during Graduation. That tackle was one that he was taught how to properly execute and has practiced many times." Now that I think about it, I have to agree with him.

"Well, he comes from an impressive military family, I wouldn't be shocked if they had taught him a thing or two about proper form when it comes to taking down an enemy." Hudson shrugs at me, this wasn't the response he was looking for.

"I guess you have a point there, but still. How well do we really know any of these people, especially the new recruits? I mean, sure, Wesley was a prick from the moment we met him at the interviews, but did either of us think that he would become a traitor against us so quickly?" Hudson has a point, I don't think any of us saw it coming. I knew he was going to be a thorn in my side from the moment I met him, but not a massive splinter wedged in deep.

"Hudson, I get it, we've both been burned by people that were close to us. People that were supposed to be our friends and our teammates, but we can't continue to let the past tarnish our future. I'll be the first to admit that what happened with them has put a sour taste in my mouth and turned me into a bit of a cynic. We can't continue to let them damage us though." I think about the walls that I build around myself. "What they did to us is horrible, but are we going to let them continue hurting us? No. We can't. It's not healthy for ourselves, our team, or any of our relationships for that matter." Hudson shrugs with irritation, *I wish he'd communicate with me*. I know he must have been hoping that I would join him in his skepticism and anger. "I get it Hudson, having people so close to us betray us on the deepest levels is a hard pill to swallow, but we're going to ruin things for ourselves going forward by continuing to let them get into our heads. I'm trying really hard to move past it too, I know how hard it is, but we have to try."

As the words come out of my mouth I realize that I'm not only lying to my brother, but myself too. I haven't tried to get myself out of this funk at all. If it wasn't for the things that happened with Ryan and the rest of The Trio I don't think that I would be fighting myself on the feelings that I have for Bentley. I could kick myself, because it feels like I'm still allowing Ryan to control me. I need to work on the things that I'm telling my brother to work on or I'm going to destroy any chance of a normal healthy relationship with Bentley, or anyone for that matter. Luggage can be a heavy burden to carry, and I definitely need to travel light if I plan on going anywhere. I need to lead by example and start making some changes. I pull myself off the couch and extend my hand to Hudson.

"Alright, come on, no more wallowing, it's time to get up and get on with our day. We're leaders, Hudson, we can't stay in here hiding all day."

Hudson starts to get up. "Are you sure?" I have to laugh; hiding does sound nice.

"Yes, I'm sure. Come on, we have an interrogation to get to anyway. Bentley and Theo should be back any moment, then we can make a plan and get down there to start this interrogation. We don't have much time and need to be quick about this; in case there's anything else in the works."

Hudson and I wander around, tidying up, and eating snacks while we wait for Bentley and Theo to return, when they finally do they look exhausted. I walk up to both of them.

"Are you two alright?" Bentley gives me a grim look. *Do I even want his answer?*

"Not really, but we could be worse. Wesley fought us the entire way and when we finally got there he tried to make a break for it." I notice a few small drops of blood on Bentley's shirt. *Bentley's or Wesley's?* "We had to fight him to the ground and put him in full body shackles. We even connected his chains to the floor so he can't move anywhere. He kept screaming about how they were going to get him and how we better let him go or they would just come get him and take us out in the process." Bentley looks perplexed as he says these things.

"So, what do you think? Do you really think that he's so important that they would come to break him out? Or do you think that they're going to be pissed that he got caught and potentially messed up their entire operation and they're going to come to get him, but only to kill him so that he can't tell us their plans?"

"I don't know, Margot." The way Bentley says my name sends chills down my spine. "Hopefully we can get a better read on him once we interrogate him. Which I think we should do sooner than later. He seems like the type to knock himself unconscious to avoid having to talk."

It takes me a minute to put together everything we just spoke about. My mind is spinning. I still can't believe how someone can be so bold and be such a coward at the same time. The nerve to break in to our Headquarters and then still show up the next day as though nothing happened, the nerve of some people. *Is he brave or stupid? Stupid.*

"Alright, let's quickly gather as much information on Wesley as possible and then head to interrogate him." This is going to be a group effort and we're going to need to use our assets to get the most out of it. "Everyone, listen up! We all need to take the time and focus on researching Wesley, the faster we can get inside his head the better. Being prepared will help this interrogation go smoothly. We need to get as much information out of him, so that we can plan our next moves. Everyone, take the next thirty minutes and then we'll gather back together to go over everything that we've found." None of us hesitate on this task, even though research only usually appeals to Emma Leigh and me, everyone is digging in.

It's almost complete silence for the next thirty minutes, other than the sound of keyboards rapidly typing and pens scratching on paper taking notes on all things Wesley Fowler and the despicable coward he is.

CHAPTER THIRTEEN
INTERROGATION

I don't know that our team has ever completed a research task so quickly, normally it takes us hours, due to the lack of interest from most of the team. Somehow we are able to find all of the information that we could possibly need about Wesley within an hour, even after extending our time because everyone was so involved. The anger we were all feeling was pushing us. Everyone seems to stop typing around the same time, looking up to see who else has finished. Without saying a word, once the last person, Emma Leigh, looks up from her notes we all gather our papers and head to the holding cell to take him to interrogation. We've all come to trust one another's abilities, so there's no longer a need to compare notes before getting to it.

The holding cells aren't anything fancy, but they do the job. There he is, sitting in the back of a cell, alone, a special cell, not with bars, but with a door. No windows and his cell is completely soundproof, no one can hear him, and he can't hear anyone. If someone was to sit in here long enough it would make them go crazy, being trapped alone with nothing but their own thoughts. I can only imagine what Wesley's thoughts might be…anger? Fear? Frustration? All of them together? He helped the wrong people and got caught, and they're nowhere to help him now and will likely never come back for him, just a pawn in this terrible game. The interrogation room that we will use is similar to his cell, no windows, no color. The only difference is that on one wall there is a two-way mirror so that the rest of us can see and hear what's going on. On our side there is a smaller bar-height table attached to the wall with stools so we can sit, watch, and take notes if necessary.

I turn to Theo, "Alright, Theo, I think it might be best for you to start things off…you're the one that tackled him and his ego is probably a little bruised." Theo gives me a single nod in recognition, he looks nervous, "Everyone is going to have their communication devices in their ears, so that if anything needs to be added to the interrogation someone can chirp in our ears to let us know. Theo, I'll go in with you, but I'm going to let you run point on this. I'll only chime in if it's needed."

Hudson starts to chuckle. "You, quiet? Okay, I'll believe it when I see it, actually-when I don't hear it."

I roll my eyes and look over to Bentley and Lee. "Could the two of you please grab our prisoner and bring him into the room? Theo and I will make our way in there once he's situated." Bentley and Lee nod and open the door to Wesley's cell which is directly across from the room that will be used to interrogate him. Wesley seems so defeated that he doesn't make any kind of defensive moves. As he stands from his bed, placing his hands behind his back to be cuffed, and walks obediently between Bentley and Lee. They sit him down in the chair at the interrogation table, even here he looks lost as he sits and stares off into space. Something is eating him alive and it's our job to find out what it is and use it to our advantage. Hopefully all of our research will come in handy with this. It is time.

I allow Theo to walk in the room before me, his eyes never leave Wesley as he walks across the room, pulls out his chair, and sits down. Wesley's eyes never leave Theo's. I can only imagine what is going through both of their minds. Both of them were brought here together after Graduation, they had a choice and chose their sides. Unfortunately for Wesley, he chose the wrong one. They sit there staring at one another for what feels like minutes, when in reality it's only been about thirty seconds. I take this as my invitation to enter the room. I do the opposite of Theo; I make every attempt to make sure that my eyes don't meet Wesley's gaze as I cross the room. I will not give him that courtesy.

The moment I am seated Theo swallows hard before launching into his interrogation. It's obvious he's been anxiously awaiting this moment, no matter how nervous he seemed before heading in here. Theo slams both of his fists down on the table.

His voice is surprisingly commanding. "Wesley Fowler, are you aware of why you are here and what your charges are?"

Wesley looks up at Theo with a blank stare but doesn't answer. His eyes are now full of sadness. I wonder if his parents, family, or friends know that he's here and what he's done. Maybe they assume that he's too busy with training and work that he hasn't had the chance to reach out to them. A part of me wonders if he's thinking the same thing, if this was all a huge mistake that he wishes he could go back on. Are his parents a part of this too? So many questions which we will hopefully get answers to. As though Theo is reading my thoughts he starts his line of questioning, even though Wesley has yet to answer his initial question.

"I take it you're not going to answer me, so I guess I'll answer this one for you. You are here because you are guilty, without a doubt, of treason against The East. You've betrayed not only your Division, but likely your family as well...if they're not in on this betrayal with you too." Nothing. No response, not even the slightest bit of movement from Wesley. Though Theo has the best intentions, it doesn't look like he'll be getting anywhere with Wesley today. Hudson has the same thought, because at this time he comes through on our communicators hidden in our ears.

"Alright, guys. I don't think he's budging and letting anything out to you two. Why don't you two come on out and swap with Auriella and I?" At this Theo gets up and leaves the room without saying a word. He looks irritated. He already proved himself once today, I really hope that he doesn't take this personally or think that we think any less of him because Wesley isn't cracking for him. This happens often in interrogations, which is why all of us are here for this interrogation. You never know who is going to be the one who actually cracks the nut. Typically, we don't all watch and wait our turns, but in this case we want everyone around to hopefully get answers faster. I get up and leave as well, not worried about Wesley following or trying to escape because his leg shackles are chained to the floor.

Auriella and Hudson head in the moment I leave the room. The thought in pairing the two of them together was that Auriella's beauty and flirtatious side might be able to balance out the amount of rage that Hudson is harboring, not only against Wesley, but against The Trio. They barely make it five minutes of trying to coax an answer out of Wesley because Hudson begins screaming at him.

"Not too chatty now, huh?! You had no problem talking when it came to giving up your division and betraying everyone who lives here!!" Hudson has made his way over to the other side of the table and is holding Wesley by the collar of his muddled gray prisoner jumpsuit. I'm ready to call him out, when Bentley places his hand on my shoulder, as if holding me back from what he knows I'm ready to do. Hudson continues screaming, now shaking Wesley by his collar, "A piece of garbage like you doesn't deserve to share the same air as us!"

Wesley stares through Hudson, unphased by what he's said, like he knows it's true and it can't hurt him because of that. His eyes blank, like looking into an abyss. This is what sets Hudson over the edge, and no amount of sweetness from Auriella could stop that. Hudson flips the table and makes a move at Wesley, fist drawn back, Lee and Bentley burst through the door and charge Hudson to stop him from beating the life out of our only witness and perpetrator. Auriella does her best to help, but in anger Hudson pushes her aside like a rag doll, still trying to get to Wesley, in a black out rage not seeing who is touching him. He is going to regret most of this later. He's done this once before and felt terrible about it for months. Theo stands by the door waiting to see if there's anything that he can do, while Felix rushes in to escort his sister out and make sure that she's okay. I shouldn't be surprised, yet here I am, stunned with my head in my hands.

Hudson can't keep allowing his anger to get out of control. As kids he was always the one to fly off the handle. Things have only gotten worse since we joined the military and our closest friends betrayed us. Mentally I know that he's struggling, but he's never going to admit that, not to me at least. I love my brother, but there's nothing that I can do to help him right now. This is something that he's going to have to figure out on his own. If I try to push him to talk about things, at least at this point in time, it's only going to make things worse. We've grown up in a world where men aren't supposed to show emotions that could possibly be construed as weakness. There's nothing weak about showing your emotions, I consider it brave, unfortunately Hudson sees it as quite the opposite.

Bentley and Lee march Hudson through the door, still fuming. He grabs the bottle of water next to me and leaves the room to cool off. *Good, nobody needs to see him losing control like this.*

Auriella and Felix walk out next. Luckily, Auriella doesn't seem to have been harmed. Felix turns around and heads back into the room with Emma Leigh, who doesn't look thrilled about having to do this. She's never been one to enjoy confrontation, which is probably why she enjoys the behind the scenes that being in the IT department entails. Felix rights the table so that the two of them can sit at it, facing Wesley. Wesley actually looks up to Emma Leigh, looking her in the eyes, as if he's pleading for her to help him. I swear they lock eyes for a moment, and Emma Leigh quickly drops his gaze, but why? Why is he trying to connect with her? She was just as much involved with sending him to laundry duty. I shake it off...I'm just overthinking and hyper aware after what just happened with Hudson.

Felix begins the questioning. Emma Leigh makes no effort to start their portion of the interrogation. "Are you alright Wesley?"

Wesley looks up at him and shrugs his shoulders, the first real reaction that we've gotten from him. Finally, an answer to a question, even though it isn't audible and it isn't an important question to answer, it is a start.

"Wesley, do you know anything about the break-in? Like how they got into the security system? They broke into systems that were so well encrypted that even the best hackers would struggle with it." Emma Leigh looks up, hoping to hear an answer on this one. An answer that could lead her to ways to better improve our technology so that something like this can't happen again.

Wesley finally decides to answer, "I know nothing about that. You're wasting your time asking me about it." He lowers his head and looks as though he's starting to drift off.

Emma Leigh decides that she's had enough of this, she pushes her chair back, and it squeals so loud that Wesley and Felix jump. She makes her way to leave the room, only looking back briefly, which Felix takes as his cue to leave too. Bentley and Lee are up next, our last hopes. They are probably our two best interrogators individually. I am interested to see what kind of force they become when working together. It isn't usual for the whole team to sit in on interrogations, so I have never seen how Bentley or Lee operates when it comes to interrogations, since my partner is typically Hudson. I only know how good they are, from their results alone. Usually, our pairs don't go into the interrogation room together, typically one sits outside and the other goes in. Bentley and Lee have been partners since the beginning. We are all in for a treat, getting to witness this.

Right off the bat it is very clear that they are going to play good cop - bad cop, and Bentley just so happens to be the bad cop. Things heat up almost immediately, Bentley stomping in and Lee coming in like a lamb. Bentley slams his fists onto the table as he begins talking to Wesley in a stern voice that I've never heard him use before. I find it alluring, but at the same time it makes me nervous.

"Alright, Wesley, listen up. Everyone is tired of you wasting their time today. You're either going to give us answers or you're going to pay for it." Wesley looks up fearfully at this, he can tell that Bentley means it. I feel a bit jumpy at Bentley's words, even though he isn't speaking to me. "So, Wesley, what's your decision? Are you going to talk, or would you rather sit in your cell while we go and have a conversation with your family?"

The color is draining from Wesley's face. They must not know what he's done. Not only did he betray his division, but he betrayed his family. What will they think when they hear the news? Maybe Wesley is actually starting to regret what he's done, and Bentley has struck the nerve to make it happen.

Lee sits up a little straighter, noticing that Wesley is visibly uncomfortable after his family was mentioned. Bentley takes this as his cue to take a seat. This is where the good cop comes into play, I guess. Lee looks across the table at Wesley, offering him a kind smile. Acting as a friend in this time where he is completely alone and being threatened.

"Wesley, please, just tell us your side of the story and how we ended up here. That's all we're looking for right now. Your family doesn't need to know anything yet." Lee stares into Wesley's eyes waiting for an answer. It's like he's turned on a faucet, because Wesley starts pouring everything out to him.

Wesley puts his head in his hands and takes several deep breaths as he begins telling his story. "I never meant for it to go this far. I was so mad after you all sent me down to the laundry department. My family would never accept that that was going to be my role, and I couldn't either. I knew that there was so much more that I could be used for. I started researching how to go about changing your job, after the initial placement period was complete." His hands ball into fists on the table, "There was nothing, I was going to be stuck doing laundry forever, unless you all decided that I was able to move on to another role. I knew that it would never happen though, that little witch out there hates me." I know that Wesley can't see me through the glass, but somehow he is staring right through the glass where I am sitting. He locks onto me briefly, before he continues on, and I can feel the hatred radiating off of him.

"I started to panic. I couldn't let my life go this way. I found a chatroom for people in situations like mine, which is where I was invited to another chatroom. I didn't realize that it was an underground chatroom meant for supporting The South until it was too late. Very quickly I was swept up into things, telling people how angry I am about the entire situation. A lot of the people there had the same amount of anger that I did. They were either angered by someone in The East or an entire group of people, either way we were all ripe for the picking by people trying to gain support for The South. People who were brought here under false pretenses, thinking it was more of a place to go and vent, not realizing that it was a place for people who supported The South to go." Wesley stops to rub his hands on his pants; I can see beads of sweat down his forehead.

"Once you're in there, you're in. They quickly find out everything about you and tell you that if you try to betray them that they will share the screenshots of everything you said. Luckily I hadn't said much, other than my disappointment and anger about being put into laundry. That was all they needed to hear though, because next thing you know The South is offering me a position in their military, an actual soldier role, not some BS role in the laundry room. They told me that my joining was all dependent on one condition, proving my loyalty to them. I was too far in now. I had already agreed to join them. I couldn't go back now that they were asking for more than I was comfortable with."

Wow, all because he was sent to the laundry department? Is this all our fault for not giving him a second chance? I shake it off, I can't allow myself to go down that rabbit hole, what's done is done.

Wesley is shaking slightly now, "Kris, Ryan, and Lena sought me out personally. Initially it was Kris who made contact with me, we spoke for hours. He told me that he had been in a similar situation, being in The East and not seeing how it would get him to where he wanted to be. That it was natural that I was feeling so worried about what I had to do, but that it would be okay, and they would make sure that I was taken care of. I made it a condition that my family wouldn't be brought into this, which they agreed to. At least there's that spot of light in all of this darkness." One lone tear escapes his eye.

"We began planning immediately, they were adamant that this would happen the next night. At this point I still didn't know Kris' true identity. If I had I probably would have backed out, understanding just how deep I had gotten into all of this. They told me that there was something that you stole from them and they just needed to get in to get that back, something that had been left behind when they left. I foolishly believed them. It wasn't until the night of the break-in that I realized who I had been working with the whole time, The Trio." He pales slightly, "I met them outside and let them in. Kris was quick to disable any kind of technology that might be used to catch us, he told me that he could do it quickly because he had helped to build it. It wasn't until after that that I realized they had stolen things and broken into your leader's office. The only precaution that they took was the cameras, we hadn't thought about covering our prints. I started to worry, a more personal attack would mean a more in-depth investigation, we were sure to get caught."

Welsey stops for several moments, as though thinking about everything that took place. Regretting every moment of it. Thinking that doing laundry for the rest of his life would be better than this.

"When they were finally done we all left together. They told me to wait at my apartment and that they would be back to pick me up the next evening. They never showed. There had been several other people like me that they had been talking to in the chatroom, I figured that they had decided to use them instead of me. Someone with much better qualifications than a wannabe soldier who was sent to work in the laundry department." His head drops, another disappointment and time being made to feel inadequate, "I was starting to panic, so I decided to head into work the next morning. I hadn't heard anything, so I figured that they had used and abandoned me, and none of you had come to arrest me yet, which made me think that we had gotten away with it all. I was shocked when you came in to arrest me, I panicked. I have no idea what they're going to do now since I'm gone, maybe they don't care. Maybe they wanted you to know all of this. I really don't know. I don't know anything anymore."

Lee can tell that Wesley is shutting down and tries to get one more answer before he's completely gone, "Wesley, what about Victoria? How does she play into all of this?"

Wesley looks surprised and takes a beat too long to answer, "Victoria? She had nothing to do with this. We only met recently. I wouldn't trust her with anything like this." *Lies. The way they were acting during placements proves different.*

Lee nods his head once in Wesley's direction, as though dismissing him. Lee and Bentley both stand and walk towards Wesley, Wesley stands and allows them to take him back to his cell without any kind of fight. Wesley is completely defeated now, I thought he was bad before, but this is worse. He is a shell of the overly confident, cocky, person that I met during placements. I can't worry about this. We all make decisions and must live with the consequences that come along with them. Ultimately this was his doing.

Once he's in his cell we all gather back in mine and Hudson's office, because that's where he had retreated to blow off his steam. Bentley quickly fills him in on what happened during the rest of the interrogation, this only seems to anger him more. He's probably feeling the same way that I do, like this entire thing could have been prevented if we had maybe been a little kinder to him or given him some more grace. None of us can think like this though, it's a waste of time. There's nothing that we can do about what has already happened, it's time to move forward and do what we can now about what's to come.

Things are about to get a lot more serious for all of us, this is just the tip of the iceberg. There were several things that Wesley said that stood out, the two major ones being that there are possibly other traitors in our midst. People that maybe have more access than Wesley does. The other was Victoria, it seemed to me like Wesley was protecting her, for now she is going to need to stay in holding. We can't risk another traitor being out there with access to The South. She will have more comforts than Wesley, we'll allow her to make monitored phone calls, but that is about it. No visitors or anything like that. Right now, she's guilty by association.

I make my way out as Lee continues to talk to Hudson about all that he had missed. I need a minute to get away and clear my head. There is so much to think about after the interrogation. I grab Jethro's leash from the wall, I'm sure that he could use a walk and this makes a good excuse for me walking away. Jethro jumps up the moment I grab his leash and starts heading for the front door. As I'm opening the front door I hear footsteps behind me, I smile when I turn around to see Bentley jogging across the entryway to escort Jethro and I outside. I forgot about the rule about moving in pairs, I'm still not used to this. I often wander off on my own or with Jethro just to get some air and think without telling anyone.

I don't mind that Bentley has decided to come along with me, I welcome his presence. It's pretty brisk outside this afternoon, so I try to walk as quickly as possible to get Jethro to a patch of grass so that we can turn around and get back inside. Bentley must be able to sense that I don't want to speak, so we both walk in silence. I am grateful for this and grateful that our walk doesn't take too long, resulting in an extended awkward silence. Today has been more than enough on its own and tomorrow is going to be even more. In the coming days we will begin to investigate who among us is ready to betray The East.

CHAPTER FOURTEEN
SMOKING OUT RATS

Even days after an interrogation like that, walking into Headquarters is daunting, but it had to be done. We have a lot of work to do and sleeping in wasn't an option. Who could sleep after finding out there are even more traitors in our midst, anyways? Once again, I spent the time that I should have been sleeping, tossing and turning, thinking about who could possibly be a traitor among us. I'm sure the others did the same. As I look around the conference table everyone has dark circles under their eyes and are clinging to their coffee as though it might be able to replace the sleep we've all missed the last several nights. If only it was that easy.

I begin gathering up all of our notes from last week, tapping them on the table in order to make the stack neat, and to get everyone's attention. Everyone slowly looks up from their cups of coffee and focuses on me, too tired for small talk, it isn't difficult getting their attention.

"Good morning, everyone. I know that we're all exhausted after this last week, but we can't let up any steam today. We have a lot to get done and we need to do so quickly." Everyone sleepily nods in agreement. I'm going to need everyone to wake up, we need to be sharp for everything that we need to get done today.

I continue, trying to rally the troops, my voice filled with any power I have left, "Thanks to the other day's efforts in interrogation we have learned that there are even more possible traitors among us. We need to find out who these people are and detain them as well. They may even be able to give us some more information about what's going on with The Trio and The South. We're going to need all the information we can get to help us win this war." At the mention of The Trio I spark Hudson's interest, he's angry again. Though I don't think his anger ever left him.

Before I can react, Hudson is standing, banging his fists on the table, yelling. "We cannot let people continue to get away with this! Why are we having all of these issues with traitors!? This is unacceptable and we need to start being more cautious about who we speak with, we can't risk accidentally saying something to someone that is actually a traitor." Hudson is banging his fists on the table like punctuation at the end of every sentence. My exhaustion, mixed with this, is going to cause a killer headache if he goes on much longer, "If they aren't sitting at this table right now, we say nothing to them. Nothing! I don't care if you think it's the most useless bit of information, if it's anything about us or our division, it's something that they are able to use against us. There are rats scurrying about in our Headquarters and it's about time that we smoke them out!" Hudson slams his fists on the table one last time. The looks around the table are mixed, some scared and others just as angry as he is.

"Hudson." I put my hand on my brother's shoulder trying to ground him, even though there's no getting through to him right now. I'm shocked that he doesn't knock my hand away. "What if we sit with Wesley again today and try to see if there's any other information that we can get out of him? See if we can figure out who these rats are and what they're up to." Hudson looks at me, face still red in anger, and nods.

I look to Bentley and Lee, "Do the two of you mind bringing the prisoner back into the interrogation room? I'd like to take one more crack at him, alone. Bentley, you and Lee can stand outside as back up. As for the rest of you, please try and focus on the things we can get done here." Hudson looks to me and opens his mouth, as if to argue about not being invited to this interrogation, but after a moment he gives up the thought and stalks out.

Everyone sleepily gets up from the table to start their day's work as I follow Lee and Bentley to the cells, so that we can get part two of the interrogation going. Wesley looks even worse today than he did yesterday during his daily check. Maybe his guilty conscience is eating away at him, and this is going to be my chance in. His conscience is the only thing eating, though, as he's refusing all food. We *have* to get more information from him, what we have so far is helpful but not enough for us to make moves on. We need to know what's coming.

Lee and Bentley support Wesley into the interrogation room, he's barely able to walk, he's shutting down. Lee stays in the room and offers Wesley some water, taking a sip of it himself first to prove to him that it hasn't been tainted. Wesley waits a beat to consider before taking a sip which turns into many gulps. Bentley comes out to stand next to me as we watch Lee taking care of our prisoner. Lee's goal only being to prepare him for the questioning that's about to come.

"You feeling okay, Margot? Are you sure that you want to be in the room alone with him?" Bentley is looking at me, arms crossed, with concern for my safety and with disappointment that he's not getting in on this.

"Bentley, I promise you I'll be fine. If I need anything you guys will be right here and able to help me. I can handle myself though, so don't feel bad if I make you feel a bit useless." I laugh and gently cup his face, as he fully leans into my hand, knowing that Lee can't see us. For a moment we look at each other and smile. It feels like forever since we've had a moment just the two of us. Even our ability to text each other is slim, we've been working non-stop and once we're home we're exhausted. The moment only lasts seconds before Lee walks back through the door, and my hand drops before he can notice. It is my turn to have a little chat with Wesley, hopefully it will go better than the other day when I didn't get my chance.

As I sit down Wesley looks up at me with a look that could kill me if his eyes were a weapon. He probably blames me for flipping his life upside down. I was the one who caught him being reckless and sent him down to the laundry department. I didn't say that it was the end of his career with us though, I even told him that he could potentially move to different departments once he proved himself as someone different than the person that we met that first day. He chose this path ultimately, not me. He should be mad at himself.

"Wesley, we need to talk, and you need to give me answers. This isn't a game anymore, we need answers or else your punishment is going to increase. What's it going to take to get you talking?" He stares at me and draws in a deep breath before starting to talk.

"Out of all of the people in this whole building are you really so full of yourself that you think I would give *you* answers!? I've heard the rumors. I wasn't with The Trio long, but even in the short amount of time I was with them I quickly learned about the person that you really are." There is pure hatred in his voice. "I believed it all the second you were a complete bitch and overreacted by sending me to the laundry department. You think because you're a woman in a position of power that you have something to prove? That you have to act like you have the biggest balls in this entire place?" It's like he's gotten a burst of energy just by hating me. "Get this through your thick skull, sweetheart, you are nothing. You mean nothing and you are important to no one."

He's saying these things with such conviction, he really means them. I do my best to not let it bother me, as hard as I try it still stings.

"The people around here are only nice to you because of your position. Ryan was only nice to you because he was trying to get information out of you and get deeper into this place to steal information. If he could get into your pants while doing so then good on him." It takes me a moment to catch my breath, hearing someone say such vile things really knocks it out of you, especially when some of them are things you've said to yourself.

Once I have caught my breath I look him in the eyes, "Are you finished?"

He is livid, not getting a rise out of me. He goes to stand but can't because Lee made his shackles so tight that he's unable to stand or even adjust how he's sitting in his chair. For this I am thankful. He looks like he's about ready to knock my lights out, but I have a feeling that Bentley is on the other side of the glass feeling the same way about him. I get up and leave the room. There is no point in me wasting my time trying to talk to him. He is never going to tell me anything. As I walk out of the interrogation room I hear Wesley spit, I look behind me to see that he was much too close to hitting his mark, me. Luckily, he decided to try it after I'd gotten up, or else it would have gotten on me, rather than the two paces behind me.

The look on Bentley's face is one of murder. I walk out of the room to Bentley fuming; hands balled up into fists on either side of him. He looks at me, "Are you alright, Margot?"

I don't know how to answer him, because I truly don't know how I feel at this moment. "I'm not sure right now, ask me later,"

Bentley looks at me with a face that is angry with Wesley, but sad for me at the same time. He quickly brushes past me to head into the interrogation room. This isn't going to be good. Thankfully Hudson isn't here because it would likely be ten times worse. Bentley barges into the room and rips the chair out from underneath Wesley, leaving him to fall onto the floor with a hard thud.

"Alright, Wesley. I'm tired of treating you with any kind of respect. You are a traitor, and we're done treating you like you're an innocent pawn in all of this." Lee smiles at me, only half of his mouth turning up with pure mischief and knowing in his eyes. Bentley lands a blow to the side of Wesley's face, leaving him spitting out blood. I gasp, I can't believe what I'm seeing. I've seen Bentley get angry, but never to the point of physically attacking someone who's not on the battlefield. I look to Lee who doesn't seem surprised. *Has this happened before?* Lee only smiles at me with a knowing smile. Wait. Does he know about Bentley and I? Is that why Bentley is attacking him, and Lee's allowing it to happen without interference, or is this truly his normal behavior in these situations?

Bentley sits Wesley back in his chair, who crumples immediately, and takes the seat across from him. Blood still drips from Wesley's mouth as Bentley begins his questioning. "Wesley, we need answers and you're going to give them to us or things are only going to get worse for you." Wesley sits in defiant silence while staring off into the distance, Bentley stands up and throws his own chair on the way out of the room.

Once Bentley is in the hallway all that I want to do is hug him. To hug away his frustration and have him hug away my hurt. What Wesley said is starting to get to me. Once again, Lee and Bentley lead Wesley back into his cell, not bothering to clean him up. The three of us head back to our area to find Emma Leigh leading a team meeting. While we were gone, her and Felix had been working on trying to find out who might be traitors within our building. Surprisingly they've turned up six different names so far. I can't believe it. Six people, in addition to Wesley, had decided to turn on our division; and this is just people that we have found so far. How many more are there?

We'd only been in interrogation for about an hour, but during that time Emma Leigh had been able to make a fake profile on a South supporter site and make *connections* with six people in the military that are traitors and ready to leave The East to support The South. Emma Leigh had asked each one for more information about the movement and what she could do to get involved. Each of the people that she had gotten into contact with had given her some type of information, whether that be that they were new and waiting for their assignment or that they had already received their assignments.

So far none of the assignments that Emma Leigh has been told about are to the extent of Wesley's. For the most part the assignments are simple things like giving the times of when certain people enter or leave the building, or if there are any major events coming up. It almost sounds like they are trying to plan another break-in, or worse an attack. The traitors among us are in a variety of positions: laundry, dining, housekeeping, even one in our Reserve unit. Very quickly we split up and head to round up all of the traitors and bring them to lockup. All of them are surprised and try to act as though they've done nothing wrong, but Emma Leigh's investigation shows otherwise.

Through all of this, though, Emma Leigh still seems to be distant and isn't acting like herself, she seems much more turned into herself than usual. I still can't put a finger on it, but something is definitely up with her. Once everyone has been put into lockup we all head back to our area to grab something to eat and relax from our already busy morning. As we finish our meals the Beta team surprises us by walking through our door: Kathrin, Terry, and Roy. It's not typical for other departments to show up unannounced, but I guess since the hack anything goes.

Kathrin greets all of us, she seems to have become the leader of their smaller team. "Hi everyone! Busy morning?" Lee lets out a laugh that's borderline maniacal.

He stops laughing long enough to answer Kathrin, "Busy morning, busy month. But who's counting?" He looks like he's hit the point of exhaustion where he either makes jokes about it or completely loses it.

"What's been going down here with you all? Catch us up!" The Beta team must have been slow for a while since Kathrin was looking to hear our stories, eager to hear something interesting. The Beta Team is composed of all new people due to promotions and retirements, so all of their tasks lately are likely routine to build their team bond.

I look to Kathrin, "Where to start? We had the break-in, and since then we've been hunting leads about it, while trying to train our team. We have Wesley in lockup right now, but he's not willing to give any of us any additional information, since our first interrogation with him. Victoria is in there as well, along with six additional traitors. If Wesley would just give us a little more information, we might be able to get a little further, but right now we're at a standstill." I clench my jaw with frustration, several others around the table share similar looks. Bentley gives me a side eye, as though to remind me to keep quiet, but I didn't say anything she wouldn't already know. Besides, it's basic information, I'm not giving away details or plans.

Kathrin smiles, "Well, we've been working on some different specialty training and mine has been in psychology. If you'd like I could try taking a crack at him." Kathrin looks eager to prove herself, and at this point what do we have to lose? We haven't gotten anywhere with him, so if she doesn't either, nothing is lost.

I shrug with defeat. *What's there to lose?* "Alright, Kathrin, you're up."

"Please, call me Kitty." She smiles with excitement, although I think the true smile she wants to wear is hidden, trying to play it cool. "We can head there now if you want, we have time." *Kitty, I like that. A good nickname for a girl like her, she is very much like a cat. She has beautiful hair and eyes which lures you in, all for her to be able to use her claws to attack.*

Everyone, except for Emma Leigh, heads over to watch the interrogation and see if Kitty can work some magic. Once again Lee and Bentley bring Wesley into the interrogation room. Bentley is not as gentle with him as he had been the previous times, basically dragging Wesley into the room and chaining him to the floor once he's been sat down. He's starting to bruise from his earlier encounter with Bentley and there's still some dried blood on him.

Lee and Bentley leave the room and Kitty heads in with Terry following behind her. The differences between them are many, if Kitty is similar to a cat, then Terry is similar to a large grizzly bear. Side by side you can see just how different they are. Kitty is smaller and agile, while Terry looks like he could tear you limb from limb without putting forth much effort. He towers over Kitty, but beneath his hard exterior there is definitely a gentle man inside, I can tell based on how he is treating Kitty, taking care of her like an older brother would. His actions towards her reminds me of the relationship between Hudson and I.

Kitty immediately initiates conversation with Wesley, "Wesley, I'm Kathrin but you can call me Kitty if you'd like. I understand that you're in here because you're accused of being a traitor. Is that what you are?" Her voice is sweet and light, in a tone that you'd use with a small child. Nothing like the sweet voice Auriella uses when trying to seduce someone into doing what she wants.

Wesley looks up, I don't think any of us have gone at him from this angle. "I am."

"Wesley, what made you choose this path? Was it your family? Are they along with you in this?" Somehow Kitty is getting through to him, maybe it is in the way she speaks. She has a way about her that makes me want to spill everything that I am thinking and feeling, and she isn't even talking to me.

"I chose this because I was angry. *She-*" Wesley turns towards the tinted glass that I'm standing behind and shoots daggers at me, pointing in my direction, but hindered by his shackles. "Yeah, I know you're out there watching me again. *She* wouldn't let me be a part of the team, so I was out to find people who would." This is something that we already knew, but he is giving it up to her so easily.

"I understand, Wesley. Anger can drive us to do a lot of things, even things that we might not normally do. Now, is there anything else that you're able to tell us?" She rests her chin on her hand. "Do you have any additional names that you can give us? What about future plans for The Trio and The South? Do you have any knowledge about that?" Kitty sits across from Wesley, patiently waiting for an answer. All the while, Terry looms over her with his arms crossed, like he's daring Wesley to slip up so that he can deal with the traitor himself.

"I didn't get much information from them, but I know that whatever is coming next is going to be big. They're ramping up their recruiting efforts, trying to get as many people as they can before launching their next attack." He starts spewing information like it's a poison that he desperately needs out of his body, "They're hoping to get as many people to change sides as possible, decreasing the other military's sizes by taking those people and adding them to their own military." His changes to a more dark and serious tone than before, "They are hungry for this and ready to do anything necessary to make sure that they can take control of the other divisions. Nothing that any of you do is going to stop them."

It's astonishing how quickly Wesley is to give up information to Kitty and how much of it he's giving her. He seems to be telling the truth too, which is both good and bad. Good, because we have more information. Bad, because our problem is even bigger than we realized. This war is coming and it is coming fast. As I've been lost in thought I missed the ending to Kitty's conversation with Wesley, she is now standing ready to leave the room.

"Wesley," she extends her hand to touch his, "it was a pleasure to get to speak to you and I appreciate your honesty. I will contact your family to let them know that you're safe, but that you won't be coming home for a while." Wesley nods his head and succumbs to all of the emotions that he's been holding in since his capture, turning into a puddle of emotion, crying out anything he may have drank today. He is completely broken.

Kitty and Terry come out and join the rest of us, everyone is patting her on the back. Each of them is just as impressed as I am by her ability to get him to open up. I speak for us all, "Thank you for that, Kitty, none of us have had much luck getting him to open up." Kitty is beaming, this must be her first big '*good job*' that she's gotten here. She earned it, I am certain that her skills will continue to come in handy throughout this war.

"Anytime, Margot. I'll take care of contacting Wesley's family now. If your team ever needs our services again, don't hesitate to reach out." Kitty shoots a wink towards Felix and makes her way back to their offices, followed by Terry and Roy. Another female leader being here makes my heart happy. In The South this is something that isn't allowed, yet another thing for us to fight for. Bentley and Lee take Wesley back to his cell and we all head back to our area. Everyone heads off to their own departments, but I still haven't seen any sign of Emma Leigh. I head back into my office and sit on my couch, Jethro is still curled up in his bed, enjoying his time at Headquarters.

My door opens and I jump up, luckily, it's Bentley so I'm able to sit back down and relax again. His face has an expression on it that I can't quite read. He looks upset but also relieved. He shuts the door behind him, a *bold move,* quickly crossing the room and plopping himself onto the couch next to me. Before I can react Bentley scoops me onto his lap and holds me as close as he can get me, his head nuzzling into my neck. His breathing is slow, yet sharp, like he is trying to stop himself from completely losing it. I quickly grab him back, looping my hands around the back of his neck, anxious to feel him in my hands, clinging to him like a last hope after everything that I've been through today.

Bentley pulls back and stares into my eyes, giving me one long kiss before pulling back again and setting me back on the couch next to him. "I'm sorry, I couldn't help myself. After the day we've had, I needed something good." He rests his hand on my thigh, the warmth that I feel coming from his hand brings me back to earth.

"Well, I'm glad I could help. Today was rough to say the least. I even saw a side of you that I've never seen before…" I don't know what else to say on the matter. Was I scared of Bentley at that moment, seeing him like that? No, but I also didn't love seeing him so angry. I feel like an idiot bringing it up and ruining this moment.

He sighs, "I'm sorry you had to see that side of me, Margot. I lost it seeing him treat you like that. Someone like you doesn't deserve to be treated that way. I care about you way too much to allow someone to act like that towards you." Bentley pulls his hand away, maybe he thinks that I'm scared of him? I grab his hand back so that he knows that him pulling away is the last thing that I want.

"Bentley, I appreciate it, I'd just never seen that side of you. But Lee didn't seem to respond at all to your reaction. Is this something that he's seen you do before? Or uh, does he know about the two of us?" Bentley takes a moment to come up with his answer.

"I'm not really sure, Margot. I mean, he and I are often partners and he's seen the way that I handle interrogations. Usually the way we play it is that he's the nice guy and I'm…not." He begins to run his fingers through his hair, "I haven't lost it like that in a while, but he most likely thinks that it was a part of my interrogation tactic. Although, he may have been thinking that there was a little more to it." He shrugs, "We've been best friends since we could walk, so I think he knows me too well to see through any lie that I might tell him. But don't worry I won't say anything to him, even if he asks. It's no one's business but ours." Bentley squeezes my hand.

One day I will get to share with the world how I feel about him, but right now it's best that we keep this to ourselves so that everyone can focus on the war that lies in front of us. I lay my head on Bentley's shoulder and can feel myself drifting off, I let it happen. I still can't figure out how we got here. Not just Bentley and I, but the state of our military, and this impending war. I wake from my impromptu nap on the couch by myself, I feel groggy and unsure how long I've been asleep for. I reach for my phone to check the time, luckily I haven't been asleep too long, but obviously my body needed that rest. My eyes finally adjust to see the small text that is a message from Bentley.

Bentley Adler
Wish I could have stayed with you but I think our cover would be blown if someone came in to us sleeping on the couch. Heading to the shop to work on my car...feel free to join me when you're up.

A small smile spreads across my face. Bentley is a great man, and I am lucky that we're getting this time together now before all hell breaks loose.

Luckily the rest of our night goes without incident, and we all walk out together at the end of the day, laughing and joking as though we aren't staring into the ugly face of an approaching war. Emma Leigh finally makes an appearance after being gone all day, she seems to be acting *normal*, but I still have this feeling that something is up with her.

CHAPTER FIFTEEN
BREATHER

I t's hard to believe that it's already been over a month since the break-in and we arrested Wesley, along with several other traitors. Things have been quiet, which is nice, but has also left everyone on edge at all times, like something bad is going to happen at any moment. Luckily Hudson stopped spending every night with me at my apartment, which was a small relief during these crazy times where everything is always changing. Everyone is still going places with a buddy, meaning that each morning someone picks me up and each evening someone drops me off. Bentley offered to be my morning walking buddy with Jethro, with the claim that he is the best morning person compared to the rest. No one argued with him, because who else would offer themselves up to get up early every day of the week to take the dog and his human out. Even Lee, who loves mornings, wasn't willing to give up so much of his personal time, which is understandable.

Of course, I still have mornings when all I want to do is let Jethro out on the patio, but those days are far and few between now because walking means I get to spend some additional alone time with Bentley. There are mornings where we can't walk due to weather or choose not to because we're too tired, but Bentley still comes over, and we enjoy breakfast and conversation together on the patio before heading to work for the day. This morning is one of those mornings where both of us are okay with sitting on the patio, rather than walking. It is drizzling and cold, being outside too long chills you to the bone.

Things with Bentley and I have been progressing, and I feel that if we weren't waiting for an impending war that things could actually be a normal relationship between the two of us. A couple who goes out on real dates and gets to share their happiness with those closest to them. Maybe one day, but for now I have to keep everything to myself.

"Margot? You there?" I'm not sure how long we've been sitting in silence with me in my own head, but Bentley's voice quickly draws me out.

"Mmm? Yeah, I'm alright. Just tired." *Not a complete lie, but enough of a truth to keep me from having to talk about what I'm truly feeling.* I don't want to burden him with my silly thoughts.

"Alright, you just seem a bit distant this morning, like you're in a whole other world." *Yes, a world where I'm not afraid to admit to myself how I feel about you. A world where I can be with you and things don't have to be a secret. Where I'm worried about the normal things that come with a relationship, rather than having a relationship in the middle of a war and someone using that against us or something terrible happening to you.*

"Oh, no. Just thinking about things with Emma Leigh, I guess. Things have been weird with her lately, don't you think?" *Hopefully this will be enough to get his attention off of me and my feelings.*

"In what way do you mean? I know she's been really busy with her work." Bentley stares at me, studying my reaction, like he's trying to hear words that weren't said.

I look down at my hands, "No, I-I know that. But haven't you noticed that she's *always* disappearing off on her own and not interested in doing anything with the team. It's been happening ever since the break-in."

"Do you think that she had something to do with the break-in?" Bentley looks shocked.

"No, I'm not saying that I'm just saying that something with her is definitely off and she's not telling us about it. It just so happens that it coincides with the timing of the break-in."

Bentley takes a moment to gather his thoughts on the matter; he's quickly running his hands through his hair. He looks almost as though he's trying to imagine any interaction that he's had with her since then, to see if he can remember anything being off with her. She's always been independent, but this is more than usual.

"You know, now that I think about it, she hasn't been willing to work with me on anything new. I've been taking everything that I'm interested in inventing to Felix and Auriella, Emma Leigh seems like she can't be bothered with things right now." Bentley stands to head inside, "Usually she'd be all over helping me come up with something new. I'll try and have a talk with her today to see what's been going on with her." He grabs my face, as I remain in my chair, kissing me with a passion that makes me not want to leave the house today.

We get up and head off to Headquarters. Headquarters seems quiet today, which isn't a bad thing. Hopefully it means that I'll be able to catch up on some housekeeping items that I have been putting off for a while. I hope Bentley's conversation with Emma Leigh yields some kind of results, but I'm not going to hold my breath on it. Emma Leigh is our friend, but she had been closest to Lena. She took The Trio's betrayal just as hard as Hudson did due to his close friendship with Ryan. Here I am hoping that Emma Leigh will open up to Bentley, while I can't even find the courage to do so.

Bentley and I go our separate ways; I begin to look for Theo and Bentley heads off in the direction of Emma Leigh, obviously he isn't wasting any time on having this chat. With today being pretty quiet, and no planned meetings, I decide to take Theo down to our archives room to go through old plans that we have laying around and see if any of them could benefit us in the war. Theo has quickly become the recruit that I rely on the most. We are very similar to one another, which means that I know I can give him a task, or have him help me with one, and not worry about whether or not the job is going to be done to my standards.

He's so enthusiastic about every task, so eager to please. "So, Margot, how old are these plans that we're going through?"

I've never really paid attention to the dates; I always just get what I need and keep going. As long as the plan does what it needs to do, it doesn't matter what year it was created. Rather than having them organized by date they are organized by the tactic style or terrain type, like water or ambush. "Honestly, Theo, I'm unsure. I would say probably back to when The Great Divide happened, maybe a little after that, around the time The East was officially established and had to start defending itself."

Apparently this is a good enough answer for Theo because he goes back to looking through the plans without further questions. It isn't until Theo finds one that was written by his great-great-grandfather that he speaks again. "Wow, this one goes back four generations, pretty close to the beginning of The Great Divide. I wonder if there are any older ones, pre-divide." Theo is now on a mission to find the oldest set of plans that he can. I let him, because you never know how or when you might come across a great idea. I continue not saying much, just like I hadn't this morning with Bentley; and just like Bentley, Theo notices.

"Hey Margot, you good? You're awfully quiet."

Again, I don't know how to answer. With Theo I can't tell him what I'm thinking about Emma Leigh, besides Bentley is already on that case. I can't tell Theo exactly what I'm feeling either, because that would mean telling him about Bentley and I, which is a no go. Besides, saying things aloud only makes them more real and I'm not ready to confront these feelings yet alone, especially not with another person. I don't need anyone thinking that I'm weak. Something about Theo though, a lot like Kitty, makes me feel comfortable spilling out everything that I'm feeling. I guess I can tell him the quick version and leave out the bits about Bentley.

"I'm feeling a bit overwhelmed by the thought of the war coming on. We already lost three people due to treason and I'm not ready to potentially lose more people that I care about." I quickly add, "Don't repeat this to anyone though, please, I don't need them thinking that their fearless leader is weak." The moment I stop speaking I regret having said anything. I can't help but stare at my feet, avoiding any eye contact with Theo.

"Margot, having feelings and being afraid doesn't make you weak. Having feelings and not expressing them can make you weak though. It's like trying to carry water in a bucket that has holes in it, you're going to need help to cover the holes so none of the water leaks out. No one can help you if you don't tell them that you're in need of help or ask for it." *Wow.*

"You know, you're right. And you know what else? You're pretty wise for just having gone through Graduation."

"Thanks. That's actually something that I learned from my Dad when I was younger." He half smiles, rubbing the back of his neck as he zones out for the briefest moment, as though he's replaying a memory of his father in his mind, "He told us about a soldier that never wanted to ask for help. One day he decided that he was going to take on a large mission, during a battle, by himself. He never came back, later they found bits of him. It's assumed that he was attacked by someone from the opposing side and then left to be scavenged by the wild animals." I shudder at the thought of this. Not only being attacked and murdered, but to then have my body attacked by wild animals, no one knowing what had happened to me for weeks. I take a deep breath to steady myself from the thought.

"That's a lot to think about."

"Yeah, ever since my Dad told me about it it's been something that's stayed with me. Definitely a graphic story to tell a five-year-old." As much as I try I can't hold in my laugh at the way Theo says this, and the image of a tiny Theo being horrified at the story his father was telling him. Luckily, Theo laughs too.

"Thanks, Theo. I think you're right. I'm going to run out for a bit, but I'll be back later, and we can work on this a little more." I run out a lot quicker than I should, but I have the courage now to talk to Bentley, so I better get it done while I have the guts. It doesn't take me long to find Bentley. He's working under one of our cars that we're going to need for the war. Bentley doesn't notice that I've come in and since no one else is here with him I decide to grab a creeper and slide under the car too. Bentley doesn't flinch when I roll up alongside him, like this is a common occurrence in his garage.

"Hiya, Margot. What brings you under here?" Bentley is covered in oil and other car filth, but his smile shines through it all.

"I lied to you this morning. Well, not exactly a lie, but an omission." I wait to see if he's going to tell me that he's upset with me or anything like that. Nothing. I'm still getting used to this kind of treatment from a man, where I can speak my mind without being immediately put down.

"Go on." He puts his tools down to give me his full attention.

"Well…this morning when you asked me about being in my own world, I wasn't only thinking about the Emma Leigh thing. I was thinking about the war and us." I look away from him, hoping it'll make this easier, focusing on the underside of the car he's working on. "It's really frustrating that we couldn't have come to this realization about each other sooner, given ourselves more time before this war starts. I know that we have bigger things to worry about, but I also feel frustrated that I have to keep everything with you a secret." I can't stop myself; everything spills out. Bentley is still smiling, as I lay there red with embarrassment. Being vulnerable is difficult and strikes fear within me. It opens you up to more feelings and a bigger possibility of being hurt, that's the most terrifying part of it all. Bentley reaches for my hand, but recoils realizing that his hands are caked in oil and grease; I grab his hand, so he knows that I don't mind. I'm not giving up a moment to feel close to him over a little grime, this is why we have soap.

"Margot, I promise you that once this is all over we can tell the world. I want people to know too, I know you don't want anyone to get hurt because they're distracted by us, and that's fine I can continue our secret for the time being. I don't want to do anything that would make you uncomfortable. Thank you for talking to me though, I promise everything with us will be okay." Bentley brings my hand to his lips and places a quick kiss on it before pushing my creeper out from underneath the car. I laugh the whole way out, partially because I'm relieved and in part because he caught me off guard. This conversation went a lot better than expected. I see myself out of the garage and find myself wandering aimlessly around the halls when I realize the time, lunch. I choose to take the long way to the cafeteria and back to our area, hoping for another chance for my mind to drift further away from anything related to work.

Today is a nice change, lately I've been feeling like I'm in a rut. During the week it's wake up, go to work, come home, eat and go to sleep. The weekends are no better, the time that I would normally spend at work is spent working on plans that I didn't have time to get to during the week and catching up on household chores. I'm sure everyone else is feeling this way too. Once I reach our area I sit down at the table near Bentley to eat my lunch. I decide that now is as good a time as any to open up about the rut I'm feeling to

Bentley as well, since I'm already on a roll with letting it all out today. Of course, he's nothing but supportive.

"I think you're right, Margot. The whole team could probably use a break from it all. Why don't we go to the ziplining course as a team? There are a couple rope courses that take you up, so that you can zipline down." Bentley's idea is brilliant. We tell the team, and everyone quickly agrees to go, even though Emma Leigh is hesitant about it. We decided to cut the day short and head over immediately, considering it off campus training.

There aren't many places left like this. Our culture is focused so much on preventing war and preparing for it that there isn't a lot of attention on leisure activities. We do have a few though, like this ropes course place and restaurants with pool tables. There's even an old arcade that used to be really popular before it was closed. There are a few games in there that still work, you just have to bring your own mechanic along to get them powered up and running. I'll never forget the first time that Bentley took us there and showed us that he was able to get some of them working. We stayed for hours playing and laughing. It became something we would do once a week, bringing a pizza and playing for hours. A smile grows across my face as I replay the memory in my mind.

Everyone is buzzing once we arrive, clearly, we are all needing a break from reality. As we begin climbing the first course I notice that Felix is lagging behind, still on the ground. "Felix? You coming?"

"Uh...would now be a bad time to tell you guys that I'm terrified of heights?" Auriella erupts into laughter, like she's been holding it in this whole time. I'd probably do the same thing if it was Hudson stuck on the ground. But since it's not Hudson stuck and Felix is my teammate, I climb down to try and give him a pep talk to get him moving.

"Felix, come on, we're all here with you. We will make sure that nothing happens to you. Plus, you have to try at least, you never know if we're going to have to do something like this while in battle. Better to do it now when we can take our time and not when someone's life is on the line." Felix says nothing, just nods his head to me vigorously. I can already see the sweat beading up on his forehead, he is not going to enjoy this. I feel terrible that we chose an outing that's a fear for someone, but it's better that we found out his fear before we get out on the battlefield.

Felix finally makes his way to the top of the first climb, not without a little harassment from Auriella and the other guys. He's covered in sweat and shaking once he gets to the platform. I put an arm around Felix, "Proud of you, kid. Now, only nine more courses to get through until the end." Poor Felix, his face goes a little green and a groan escapes him.

As the afternoon goes on Felix seems to be becoming more comfortable. Everyone is laughing and having a good time with one another. Emma Leigh hasn't said much the entire time though, I wonder if Bentley had his conversation with her already. Auriella seems to be enjoying it the most, with every zipline she spreads her arms and legs as though she's flying or freefalling. Her hair, in braids, whipping through the wind. The whole way down she's screaming and giggling to the point where the rest of us can't help but laugh along with her, it's infectious. It feels good to laugh with everyone. Once a group of mostly strangers, now friends.

Once we finish with the course, we sit together at the picnic tables enjoying snacks, at this moment I realize how badly my cheeks hurt from smiling so big and laughing so much. *Thank you, Bentley, for coming up with this idea.* We all needed this break today, preparing for a war and constantly being on edge, not knowing when it's going to happen weighs heavily on a person.

As I look around, everyone is smiling and laughing, enjoying conversation and sharing snacks. Emma Leigh is at least contributing to the conversation now, but she still doesn't seem happy about it. I decide that it's time for me to try and engage her and see if that helps any. "Hey, Emma Leigh, did you have fun? Maybe get any ideas for new inventions being out here?"

Emma Leigh looks up at me from her sandwich, seemingly bothered that I interrupted her eating. She replies with a short and curt, "No." and returns to eating her sandwich as though it is more important than anything else. Bentley and I catch each other's eyes and share a concerned look. Something is going on with Emma Leigh, and we need to find out what is going on with her before it turns into something too difficult to handle and deal with.

Before I get the chance to ask any additional questions to Emma Leigh, Felix interjects himself into the conversation, "You know, Margot, I've come up with a few ideas thanks to the terrifying day that you guys planned for us." Our entire table bursts out into a symphony of laughter startling a nearby bird, at least Felix is willing to make jokes about himself now. Good for him, beat the others to the punch and they can't use it against you.

I give up on my conversation with Emma Leigh and throw Felix a bone. "Alright, Felix, what are the ideas?"

"Well, even though I hated it, ziplines could actually come in handy for us while in battle. Think about it, there could be times that we're stuck in a high place and have no way to get down. Sure, if we're up on a cliff we could scale down, but that would take a fair amount of time." He looks towards the trees' canopies and shudders sightly, "My thought is that I could design some kind of drone that I could fly to the ground that would stake the other end of the line in the ground and then we would be able to zip down a lot faster than scaling down the side of a cliff." Everyone takes a moment to think about the idea that Felix has just proposed.

Hudson is the first to speak up, "It sounds great in theory, but then you're also carrying around a drone with you in the field. And, what about the enemy cutting our lines? Then you're mid zipline and fall possibly to your death."

Felix doesn't miss a beat to defend himself and his idea, "If someone cuts your line as you're scaling the side of a cliff you're likely to fall to your death as well. It's no different, but if the zipline doesn't run into any issues with enemies then everyone is to the ground faster and you waste less time than you would scaling." There's a hint of irritation in his voice.

It is a nice change of pace to see someone challenging Hudson right back. So often people will immediately fall back when Hudson challenges their idea, due to his size or status, or both. At this moment I am proud of Felix for standing up for himself and his ideas. He's given me so many reasons to be proud of him today. I'm glad that he's really starting to hold his own on our team. The look on Hudson's face when someone stops him from walking all over them is oh so satisfying. It's good for him to be checked every so often, you can't be a great leader when you set yourself on a pedestal far above everyone else.

Hudson knows he was wrong to shut Felix down so quickly, I can hear it in his voice as he continues speaking with Felix, "Good point, Felix. I guess if we're screwed we're screwed, but if we're able to get down faster when we already have a lead it could maximize the lead we would already have. Add that to your list of things to do once we're back." He pauses.

Felix smiles, as does Auriella. They have an interesting relationship built on a lot of teasing, but I can tell that they truly care about each other. Just a few minutes ago she was laughing at her brother's expense, now Auriella is beaming with pride for her brother. In fact, everyone seems to be proud of him and his idea. This really could be a game changer if he's able to make it work how he's imagined. After this we all wrap up our food and trash and start to head out. I drove alone, so that Jethro could nap in my car while we were at the course. Luckily my car has a function that allows me to keep the air on for him at the perfect temperature and monitor it from my phone when I can't be there, a gift from Bentley last year. It's perfect for days like these, and he doesn't mind the opportunity for an uninterrupted nap.

As I drive home I am alone with my thoughts, what a day today has been. I am thankful for the new members of our team; they've brought something to the table that our team has been lacking. New ideas. The day started with Theo giving me the idea of how to handle my relationship with Bentley, without knowing for certain what I was talking about. He is pretty skilled when it comes to handling people, this is something that we could utilize, especially if we team him up with Kitty.

Then, there was Felix's performance today. He was terrified and yet he still managed to get out there and enjoy himself. Not only enjoying himself but using this experience to his advantage to invent something that might be able to help us when it comes to battle. He kept a positive attitude the entire day, which inspired me.

Lately I've been so down in the dumps about everything going on. Thinking about how unfair it is that this war has decided to crop up right when I realize there are some deeper feelings lingering near the surface for the guy who's been my friend for as long as I can remember. Thinking about how I wish that I had more time to read or just do nothing. I have to stop thinking like this. It's about time I become a lotus flower, growing out of the mud. Today

I start living with a more positive mindset. I need to grow through everything that we're going through; take a page out of Felix's book and use something that might be bringing me down and turn it into something positive.

CHAPTER SIXTEEN
PLANNING

Even a week later everyone seems to be doing a lot better, more relaxed and better able to focus after going to the rope climbing course. I know I can feel the difference in myself. I can tell especially when I lay down at night for bed, before I was struggling to fall asleep, thinking about all that was going on, but now I am able to fall asleep quickly. Tonight is like any other night in the last week; the moment my head hits the pillow I pass out. But this time I am transported to another world, one that looks familiar to mine, but everything seems wrong.

Before I can register anything in this world, I wake myself up, screaming. I can't remember anything from my dream, except that Ryan was attacking me. Blurry eyed I make out the time on my phone screen, it's almost time for Bentley to get here to walk Jethro. I head to the door to await Bentley's arrival, opening it after a single knock. The moment Bentley is inside my apartment I cling onto him searching for his warmth to ground me. Hoping that his touch will replace the phantom hands that I continue to feel attacking me even while I'm awake thanks to the dream that felt so real. Bentley doesn't say anything at first, he holds onto me tightly, sensing that I need this.

He whispers into my hair, "What's going on Margot?"

I speak into his chest, "I can't really remember what happened, but I had a nightmare and all I can remember is Ryan attacking me and I woke up screaming." I look up at him as Bentley looks down at me with anger and sadness. *Should I have told him? Is he upset that I still dream about someone from my past, even though they are nightmares?* I choke out a whisper, "Bentley?"

Bentley runs a hand through his hair in an aggressive manner while keeping the other on the small of my back, then shakes off whatever it is that he's thinking about and pulls me back into an embrace. It's warm here and he always has a smell about him, like a mix of salt water and smells from his garage, a combination of gasoline and heated metal from welding together his latest project. Everything about this makes me feel so comfortable and at peace. "I'm sorry Margot, I needed a moment. I can't stand how much pain he's caused you and how much pain he's still causing you. You should have never been treated so poorly, and he shouldn't be targeting you now." I feel his hands on my back turn into fists.

Bentley's changed so much since I first met him. He used to be full of jokes all the time, never taking anything too seriously. Now he is older, more mature. Still full of jokes, but he's also had time to develop his emotional side and embrace it. I appreciate both sides of him, like a sweet and salty snack. I take his face in my hands, skimming his cheek bones with my thumbs, "Thank you, Bentley. I'm truly okay. Getting better all the time, and I'm glad that I have you now, so I don't have to go through this alone." I move to fix his hair that he ruffled in frustration, "The rope course helped a lot, but I still find myself worrying about the war quite often. I can't help it, no matter how hard I try." I say into his chest.

Bentley continues holding onto me, now smoothing the back of my hair while his chin rests on the top of my head. I'm not sure how long we stay like this, but it is long enough for Jethro to take notice. Our moment is interrupted by Jethro whining and patting me with his paw, he must really need to get outside. Both Bentley and I give Jethro a pat on the head as an apology. We quickly get him geared up and head outside for our walk. This morning is brisk, but not unbearable, a reminder that winter is right around the corner. I figure now is the perfect time to ask Bentley about his conversation with Emma Leigh and how it went. I don't want to nag him about it, but it's been long enough.

As we make our way toward Jethro's favorite spot, I play different ways to bring up this conversation and the different outcomes that may come of it in my head. Rehearsing, as though I might actually be able to get out the words that I am thinking. Being a military leader comes easy to me, coming up with what to say in those instances too. Something about conversations in my personal life though, those are the conversations that I struggle with. I always go into it thinking about what I'm going to say, and once I start talking I promptly stick my foot in my mouth. Without fail after the fact I always think of things that would have been better to say.

"So, Bentley. Have you been able to have your conversation with Emma Leigh to see what's been going on with her lately? She still seems to be in a funk, even after the team outing, when everyone else seems to be doing a lot better. Though, no one had been acting as distant as her before the rope course."

I look at Bentley out of the corner of my eye to see if his face will give anything away before he begins speaking. Bentley takes longer than expected to answer. "I did."

That's it? No explanation of what the conversation entailed? Just that he did have the conversation? This conversation already feels like it's going to be a challenge.

"Well? How did it go?" Again, I give a sideways glance at Bentley to see if his face is going to let anything slip. Still, really nothing, he's mindlessly watching Jethro sniff around while running his fingers through his hair again. Either he's about to weave a web of lies or he really doesn't like the answer that he's going to have to give me. I try to prompt him, but I'm so nervous that it comes out as a whisper, "Bentley, please?"

"Sorry Margot, I was trying to figure out how to say it. I did talk to Emma Leigh, but she didn't really say anything of importance. Something that she said to me during the conversation has stuck with me though." He breathes deep as though taking a moment to fully remember the conversation, "She mentioned that she's just different from all of us, so that it's expected that she'd be an outcast among us." *An outcast?* "I don't know about you, but I've never thought that about our relationship with Emma Leigh. In my opinion she's always been really close with us until right around the time The Trio left, but it's gotten worse since the break-in."

The more I think about it the more I realize that Emma Leigh *has* always been a little in her head, always focusing on her gadgets. There were times though that she came out of her shell, like the night after selecting our new team when we all went to dinner at Bentley's parents' house. I remember laughing with her and feeling like things were going to be different with her this year. I guess I was wrong. She's always been our quiet friend, and that doesn't bother us.

"Bentley, I hate to ask this. I'm only asking because I have to." He looks nervous about what my next question is going to be. I speak quickly before I lose my nerve, "Do you think that Emma Leigh could possibly be associated with any of the traitors? She's been more distant than ever before and pulling away from us. This is different from her just being in her head thinking about new inventions, she's actively pulling away from us. It makes you think..."

Bentley looks at me like I just kicked his dog. Like me asking him if Emma Leigh could possibly be a traitor is a personal dig against him. *Is there some kind of history between them?* I shake the thought, because I don't have time at the moment to be thinking about that kind of thing. I'm sure Bentley doesn't want that to be my follow up question either. To the back of my mind it goes, eventually I will need to ask him about it or the unknown will drive me mad.

Finally, Bentley answers, "I don't know, Margot. We don't have any evidence proving otherwise, so I think for now it's best that we trust her."

Our walk now is accompanied by silence; a deafening silence that leaves me far too alone with my thoughts. I need to focus. This is exactly why I shouldn't have put myself in this situation with Bentley, I'm setting myself up to get hurt. *Shut up!* I cannot allow myself to get caught in my head. It's dangerous there, especially when I head down the rabbit hole. The silence continues as Bentley drops me at my door, and the morning continues to feel silent even heading to Headquarters.

Once we all arrive at Headquarters I make the last-minute decision to call a team meeting. It's been a while since we've had one and it will be good to catch up on everyone's progress and to see if anyone's heard any whispers lately. For the most part we tend to blend in with society, so catching the latest gossip isn't too difficult. There are also certain departments here that are chattier than others, like Renee up in Human Resources; bring her a batch of cookies and she'll tell you the latest gossip while eating the cookies with you. Some people just need a little buttering up, and then it's as though you've broken the dam.

"Good morning everyone, I know we haven't really had many formal meetings lately, but I chose to call all of us together to discuss anything that anyone may have heard lately. Before the break-in we had heard that there were sightings around town, so I'm wondering if anyone has heard anything similar lately?" Everyone is silent as they rack their brains to try and remember anything that they've heard lately. I look towards Emma Leigh, studying her. My earlier conversation with Bentley flashes through my mind.

Finally, Auriella decides to speak up, "You know I've heard a few things…" Auriella stands there, propped against the table, looking like a killer beauty; someone who could easily lure you in with her beauty and then kill you with her bare hands. The more I get to know Auriella, the more I like her. Although she's the one whose bad side I would least like to be on. In typical Auriella fashion, she stands there, twirling her hair and playing up the dramatics of leaving everyone hanging. Not a moment before I go to call out Auriella for being dramatic, a notebook flies past my head. I don't need to turn my head to know that it was Felix who threw it. Auriella jumps over the table to get to her brother, before any of us have a chance to intervene. It takes both Lee and Bentley to pull her off of Felix. *Good for her.* Maybe if I had stood up to Hudson sooner he wouldn't have continued bothering me for so long.

Auriella stands up and saunters back over to her spot at the table, as though moments ago she wasn't sitting on top of her brother whacking him in the face. She looks gorgeous, not a hair out of place. Felix on the other hand looks disheveled, every curl on his head is out of place, sticking up every which way. It looks like Auriella may have even caught Felix with a nail during their scuffle, there's a faint red line across his cheek. As much as I want to send him to the infirmary to get patched up and get some antibacterial ointment on it, I know that I can't without further bruising his ego. He's a big boy; he can handle himself. I quickly act to take the attention off of Felix.

"Auriella, what was the information that you had been hearing?" I stare at her with my arms crossed, this could have been avoided.

Auriella flips back her curls, as though mocking her brother's curls that are all over the place before speaking, "Well, I heard from Ellen who heard from Clarence, that there are people from The South here in The East. They even set up a camp and are attempting to recruit people from The East to join them." *Such a bold move by The South if this is true.*

"Anything else, Auriella?" I look around, "Has anyone else heard anything similar to what she's heard?" Everyone looks around at one another, shaking their heads. I noticed Emma Leigh staring off into the distance, towards the doors, like she wants to run out of them; or as though she's waiting for someone to come walking in, but we're not expecting anyone today, just another thing to add to the list of her odd behaviors.

"Margot?" It's Theo that pulls me from my line of thought. It's funny how such a small voice can be coming from someone that's built like a linebacker I've seen in history books.

"Yeah? Theo, what's up?" I'm struggling to focus.

"Well, it's just that I was thinking that maybe we need a bigger net." *Huh?*

Confusion is painted across my face, "Um…what do you mean, Theo?"

He's eager to share, looking elated when I ask him to explain further, "Think about it this way, we're fishing using nets, and there's only eight of us with relatively smaller nets. Sure, we have people here and there that might feed us some information, like Renee or Ellen, but that's only when they feel like doing so or we try and coax it out of them. If we had a bigger net we'd be able to catch more fish, much bigger fish."

Ah, not actual nets…I need to focus, because all I could imagine was giant nets to replace some of our security traps. I look over to Auriella to see that this bit has gone right over her head. Her mind is elsewhere, and she looks as though she's trying to figure out when we went from talking about traitors to fish, since she hasn't been focusing either. "Alright, Theo, what do you have in mind?"

Theo smiles a big toothy grin, like he's been waiting for his opportunity to make a difference. "Well, in the past whenever someone was looking for information they would turn to the public and try to find it from them. What if we release a most wanted list that includes The Trio and their photos. We can go ahead and include a photo of Wesley as well, so that they don't know we've captured him. Lead them to believe that Wesley has simply betrayed them as well." *Brilliant.*

"Alright, team, you heard the man. Let's get to work on this idea and see just how many fish we can catch."

Everyone quickly disburses and starts working. I love that there's no need for us to sit around discussing who's going to do what; we've become a cohesive team in this short amount of time. As I make my way back into my office I can already see Auriella at work with Felix setting up a phone system for people to text or call in their tips to a direct line, that doesn't affect our office lines, as though they didn't just fight in front of everyone. Emma Leigh is working on setting up a website and an email box specific for it too, she seems to have snapped back into the game.

Theo is working on printing photos for the news release and Hudson is with Lee already on the phone with the local news station to make sure that this gets out as quickly as possible. Bentley walks by my office without making an effort to look at me, even though he knows that Hudson isn't in here with me, he's holding on to the same silence from our walk. This is why I build walls up and don't allow people to get in, because when I do let people in it always ends badly. Every time I end up hurting, even though there's no reason for his actions. I wish he would talk to me about whatever's on his mind. Maybe I shouldn't have let Bentley in...

Within an hour a news crew is at Headquarters and ready to have a press conference with Hudson, and myself apparently. I don't like attention being drawn to myself, I didn't like it when I was the standout at Graduation and I don't like it now. Hudson and I get changed into our formal uniforms and make our way to the front doors of Headquarters. We decided to hold the press conference outside of Headquarters, our heavily tinted windows add an extra layer of protection, so that no one can see what we have going on inside or end up on camera.

The press conference goes without incident; we are able to quickly get the information out there and not have to give out too much information that may compromise our investigation. Not even an hour passes after the press conference, and our tip lines are overloaded with people trying to get information to us. I know that not all of the information coming in is going to be credible, but even if one in every fifty contacts turn out to be reliable, we'll still be in better shape than we had been earlier. With all of this new information coming in and The South being aware that we know that they're up to something it's time to make sure that we're prepared for this war that's going to be coming a lot sooner than any of us imagined.

Hudson is working on something at his desk as I roll my chair across our office, towards him, to bother him with what's on my mind. He looks up at me with a glare that cuts into my already wounded self, thanks to Bentley's antics today, as I bump into his chair with mine. He snarls at me, "Can I help you?"

This day is getting to him worse than I could have imagined. It probably isn't helping him having to talk about Ryan so much, having to retell the betrayal to the news. I make a mental note to talk to him about it later, I don't have the mental capacity right now to take on someone else's baggage as well. "Hudson, I think we need to have a real conversation with the team about what today's events mean in the timeline of this war. We need to discuss our next move with them and make sure that everyone's on the same page." Hudson nods his head at me in agreement, guess that's one more person not talking to me today.

I wonder if he's thinking about the war and what his role is going to look like in it? Before, a battle meant having Ryan at his side as his backup, this time it is going to mean fighting against Ryan. Hudson might even be put in the position that he has to be the one to kill him. I shake the thought. That might be too much of a burden for Hudson to bear. I try once more to engage him, "First things first, we need to get out a plan to the team and ramp up training. We need to be war ready in a matter of weeks." Again, Hudson says nothing to me and simply nods his head. I guess all of this is going to be on my shoulders, which I'm more than capable of handling, but I wish that Hudson was offering at least a little bit of help.

He trusts my judgment, so I work quickly to come up with a rough plan before lunch time. Everyone gathers for lunch, and I decide that there's not going to be a good time to discuss the next steps with them, so why not now? The whole team is still eating as I stand from my lunch and clear my throat. Bentley notices but barely looks at me. He's either hiding something or he's still frustrated with me. I have to ignore it. I don't have time for this.

"Team, after today's events and press conference it's come to our attention," I glance at Hudson, "that this war is going to be here a lot sooner than later. It is time for us to take charge and get ready for the battle of our lives. One that could completely change our way of life, and the lives of those we care about." Everyone looks around nervously, especially the new team members who have yet to see a battlefield. "Everyone will need to start getting their arrangements in order, we are going to be setting off soon, it could be in as little as a few weeks, but hopefully we have some more time than that."

Everyone is looking between myself and Hudson, trying to figure out where we're going, as Hudson looks back to me to let me finish. "Our first stop will be The District. This is going to be the first part of our mission, and something that I think our team can handle on its own. We will be heading there to scope it out and to find any possible supporters of The East…or even The South.

After this our next step will be heading to The South, to begin the war officially, if it hasn't already started."

Everyone looks fearful. Bentley is finally looking at me, he has fear in his eyes. It's almost like he's staring through me, trying to find some kind of comfort that I unfortunately do not have to give him, since I'm on edge myself. Even if I did it wouldn't be something that I could give here in front of all of these people who think we're nothing more than teammates. Even then, he's decided to be icy today ever since our conversation on our walk, so why should I be warm towards him? He can't just flip back and forth about how he's feeling about me when it's convenient for him and he needs something from me.

I force myself to start talking to the team again, I've been in my head too long. "With all of this coming we also need to vamp up our training. There are a lot of gaps in our knowledge, especially in fighting together as this team, and we need to work on that before leaving. But, for now, I think it will be best for each of us to really prep our own departments, so that we have everything ready for when it's time to go. We also want to make sure that we have as much ready as possible, quickly, in case we need to head out at a moment's notice, sooner than later."

Everyone still looks shocked from the news, but they had to have known that this was coming, especially the senior members. Still, I know that it's a lot to process. Heck, even I'm still trying to process it, "Alright, everyone, why don't we take the rest of the afternoon to catch up on things that we need to work on without any kind of formality. I think we've had more than enough meetings for the day and could use some time to ourselves. Felix, could you please run over to the Beta team and let them know what's going on? Kitty can call me if she has any additional questions. We're going to need them to hold down the fort while we're in The District." A sly half-smile grows towards one of Felix's ears and he quickly heads off to talk to Kitty. I smile to myself, I thought seeing her might brighten his spirits a little bit. At least I can make one person's day a little better. Everyone heads off in their own direction; Bentley is the last one sitting at the table. I pause for a moment and glance at him in a sort of sad way after the way he's made me feel today. I look away quickly and walk off to take some time wandering the halls to try and clear my head.

The back half of the afternoon means that the halls are empty since most people are in their offices trying to get as much work done as possible before calling it a day. I hear footsteps behind me, definitely following me. I can still hear them behind me as I turn down a hallway that's seldom used. I choose not to turn around to look at the person in case it's nothing. Today's conversation of war and knowing there are still traitors among us has me on edge. I feel my body tense up, their speed is increasing, the panic rising in me is unavoidable, not having a weapon on me either is making it worse. I see a janitor's closet up ahead and decide that, if needed, there is probably something in there that I can use as a weapon. As I get closer to the closet I slow my pace, so that I don't pass it and render myself helpless, but the person behind me is speeding up and now almost on my heels.

I don't dare look behind me, doing so could waste precious moments. As I slow my pace to slip into the closet the footsteps behind me stop as the person who's been following me spins me around to face them, placing their hand over my mouth before I have the chance to scream. My heart was racing already and now begins to pound even harder as I realize that it's Bentley who's been following me and has now subdued me. My eyes widen, terrified of what's happened. Is this why he's been treating me so poorly all afternoon? *Bentley, a traitor?* With my back pressed against the door and one hand over my mouth Bentley uses his free hand to reach around me and open the closet door behind me, pushing us both into the closet, his hand still over my mouth.

CHAPTER SEVENTEEN
TRAINING INTENSIFIES

I can't breathe. Bentley's hand isn't covering my mouth in a way that is making it so that I can't breathe. No, I can't breathe because I am in such a state of panic over the fact that I can't believe this is happening. As quickly as he grabbed me, Bentley releases me, removing his hand from my mouth and quickly replacing it with his mouth. He's kissing me quickly, like he's putting every emotion that he's ever felt behind it: anger, sadness, joy, need, hurt, fear, want…love? *No. This can't happen.*

I push Bentley off of me and slap him before I can think of any other way to react. He looks at me, hurt. I can't believe I hit him, but how could he possibly be surprised? He just stalked me down and dragged me into a closet with his hand over my mouth. He made me feel like a gazelle being hunted by a lion. What was he thinking?! He goes to lean in on me again and I push him back.

"Bentley! What the *hell* are you doing?!" He stops moving and stares at me, confused.

"Today's been a rough one, Margot. I thought that we could both use some time alone together." He looks so sad and innocent.

"So, you decided to stalk me and drag me into a closet? Are you stupid?! Had I had my weapon on me you could have been killed!" I rub my temples, trying to relax my mind.

Realization hits Bentley. Realization hits me. Bentley wasn't trying to scare me or have me hurt him, he was so caught up in emotion that he wasn't thinking. He acted purely on primal instincts. The need and desire to have another person close. To have *me* close. Everything from today has been building up and it's finally hitting the surface. I don't even try to stop the tears from spilling, Bentley begins to wipe the tears away from my face, looking nervous and apologetic that he dragged me into a closet to try and have a moment alone and it's turned into me crying. A plan with good intentions, gone horribly wrong.

He cups my face in both of his hands, still wiping away tears with his thumbs, "Margot, I am so sorry. I thought that it would be fun, a little spice to contrast this day that has done nothing but go from bad to worse…and I've now made even worse than it already was…"

Oh Bentley. I move forward and wrap my arms around his waist, resting my chin on his chest as I look up at him, "This might be the stupidest thing that you've ever done. You've been so cold to me today ever since our conversation about Emma Leigh during our walk. You've made me feel alone today, when I've really needed you."

Bentley squeezes me tightly, "Margot, I'm sorry. I needed to be alone today for a bit. I was upset after this morning's talk and didn't want to take any of my feelings out on you. I thought it would be better just to stay away." *Seriously? Horrible idea. I'd rather just fight it out.* I hate silence and not talking about the issues at hand.

"Well, please don't do that ever again…and if you're needing some time alone to cool off, let me know so that I don't have to feel like this ever again." I squeeze him back, "Oh, and add to your list of things to do next time…asking me to be alone with you rather than stalking me and dragging me into a closet." Bentley doesn't laugh out loud, but I can feel his chest bouncing under my head from his silent laughter.

Before I can say anymore Bentley is cupping my face in his hands once again and bringing it towards his. This conversation is far from over, but I need this distraction just as much as he does. I don't want this moment to end and I could spend hours here with him, ignoring all of my problems that wait outside that door. As he kisses me I feel my body melt into his. When we finally pull away from each other I'm not sure how much time has passed.

"Bentley, we can't just kiss away our problems…we do have to communicate with words too you know." Bentley smiles at me and begins kissing me again. I pull away, this time not from anger, but because I have no idea how long we've been gone. I'm sure that someone is going to notice soon that at least one of us has gone missing. We *really* don't need anyone realizing that we've gone missing together either. As though reading my mind, Bentley presses his lips to the top of my head before opening the door and making sure the coast is clear. He waves me forward and we both head back down the corridor towards our offices.

My mind is racing back and forth between moments ago in the closet with Bentley and the thought that someone could have been watching the cameras and saw us enter or leave the closet together. I am able to calm down realizing that if someone was watching the cameras, when we went in at least, they would have come running. All of us are on edge due to the thought of more traitors being on the inside. Someone watching could have easily believed that Bentley was a traitor and had completely gone off the deep end, kind of like I did for the briefest moment.

Oh well. I don't have time to worry about this now, and honestly it would probably make things a lot easier if this was just out in the open, although the initial reactions might be a bit dramatic, and I'm still not ready for that step in this relationship. We stagger our entrances back into our area, so as to not make anyone suspicious. Fortunately, the rest of the day goes on without incident. No one gives us a second look, so it seems like no one saw anything or noticed our extended absence. We all head home for the evening and I continue to replay the series of events which led me to the time spent with Bentley in the closet, wishing that our relationship could just be normal, but I'll take what I can…for now.

Especially because a part of me won't even admit to myself the feelings that I have for Bentley, out of fear, so admitting those feelings aloud to others is even more daunting. It would make this whole thing real, and real feelings cause real hurt.

The following day comes quickly, as we all enter the building it feels as though the energy has shifted. We went from being somewhat on edge to having the nerves of someone tightroping across a canyon, everyone worried about what the next steps might be and what might be thrown at us next. I decide to let everyone head off into their own directions while I float around checking in on everyone. Right away I notice that everyone has gone straight right to their comfort zones. I check in with the technology department first.

Felix and Emma Leigh are working with their computers and gadgets, while Auriella lingers nearby. As I get closer I can overhear a bit of their conversations, Emma Leigh is actually snapping at the both of them, "How about you both go find your own things to work on. I don't need the two of you hovering over me while I'm trying to get things done." Both Auriella and Felix give each other a look, in a language of unspoken words between siblings. They walk off together to find something else to keep themselves busy, obviously irritated.

This is completely out of character for Emma Leigh. Every little thing has me feeling more and more concerned about her. I guess if Bentley thinks that everything with her is fine I'll just roll with it for now, until I have some more evidence against her to bring to his attention. I take this as my cue to leave, I don't feel like starting a conversation with Emma Leigh while she's acting like this.

I head over to Bentley's garage to take my mind off of things. It's amazing how big his space is, from the outside you wouldn't think that this office building on the main downtown street could house an entire garage, it looks more like it holds cubicles from wall to wall. When this place was designed it's like they had Bentley and his cars in mind, there's even a garage door at the back of his shop which allows him to easily take his vehicles in and out.

It's like Bentley can sense my presence as I walk into his garage, he turns and his eyes immediately meet mine. He's beaming at me seemingly excited that I've made the effort to come see him. "Margot! You busy?" I quicken my pace to get closer to Bentley so that we're not shouting across the building to one another, drawing more attention to ourselves than necessary.

"Uh…kind of? What's up?" I nervously look around to see if anyone could possibly be listening in to our conversation. Bentley is smiling and swinging a set of car keys around his finger. He's up to something.

"Wanna take my newest baby for a quick spin? I need to test out some of the new gadgets that Auriella and Felix helped design and install." Bentley is always getting new vehicles to modify and personalize for himself and our team.

"Alright, but we have to be quick! I have to get back and get some work done." Bentley smiles at me and makes his way over to one of the sleekest cars I have ever seen, its exterior and interior are completely blacked out, it's gorgeous. This car looks like it *only* goes fast. Bentley throws me the keys, and I defensively smack them out of the air. Growing up with a brother constantly throwing things *at* you causes this to be a natural reaction of things being tossed in your direction. We both burst into laughter. I pick the keys up and go to get in the vehicle...*stick shift. Crap.* I never learned, especially since it's more of a historical car trait, although this car doesn't look historical at all. I guess it makes sense that Bentley would have a manual car, he loves being in control, his car is no different.

I give Bentley an embarrassed look as I walk over to the passenger side, with my head hung in shame, where he's already settled in the passenger seat, he gives me a confused look with one eyebrow raised, "What?"

"I'm not sure how to tell you this, without breaking your heart, but I have zero clue how to drive this thing..." Bentley rolls his eyes at me and gets out of the car, taking the keys from me.

"Come on, Margot...I was hoping to sit back and relax while you drove me around the division. Guess I have to do all of the work." He winks at me and heads over to the driver's side; he gets in and immediately starts the car. Like that we're off; cruising around the division without a care in the world. Bentley rests his hand on my thigh, since there are no prying eyes around, I allow it, especially since it's only a brief moment as he needs both to operate this vehicle. With the windows down I can feel the fresh air breathing life into me, I wish it could last forever because I've needed this relief. There's a crisp chill in the air reminding us that December is only days away, so the windows can't stay down long, no matter how much I'm enjoying it.

This car rides smoothly, even the bumps that we're hitting don't make any kind of impact on us inside the car. I could probably ride in this car with a bowl of soup on my lap without a worry. I smirk at the idea. Our ride has me thinking about how I don't know much of anything about the vehicles that we have in our garage. Now that I think of it, I really don't know much about anything that's outside of planning, leading, and fighting. Not that it's a bad thing to have specialties, but it's important to understand all aspects that go into fighting a war. With me being one of the leaders, I really need to set a better example.

The drive ends too quickly, leaving me wishing that the ride could have lasted all day and that there wasn't so much time left to work. I try to busy myself to make the time go quicker, by continuing my rounds, peaking in on everyone. Lee's office is next to Bentley's, so I make my way there next, before heading to the other side of the building where Hudson and Theo are working in the firing range. Lee's office is next to Hudson's gym, but Hudson has to split his time between here and the firing range across the way. Lee is working on packing up his first aid kits that will come along with us on our journey, along with several totes full of spare supplies.

As I approach Lee I notice Auriella pop out from behind a closet door, her arms full of supplies. "Auriella? What are you doing here?" She looks almost too excited to see me.

Auriella drops her supplies onto a nearby countertop without any kind of grace, Lee rolls his eyes out of frustration. Lee already doesn't like people touching his things, so her throwing them around isn't helping matters. "Well, Emma Leigh didn't want Felix or I hanging around, so I decided to see what else I could get myself into and I found myself here with Lee." Auriella smiles at Lee and he quickly turns away, clearly she is feeling happier about this arrangement than he is.

"Oh, well, are you at least making yourself useful?" Auriella nods her head vigorously, as I look to Lee to get his genuine reaction, he is shaking his head like he can't believe that he got stuck with her. I have to hold in a laugh at their polar opposite reactions. I look back to Auriella, who has the complete opposite look on her face while tinkering with the materials in front of her. The speed that she is working on her little creation is fascinating. *What is she working on?* She takes about three minutes before answering my silent question. I don't try to rush her, I can clearly see that she's up to something. She has my full attention and I'm desperate to know what she's working on.

"Finished!" Auriella holds her hand out to me. It's a little bead looking thing next to a syringe. Auriella is beaming over her little creation as I stare at her like an idiot, with zero clue as to what she is holding in her hand or why she's so excited about it. Before I realize what Auriella's doing she's loaded the bead into the syringe and injects it into herself! Both Lee and I realize too late to stop her.

"WHAT ARE YOU DOING?!" Lee screams at her while grabbing the syringe out of her hand. Auriella smiles at him and points at the computer screen that's nearby. It's now got a scan of a body on it with a blinking dot moving about the screen. *Is that...the bead?* Lee is now watching the screen with an intensity that matches Auriella's. Now he's smiling too! *What is going on?*

"Uh...earth to Auriella and Lee?" I snap my fingers with impatience, trying to get their attention. "Either of you care to explain what's going on here?" I feel a twinge of irritation, being left out. They both finally snap up from the screen, a couple of goobers with giant smiles clearly excited about whatever just happened. My expression goes blank as I wait for someone to clue me in on what's going on.

Auriella is bouncing on the balls of her feet, ready to tell me, I've never seen her so excited. "Well...Lee had been talking about the inability to control internal bleeds when we're out in the field, so I came up with this little guy." She's actually using the syringe to point at the dot on the screen. The more I see the needle flailing around, the more queasy I feel.

"Okay, I see that…but do you mind breaking this down and explaining it?" Oh man, I just said the magic words. She's practically vibrating with excitement as she launches herself into her explanation, talking almost too quickly for me to wrap my head around any of it.

"So, Lee had the problem of not being able to control internal bleeders in the field. He told me that during battle this can be a large issue. It leaves medics with a choice; whether or not to save the person, hopefully, by performing a lifesaving surgery in the field or trying to get somewhere safe and sterile first to perform the surgery while they continue to bleed out." She comes up for a quick breath before diving back in, which allows me a second to swallow down the nauseous feeling that I'm getting from seeing the needle. "Time is everything when it comes to an injury, especially one like that. I've come up with something that makes getting out of the area first and then performing the surgery an option. An option where you don't have to risk being too late to operate, but also don't have to risk operating in the middle of a battlefield, where you end up risking multiple lives."

I look to Lee who's nodding along like a puppy following a treat that's moving up and down. I can't tell if he's obsessed with this girl, her idea, or both, even though moments ago he was irritated about being stuck with her. I have to hold in a laugh as Auriella continues.

"So, this little guy," she holds up her syringe, like a proud mother, "is the solution. Using the syringe, you inject the little bead into your body, the bead can detect where major blood loss is coming from. It then travels to that area and expands, creating a barrier where the blood is coming from, by expanding to fill the tear or hole." She's back to using the syringe as a pointer on the screen, tapping the screen with it as she continues to explain. I move my focus to only the blinking ball moving around the body.

"It's also got a tracking device in it, so you're able to see on the screen exactly where the bead has traveled to. This way we can identify any organs that might be involved and decide the best course of action based on that. Once in surgery we're able to safely repair it and remove the block that the bead created. Afterwards it must be disposed of, but I'm really hoping to create something that can be used over and over again."

Now I'm wondering about how we're going to remove the one that Auriella has just put into her body that I can still see blinking around on the screen, though I think that the blinking has slowed since she started her explanation. As though she read my mind, Auriella answers my unasked question, yet again.

"Looks like you've noticed that blinky isn't so blinky anymore. This little guy can not only find bleeders, but he also can tell when there isn't one. So right now, it has determined that there isn't a bleeder that it needs to fix and will start to essentially self-destruct and dissolve in my body, causing no harm to me." *Wow.*

"So how long have you been working on this, Auriella?" She looks to Lee, who looks at his watch.

"Well, she got here about an hour-hour and a half ago? We talked before she began working...so maybe an hour or a little less?" He says this as though this kind of creation in that short amount of time is a totally normal occurrence.

"Excuse me what?! Auriella, you came up with this in just an hour?!" I high five her, I am in complete awe, "You're amazing!" I could never come up with something half as amazing in a whole year, let alone an hour. I really know nothing about technology or health, not like these two do. The more I get into this afternoon, the more I'm realizing just how narrow my scope of knowledge is.

As I make my way to our other wing where Theo and Hudson are located I replay over and over in my mind Auriella's creation. I enter our miniature library, where we keep older plans and books on war. I find Theo crouched over a large table that sits in the center of the room. Bookshelves surround the entire room, except for one corner where there's an oversized chair that I love to sneak to to read my books. The chair is currently occupied by Jethro, who looks up when I enter and gives his tail a little wag before putting his head down and going back to sleep, Theo doesn't notice me. At least here I don't feel like a fish out of water.

Theo doesn't bother to look up at me; he's engrossed in the battle plans that he's looking over. I clear my throat to alert Theo of my presence. He looks almost panicked as he shuffles the papers he's been looking over, as I walk towards him. I notice that he quickly moves the paper on the top of the stack to the bottom, out of my view. I make my way over to say hello to Jethro. Theo looks up as I pass and merely gives me a nod, making no effort to engage in conversation. I take this as a hint that he would like to be left alone. As I make my way out Jethro jumps down off the chair to follow me as I go off to find Hudson. As I leave I swear that sticking out of Theo's stack of papers he's reviewing are different pieces of evidence from the break-in. *What is he up to?*

The moment I open the door to Hudson's armory I can hear faint gunshots; he must be in the shooting range. Luckily the viewing area is pretty much soundproof, so I'm able to take Jethro with me to watch. Hudson had designed it himself to make it so that people could watch and learn without having to be in the room with him. When you're in the viewing room even the most powerful gun only sounds as though someone is knocking on the wall. I cross the room to take my seat, and I am taken aback when I see what Hudson is using for target practice. I am almost positive that it is a shredded image of Ryan.

After the thought sets in I begin laughing at the fact that Hudson has chosen to use this as his target for shooting practice today. My laughter ends abruptly, though, when I begin to think about what it's going to be like when the two of them meet face to face during the coming war. It isn't a matter of if but when. A shudder runs down my spine with the understanding that one, if not both of them, won't walk away from their encounter. Ryan, and the other traitors, are going to want to take us on personally and I'm sure that most of us on our team feel the same way about them. Things are going to get ugly, that is one of the only guarantees going into this.

I choose not to interrupt the man with a loaded weapon who is clearly angry and instead wait for him to notice me and come out to talk. Today's events have really opened my eyes when it comes to training, and as leaders this is something that Hudson and I need to improve upon. Hudson finally makes his way out to the viewing room holding on to the shredded target, which I can now confirm is in fact an oversized picture of Ryan, almost unrecognizable now with the number of holes that Hudson has put in it.

Hudson gives me a quizzical look and sits down beside Jethro to pet him; Jethro can always calm Hudson down. Jethro quickly adjusts himself so that he is sitting with his head in Hudson's lap. I guess now is as good a time as any to talk to Hudson about my findings. Even watching him handle a weapon makes me realize that I should take some time to improve my skill in this area too. I'm pretty handy with weapons, but nowhere as good as Hudson, especially not when it comes to repairing them or anything like that.

"Hudson, I spent some time today floating around between different departments and it really got me thinking about how much none of us know about other people's specialties. I watched Auriella make a new medical device in just an hour, something that I would never be able to accomplish, even if you gave me all the time in the world. I spent some time with Bentley in the garage and found that I have no idea how to drive a manual, that if it comes to that I'm screwed. I would have to rely on someone being there that knew how to drive it." I wince at the thought of having to lean on someone else to save me. What if I was the only one there...*or left?*

"This is entirely unacceptable, especially as one of the leaders of the team. I know that if you started to wander around to the different specialties that you would feel the same way I do. We both need to take the initiative to learn more about other specialties and not be so narrow-minded when it comes to our knowledge."

Hudson takes a moment to digest what I've said, "You're right, Margot. But how do we go about fixing this?" *Did he just admit I'm right...that easily?*

"Well, I haven't gotten that far, but I'm going to get a plan together and then I'll call a meeting with everyone to discuss how we're going to do things going forward. I think it'll help. We've probably got a little over a month before we pack up and head to The District. That gives me a few days to come up with a plan and a few weeks for us to execute it, and hopefully the holidays with our families too so long as nothing changes."

"Sounds like a plan, Margot. Let me know if there's anything that you need help with." We only sit here for a few minutes, before realizing that it's time to head home for the night. It's been a long day and I'm ready to get home and into my bed.

CHAPTER EIGHTEEN
STRENGTHS AND WEAKNESSES

ometimes, I tell myself that it's the intention that counts, especially when I was supposed to come home after work and begin working on a training plan. On top of that, creating the meeting to go along with it. The moment that I step through the door of my apartment I change into my comfy home clothes and make my way straight to my bed and pass out. I wake up to Jethro moving around in my bed, trying to get comfortable. My bedroom light is on, but I'm still having trouble seeing as my eyes are blurry, not quite ready to be open. I'm squinting just to try and make out the time on my alarm clock. *3:00 am!* I can't believe I let myself fall asleep so early without eating dinner or setting an alarm.

I set my alarm and turn my light off to go back to sleep for a few hours before it is time to go to get up again. It takes a while to get back to sleep because now I'm thinking about all of the time that I wasted by falling asleep early. I didn't get anything done for training or the meeting plan and this is something that needs done immediately. Finally, my brain decides that we can go back to sleep, though I'm not sure how long I lay there awake overthinking everything.

When morning comes I realize that walking with Jethro isn't going to be an option for a couple of days, not until I figured out this plan. I need to focus, so this means no mornings on the balcony with Bentley either. I'll see Bentley at work and Jethro will still be coming with me to Headquarters, so at least he'll get a walk during the day there. I decide to sit outside this morning to work on planning while Jethro gets to enjoy some time outside. It's quite chilly, I can feel the season starting to shift. My skin pebbles, making me wish I'd dressed a little warmer for our time outside this morning. Jethro is happy about it though, his thick coat is perfect for this kind of weather.

The next few days feel like someone is rewinding my days and playing them back over and over again. Every morning when I wake up I work on planning while sitting outside with Jethro, then it's off to Headquarters to work on it some more and then it's right back home where I inevitably end up passing out almost immediately surrounded by papers I had attempted to work on. To top it off I wake up every morning starving because I keep missing my dinner. At the end of the fifth day of this seemingly never-ending cycle I *finally* finish my plan. It's the best it's going to get and I know I'll need to tweak it as we go, but ultimately it will make our team even better. I decide to text Bentley and invite him over for the next morning's walk with Jethro since it's been almost a week since we've had any time alone. I don't need him stalking me and dragging me into a closet again, although it would be a nice break from reality.

Looking back, I can laugh to myself about that whole incident. It's funny now, but things could have ended so much differently. I'm glad that I realized who he was and didn't have a weapon on me, or else my walks would be accompanied by a different partner. We still never really spoke about that day, but at this point I wonder if it's even worth it to bring it back up. Tonight, I actually put myself to bed, after eating dinner, and without a bunch of papers around me. A welcome change I wish I could get used to.

Morning comes just as fast as any other, but I don't feel as rushed. This morning will allow a little bit of time to relax and just be. Bentley arrives with a muffin in hand; he knows that I haven't been eating as much as I should, the last week, due to the constant work I've been putting in on these plans. He gives me a quick peck before we take Jethro downstairs and head outside to talk, walk, and eat. Much better than how my past few mornings have been, even though a war could break out at any moment I feel ease wash over me.

"So, Margot, do you want to tell me what you've been working on so hard the last few days? I was starting to get worried that the whole closet incident had thrown us off." *Oh, are we talking about this?*

"I mean, the closet incident was *definitely* something else. I was just thinking about it last night."

Bentley raises an eyebrow at me in a mischievous sort of way, "Oh?" He's smiling like a cat with a mouse.

"No, Bentley, not *'Oh?'*. We should be lucky that that whole event ended the way it did. I was already on edge and thankfully I didn't have a weapon on me. I had turned into that janitor's closet to find something to attack *you* with. I assumed that you were some crazy traitor that was amongst our ranks." I didn't mean to come off so harsh, but once I started, I couldn't stop myself.

Bentley's face drops, I don't think he thought about it that way or even knew where my mind was before we entered the closet. I press on, "*And,* while we're on the subject, we can't just kiss away all of our problems. You really upset me that day, how you treated me wasn't okay just because I had an opinion different from yours." I wish I could swallow back that last part. I really like Bentley and don't want to push him away, but I owe it to myself to be honest.

Bentley takes a minute to register what I'm saying before trying to kiss me, I allow it but only for a moment before pushing him away. One, because someone might see us and two, because he's being a smart ass about the whole not kissing away our problems thing. He looks down, "I'm sorry, Margot."

"Thank you." He slowly blinks at me, looking a bit lost by my response, since I don't use the common *it's okay* in response to his apology.

Bentley seems ready to change the topic but lacks the segway to do so, so his leap from the current topic to the next is anything but graceful. "So, you wanna tell me about this project that you've been working on that's kept us from our walks?"

I really don't feel like diving into the whole thing just to have to repeat it again once we're at Headquarters. "Uh, you'll see later today." I want to catch everyone by surprise with this meeting. I think I might get more honesty from the team without them having time to prepare answers ahead of time. I can tell that Bentley wants to know more, but isn't going to press his luck, not today at least. We make it back to my apartment where Bentley walks us inside to say goodbye to me. He gives me a kiss; a sigh escapes me as he walks towards the door.

He stops short of leaving, his hand on the doorknob, "What?"

"It's nothing, I wish that we had more time together. More time to just be, rather than focusing on this freaking war. I want it to be over already and live a normal life." My hands are balled into fists at my sides, with my fingernails digging into my palms reminding me not to cry. "I really hope that this war brings about a change, maybe even reuniting all of the divisions." Bentley smiles softly and gives me another quick kiss on the forehead before making his way back to the door.

He places his hand on the knob and turns back to me. "Margot, I promise you that once this whole thing is over, I'm going to take you on a proper date. There will be plenty of time for us. Oh, and I'm definitely going to tell Hudson that I've been kissing his sister." I throw a pillow at the door as he leaves, both of us laughing. This morning has been the reawakening that my soul needed. Something different in the midst of the mundane last few days I've been doing nothing but planning. I quickly grab my things and head out the door, hopefully I can get there early enough before others and have a few moments alone, with Jethro of course, to set everything up for the meeting.

With the way things have been going lately, and being on the brink of war, I normally wouldn't come in early and risk being alone, but Jethro is with me, and I know that he'll do whatever it takes to protect me. It's dizzying, keeping my head on a swivel. Being in Headquarters alone, every little noise that I hear draws my attention and makes me jump a little bit. I've wheeled two whiteboards into our rarely used conference room; most of the time our meetings are informal and we meet wherever the opportunity for a meeting presents itself.

I write in bold letters on one board *"strengths"* and on the other *"weaknesses"*, along with a list of everyone's names on each of the boards, including my own. Hopefully this will get everyone thinking as they enter the room, so that we can start the discussion almost immediately. I give the room a quick look around to ensure that I'm happy with the set up and then begin walking around the building to remove things that are essential to everyone's jobs, leaving notes telling them to come to the conference room if they'd like to get them back. Just a fun joke to start the day, it's not out of the norm for us to trick one another. My favorite will forever be when Bentley, Lee, and Hudson all came in early a few days before Christmas and wrapped every inch of my half of the office in wrapping paper; it took me hours to get everything unwrapped and cleaned up enough that I was able to start my day.

People slowly start to trickle into the conference room. I'm currently joined by Lee, Theo, and Bentley all chuckling about their missing items: Bentley's toolbox and both Lee and Theo's tablets. The laughter is quickly silenced by yelling.

"Who the hell thinks they have the right to touch my stuff? Is this some kind of joke!?" Emma Leigh is actually screaming at the top of her lungs, pissed off that her keyboard, of all things, is missing. No one else took it this seriously, the guys came in laughing about it. Emma Leigh is pissed and seems to be on a rampage. I can actually hear her feet stamping as she makes her way to the conference room. She doesn't even come through the door of the conference room. She merely stands at the edge of the door giving me the dirtiest look that she can muster up. I don't have time for drama today and I'm really not sure what her deal is.

"Care to join us, Emma Leigh?" There is a pileup forming behind her now, the rest of the team is here and ready to join in the meeting. A death glare from Emma Leigh precedes her entering the conference room, aggressively pulling a chair out, and taking her seat. Everyone can feel the tension in the air and have been made to feel uncomfortable by this situation. Now is not the time for our team to start falling apart from within. I decide to leave it for now but based on the look that Bentley is currently giving me, this is definitely something that's going to get brought back up later. He takes a deep breath, and I follow his lead before beginning.

"Alright, so I'm hoping that everyone has had a moment to look at the board and think about the first thing that comes to mind when they see these words alongside their name." I'm met with silence. Bentley notices that no one is going to be the first to speak and decides to offer himself up.

"Uh, so some of us here have only strengths and no weaknesses." Bentley winks at me as he elbows Lee and they both start laughing. At least there's someone talking other than myself. I turn to the weakness board and next to Bentley's name I write *"everything"*. Lee and Hudson are rolling with laughter; Theo, Felix, and Auriella are holding their laughter back, trying to not upset their seniors. Even Bentley has joined in the laughter, but there sits Emma Leigh looking like someone took her keyboard and bashed her over the head with it, rather than just taking it as a joke. I need to bring everyone back together. I clear my throat.

"Alright, since the room feels a lot more alive now, let me dive into why I've brought you all here today. The other day I spent time wandering from department to department to check in and see how everyone was doing. I very quickly realized that there are a lot of things that I don't have much of a clue about." I write down each department I had visited that day next to my name on the weakness board, "This got me thinking about how everyone around here has their niche, their specialty. Which is great but could be problematic when we get into the thick of the war. For example, I don't know how to drive a manual. If we ever got into a situation where Bentley was hurt and one of us needed to drive his vehicle, I know that I personally couldn't. This sent me down the rabbit hole wondering if anyone else would be able to do that." As I look around the room I see a lot of heads shaking, it brings me to the scary realization that no one here, other than Bentley, is able to drive the manual vehicles.

"The more knowledge that we have, the more powerful we can be. We are only as strong as our weakest link, and I would prefer we have none of those, only equally strong ones. This brings me to my boards, obviously we know what our strengths are based on our departments." I jot down each person's department next to their name on the strength board. "Now, I know that our newer folks haven't really settled in yet, but I think that based on what I've seen here I know what each of your strengths are. Auriella, your creation the other day showed me that you're meant to be with Lee in the wellness department. Your knowledge of technology and the body are going to prove a great asset there." Lee looks at me rolling his eyes, probably thinking that I'm up to something with this assignment, but he couldn't be more wrong. Right now, I'm looking to make a stronger team, not to annoy him by making them partners.

"Felix, I think you're doing a great job in our technology department, and I would like you to really focus on that. Later on, I'll explain more of what I'm looking to see from you. Last, but not least, Theo. You've been doing a great job studying plans as well as your physical strength and weaponry. Continue to work on those." Felix and Theo nod, looking unsurprised by what I've requested of them.

"Now that everyone knows where they stand as far as strengths go, I would like to discuss our weaknesses. Honestly, I think that anything that isn't our specialty is our weakness." I point to where I wrote any department that isn't my specialty, "Over the next five days we are going to work on our improving weaknesses, each day we will be focusing on a different specialty and following their lead. Our veterans will be taking charge of teaching us each day." The veterans start looking around in complete shock, seemingly nervous about this challenge that I've set forth for them. We've never truly prepared for war before, not formally at least, and no one has ever put much into learning something that isn't their specialty. It's a new challenge for all of us.

"Don't look so nervous, this is going to be great. Today will be used for planning your teaching sessions. We will start off with me in tactics on Tuesday, since I knew that this was going to be coming. The rest of the week will go as follows: Wednesday will be vehicles with Bentley, Thursday will be health and wellness with

Lee, Friday will be weapons and combat with Hudson, and the following Monday will be technology with Emma Leigh. Next Tuesday we will have a brief meeting about how everything went and get a feel on how everything is going. Does anyone have any questions?"

I look around the room at my team, and everyone is shaking their heads, except Emma Leigh who still isn't being very responsive. I'm really over her attitude today. "Well, if there aren't any questions, everyone feel free to collect your things," I place the box on the conference room table with everyone's *stolen* goods, "and get to planning." Everyone grabs their things and makes their way out without saying much. It could have gone better, but at least there weren't any more outbursts from Emma Leigh.

I'm too lost in thought to realize that Bentley has hung back from the mass exit. He stops in front of me and speaks in a low, dark tone. "I think you may be right." I'm not sure what he's talking about, so I raise an eyebrow at him and tilt my head hoping that he'll continue with his thoughts. "About Emma Leigh." *Oh!*

"Really?" I can't believe he's actually coming around.

"Yeah, today was eye opening, she's not her usual self. I think that everyone in here noticed it too. We really need to-" Bentley trails off from his thoughts as Felix enters the room but quickly turns to leave when he notices that we're clearly in the middle of something. Bentley walks out after him, to not draw more attention to the fact that the two of us were alone, talking much too close to each other. Everything is peacefully quiet for the remainder of the day, it seems like everyone is taking this project pretty seriously.

Tuesday comes quickly, and everyone has settled between the conference room and the library for my day of training. It goes on without much issue. Planning doesn't have to be complicated, if I can just teach everyone to understand the plans and maps that we already have and how to read, then they will be able to use them if I'm not around.

Everyone starts to pick up on them pretty quickly. A lot of our newer plans are paper copies, since the break-in, to avoid hackers being able to steal them in a breach. They also can be easier to destroy if someone is attacking us, simply light them on fire and they're gone. I quickly start to teach everyone what the different symbols on the plans mean, so that they have better luck reading them. There aren't any keys on our plans either; in the event that they're stolen this will make it more difficult for an outsider to decipher.

Theo slowly raises his hand but before I can acknowledge him, he begins speaking. "Uh, Margot. I have a question. I'm not trying to sound like a negative Nelson, but what happens if someone from The Trio steals our plans or they are stolen by someone else and brought to them? Wouldn't they understand what the symbols mean?" *Crap.*

"Theo!" Theo jumps, I don't think he expected this response from me. "I didn't even think of that, you're totally right. Alright, everyone, I'm sorry, training is going to be changed up a little bit." We all spent the next two hours changing the symbols and redoing all of the plans, throwing the old ones in the shredder. Many are rubbing their now cramped hands; there was a lot to be done.

"Thank you, everyone for your efforts on that and I apologize that training took a little sidestep." I stare at my thumbs, having a thumb war with myself, feeling a bit down about how my training day went.

Auriella perks up. "Actually Margot, it's probably for the best that we did it this way. Even though it took a little longer it's actually proven that if you have some kind of repetition you're more likely to be able to recall it. This will make it easier in the end for all of us to remember these symbols, especially in the heat of battle." Leave it to Auriella to find a positive spin that relates to her knowledge of how the body works. This just makes me feel even better about my decision to move her to health and wellness with Lee, she's going to do great things there.

The rest of the week goes on better than I could have imagined. I am impressed by how willing everyone is to teach each other and learn from other teammates. Of course, each day brought its own challenge, but each person took them head on. Even when Auriella destroyed the transmission on one of Bentley's cars while he was trying to teach her how to drive stick, he took it pretty well, all things considered. Emma Leigh was the only one the entire week that seemed to be completely out of it. Of course it's now her day to teach, and she's nowhere to be found.

It seems pointless to address the team, as they can all clearly see what's going on, but I do it anyway. "Well, as you can all see Emma Leigh has not shown up yet today. I've tried getting ahold of her with no luck. Has anyone else heard from her this morning? It's not like her to not show up and not let anyone know." Everyone pulls out their phones to check but ultimately ends up shaking their heads.

"Alright, well would someone mind just trying to call her real quick to see if we can get ahold of her and make sure she's okay?" *What is going on?*

"I can do it, Margot." Felix is already holding the phone to his ear as he says this. He looks more and more frustrated and concerned as it continues to ring, with no answer. I don't know if I should be worried or angry. I guess for now being worried is the safe bet, I can be angry later once I know that she's safe. This goes on for almost two hours before Emma Leigh slowly saunters in as though we all haven't been waiting for her and trying to get ahold of her, worried that the worst may have happened. She looks disappointed when she realizes that we haven't moved on from her department and are clearly waiting for her to show up.

"Emma Leigh, where have you been? We've all been worried about you and trying to contact you!" I can't help but yell slightly as my nerves start to relax and I go from being worried to pissed.

"I overslept this morning, nothing serious. Since I'm here late we can just go ahead and skip my training day." *Is this what all of this was about? She had the longest amount of time out of everyone to prepare!*

I take a deep breath before responding to her, as to not completely lose my head. "No, that's okay Emma Leigh, we've been waiting for you to start our day, so you might as well go on with your plans. If we need to carry it over into tomorrow morning to have enough time, we can do that." Emma Leigh is visibly pissed that her plan to get out of this didn't work.

Her foul mood is brought into her training time. The entire time is spent teaching everyone things that they already know. She started by showing everyone how to turn a computer on, treating this entire exercise as a joke. The day continues like this, showing us simple things that if someone didn't already know how to do they could figure it out easily. I don't have the energy to try and correct her, even if I did I don't think I'd be able to stop myself from going off on her. I think her actions today are making everyone around her notice that something is definitely off with her. We get to the end of the day, and I am relieved when she tells us that that was all she had planned for our training session.

I call the group together. "Thank you everyone for putting forth *full* effort this past week on our training project, I really appreciate it. Going to go ahead and cancel tomorrow's meeting as I don't think it's needed. As we move forward let's continue on this path of trying to shadow others to learn more about specialties that aren't our own. Hudson and Lee, I would like to make sure that everyone is involved in combat and shooting training multiple times a week. I know we've typically handled this on our own, but I think we'll get a lot more out of it working on it as a group." They both nod, looking as though their gears are already turning on the grueling workouts that they're going to put us through. This past week truly was great, and other than Emma Leigh's performance, it gives me a glimmer of hope that we may actually have a shot in this war.

CHAPTER NINETEEN
WHISPERS IN THE WIND

After the drama that Emma Leigh brought along with her today I am thankful that this work day is over and I can go home and relax. The moment that it's time to leave Emma Leigh quickly gathers all of her things and hurries out of Headquarters, disregarding the buddy system in place, leaving the rest of us walking out together with Jethro. As we make our way towards our cars I notice a group of people talking across the street. They are whispering in a fearful type of fashion, clearly, they've been spooked by something and are now gossiping about it.

No one in our group notices and continues chatting amongst themselves as we walk by this other group. I decide to remain silent in an attempt to listen to as much of what they're saying as I can, to see if it's anything of use. I can only make out bits and pieces of what they're saying, something about The South and that they're preparing for war along with starting to try and convince other divisions to join them. *This can't be.* Then the worst bit of it rings out loud and clear.

One of the girls who looks like she is of school age gets overly excited about the news that she is sharing and sort of blurts it out loudly. "Did you hear about President Madden? Apparently, her husband's gone missing and they're all being blackmailed..." Unfortunately, the girl's voice trails off as we walk further away from them. I consider, for a brief moment, to stop and pretend like I need to tie my shoe, but I figure that it would be too obvious, and they would suspect me. I can't believe what I've just heard, then it hits me. I remember back to the strange behavior President Madden was exhibiting at Graduation. Unfortunately, there's been no update to this, the Presidential Security team works by themselves and keeps everything secret. They don't trust anyone outside of their team with private information about her. *But how would she know this? Another rat somewhere?*

"Uh, hello? Earth to Margot?" *Huh?* It's Hudson's voice. The problem with spacing out to listen to other people's conversations is that I have to concentrate extremely hard on what they're saying and miss out on whatever is going on around me. I have to shake myself back into the conversation that I'm supposed to be paying attention to, unfortunately I haven't the slightest idea what any of them are talking about.

"Sorry, I was just, uh never mind, I'll explain later. What's up?" Hudson rolls his eyes. This is something that I've done since I was little, listening into other people's conversations. He knows exactly what happened, and by the look on his face he's realized that I've heard something of serious importance.

"We were just talking about heading over to Bentley's parent's house for dinner, you down?"

"Yeah, sure, sounds great!" I probably sound too eager. We all disperse and make our way to Bentley's parent's house, luckily, they love Jethro, so I can drive straight there with him and not have to stop to drop him off. The entire drive over I keep replaying the conversation that I just heard. Thinking back on it, I remember seeing President Madden at Graduation surrounded by unfamiliar faces and her husband was nowhere in sight. *Maybe* the rumors were true. Hudson and I should have looked more into it.

Being around Bentley's parents has always been a pleasant and comfortable experience. Tonight feels a bit different, since I've started forming some kind of feelings for their son. I'm sure Bentley hasn't told them about anything that has been going on between the two of us, but I notice that Mrs. Adler's eyes are following me a little closer than they normally would. I shake it off, because there's no way that he would have told her, or anyone.

As we begin to gather around their kitchen to make our plates the Adlers begin talking to us about their work and the current state of The East and the rumored impending war. Mrs. Adler, who is tiny in comparison to her towering sons and husband, teaches lower-level school children and always offers a unique perspective of everything that's going on. "I know you all have to keep certain things a secret, but I just wish you would give me a little insight as to what's going on with this supposed war. I swear, the kids I teach give up more than you bunch. Just yesterday one of my littles told me that their mom and dad are scared and have been talking about moving their entire family to The North." Her eyes beg us to give her even the smallest scrap of information.

Bentley shakes his head, "I'm sorry mom, you know we can't disclose anything other than if we're going to be shipping off. Even then we can't tell you what the mission is, just when we're leaving and when we're hoping to return." Bentley places his hand on his mom's shoulder. "Don't worry, though, everything is going to be okay. You have the greatest soldier there ever was fighting for your side." Bentley stands there grinning, looking towards his mother, waiting for some kind of approval, when she turns to Lee and smiles.

"I know, honey, Lee is doing a great job and will continue to make our division proud." Everyone erupts into hysterical laughter as Bentley stands there, dumbstruck, rolling his eyes. I have to hand it to Mrs. Adler, she is quick. Must be where Bentley gets it from. When we all quiet down long enough Mr. Adler decides to add to his wife's point about the war. I think he's hoping to get one of us to slip up and either confirm or deny what he's heard at the auto body shop that he owns.

"You know how many different people that we see each day in our shop? Ashton was there with me the other night and told me that he overheard a customer dropping off their car for a full routine maintenance, that wasn't even due for another eight months!" We all look at Mr. Adler, wondering how this is anything in comparison to what his wife had heard, when he continues with his story. "They said they wanted to make sure that their vehicle was in top condition to make a trip to The North." Bentley is just as quick to divert his dad as he was with his mom.

"Dad, Ashton is only nineteen, are you sure that he heard them correctly or was even paying attention to something other than his phone?" I feel something whizz past my head, a ball of mashed potatoes smacks Bentley in the back of the head. We all laugh as we turn back to see the obvious suspect, Bentley's younger brother Ashton, standing there laughing maniacally.

"Talk trash, get mashed bro...get it? Mashed potatoes." Everyone is rolling with laughter over how corny he is. Even at nineteen Ashton is almost Bentley's height, looking so much like him only with less muscle definition. He runs upstairs before Bentley can get his hands on him.

Mr. Adler continues as though food throwing is a normal occurrence in their household. "As I was saying, we see a lot of different people there each day, so that wasn't the only thing that we heard. We also heard one guy telling his buddy that The South is increasing recruiting tactics in all divisions, including The District."

"Dad, you guys really can't believe everything that you hear. It could just be a ploy to get everyone into a frenzy, panicking about everything that's going on." Bentley is talking about such a serious topic, all the while trying to get mashed potatoes out of the back of his hair. It's quite the contrast to witness. I find it quite endearing that Bentley is trying his best to play it cool for his family, while we all know that The South is for sure on the move and making advances in this impending war. So much of what we do is top secret, so he wasn't able to talk about the break-in with his family or even what we know as far as The South's plans.

With that, the conversation of all things related to The South and a possible war come to an end. We all sit down to eat our dinner, and other than words of appreciation to Mrs. Adler about her cooking, not much is said. Next to being starved from a long day of training and dealing with drama, I think that all of us are trying to avoid any possible conversation about the war. The entire meal Jethro circles the table like a shark, waiting for someone to drop a piece of food, whether it be accidental or on purpose. Once we've finished eating everyone pitches in to help clear the table and clean everything up. I offer to take the trash to the bin; hopefully Bentley takes this as an invitation to follow, like he had the last time that we were all here for dinner and whatever this relationship we have now started.

I'm about halfway to the bin when I hear footsteps behind me. Before everything started to hit the fan I probably would have blindly believed that it's Bentley, but now I can never be too sure. I stop walking to turn back and make sure that the footsteps belong to Bentley, my heart does a little flip seeing that it is him. I smile at him and continue walking to the bin with the overly full bag of trash. We hadn't been able to steal a moment alone with each other all day, and after Emma Leigh's performance today I was more interested to see what his thoughts on the matter were.

"Can I help you, Mr. Adler? Do you not think that I can't take the trash out on my own?" I say as I hoist the bag into the bin. Bentley laughs and grabs me around the waist from behind and just holds me there for a moment, resting his chin on my shoulder. If only it could always be light and playful like this. I wriggle free and turn to face Bentley, as much as I'd love to go off and be alone with him right now, I know that someone is going to be looking for us sooner than later. I place my hands on his chest, with my arms straight, to make sure that he doesn't try and do anything to distract me from the real reason that I led him out here.

"Sorry, Bentley. I thought that we could enjoy another trash walk talk." *Did I really just say that?* "What was Emma Leigh's problem today? Something is going on with her, and I think that it's time that we all address it; you, me, Hudson, and Lee. Thoughts?" His shoulders sink as he sighs.

"I agree, something is going on with her, for sure. As if last week wasn't enough, today solidified it. I'm just not sure if we should bring it to everyone else yet. If we're wrong about this we could really stir the pot, and that's not a spoon I'm willing to lick just yet." *What an interesting expression.*

"Alright, but what are we supposed to do in the meantime?"

"I guess we continue on how we have been and stay vigilant with everything that's going on around us. We'll want to pay close attention to anything that Emma Leigh is doing and note anything else that seems fishy." He shakes his head as though he can't believe we're actually having to have this conversation, "No point in bringing our suspicions to the forefront when we don't really have any proof to back it up right now. She could just have something going on personally and brought it into the office, but better safe than sorry and make sure at least you and I are watching her." He shrugs his shoulders, out of ideas.

"That sounds like a good plan. Although, I don't think it's just you and I that are watching her. A couple of weeks ago when I was making my rounds I swore I saw Theo looking at all of the evidence again, from the break-in. I think he might be having some suspicions as well." Bentley looks puzzled and I'm not entirely sure why.

"Why didn't you tell me about this until now?" *What?* I raise an eyebrow at him.

"I guess I forgot about it until now when we got to talking about it. That was the day that I had decided that we all needed to have better training and learn everyone else's specialties. That night I got right to planning and I haven't seen you alone until the morning that I launched the plan, and we had our meeting. I really didn't think much of it until now."

"Oh, right." Bentley looks down and starts kicking at the rocks below his feet. Clearly embarrassed for trying to call me out on something that was entirely an accident. "Sorry, I think I'm just feeling a bit stressed about everything going on. Especially with

Emma Leigh, I mean she's supposed to be our friend just like The Trio were and I just have this awful nervous feeling that something like that is going to happen again." He's talking a mile a minute, his voice filled with anxiety, "We don't need that again. It makes it that much harder for us to trust each other, tears our team apart from the inside out."

Bentley is right, although what he said has left me feeling a bit helpless. I don't have anything that I can say that can really change how things have gone and could possibly go again. When I look at him I don't see the goofy guy that I became friends with, not even the guy that all of our recruits met just a few months back. He's much more serious now, occasionally the goofball that we all love shows, but usually it's the more serious man that stands before me tonight. Maybe he can sense that I've become lost in my own mind, because within a blink he's closed the space between us and holds onto me, seemingly like I'm the only thing holding him here.

I don't fight it, even though I swear I hear the back door of Bentley's house open, but I hear no footsteps, just the door shutting again a moment later. Someone definitely saw us, I'm just not sure who, but right now at this moment I don't care. The height difference between Bentley and I allows me to easily rest my ear on his chest, right at his heart. I wait until I hear his heart rate drop back down to something calmer before releasing myself to look at him.

"Bentley, it's going to be okay. We're going to be okay…as long as it wasn't Hudson that walked out here and saw us together." Bentley whips around to check the door, no one is there though, they're long gone. I laugh, a little out of nervousness and partially due to Bentley's facial expressions. He knows better though, if it had been Hudson we would have been broken apart as quickly as Hudson could get to us and throw Bentley away from me.

"Well, now that I'm paranoid about Hudson coming out here to murder me, let's go on inside. Someone must have noticed that we're missing by now." Bentley cups my face to draw a breath from me as he kisses me. When he pulls back I nod to Bentley and we both head back inside. December is here, and without Bentley distracting me I notice just how cold I was getting outside. Bentley lingers in the kitchen for a moment as I make my way into the living room where everyone else is hanging out. No one even notices as myself or Bentley come into the room as Theo and Auriella are in a heated argument about some video game that they're playing. I feel a bit sad as I look around, realizing that this is probably going to be our last night here for a long while, possibly ever.

Without saying anything everyone starts to pack up their things as we get ready to head out for the night. Everyone thanks the Adlers on their way out and Mrs. Adler even hands each of us a brown paper lunch bag with leftovers in it for us to enjoy tomorrow for lunch, she even hands me an extra one with some scraps for Jethro. Tomorrow is going to be another long day, and we can use all the help we can to get through it. A home cooked meal always helps to boost your mood.

As I lay in my bed thinking over the events of today I start to realize that even though I keep saying that a war is coming, it's not. It's not coming because it's already here. Whether or not we're ready for it, we're going to be forced to be. I know the time is coming that Hudson and I are going to have to make the decision to start moving towards The South. This is probably the worst part of my job, making the decision to put myself and those on my team into danger. Before, it's been minor battles. This time it is a war, with much larger stakes. Typically, our battles that we were involved in were helping other divisions to make sure that they could keep living their ways of life. Oftentimes, though, we ended up dealing with smaller petty issues, like people trying to hop divisions and commit crimes here or escape the crimes they had committed in a different division.

These people are my friends, and I don't want to risk losing any of them. I feel guilty that I have to tell them that we must enter this war, formally. I feel more and more anger towards those in The Trio. We wouldn't be at this point if it wasn't for them. They've caused not only issues for us within our team, but for every single division, even The District. Every division is going to suffer due to them, some more than others. Unfortunately, our divisions don't really have much communication, so I'm not sure what they're planning to do about this, if anything.

Although, I can't entirely blame The Trio and The South for these problems that we're currently facing. A huge part of this all stems from the original problems that started over two hundred years ago. Had The United States not turned against each other and ended up dividing I might have had the chance to live a normal life where I wasn't worried about impending war and those around me dying as a result. Now, I know I wasn't there, but I don't see how any differences that are listed in our history books could have ever led to them dividing and fighting amongst themselves. A domino effect can only start if the first domino has been pushed over.

As I continue to go through the scenarios in my head, I know that there isn't any good way to go about announcing to the team that we're heading out to try and fix the problem at hand. I know Hudson is probably having the same thought as me and it's something him and I will need to discuss at length, before making any kind of announcement to the rest of the team. Unfortunately, we will need to move quickly with our decision this time due to the possibility of any number of traitors still being among us. We can't be too careful.

I go over every possible way to word the phrase 'We're going to war.' The second we're spotted moving our troops towards The South it will be considered an act of war, which is exactly why we'll start with a small group to scope it out. There isn't going to be an easy way to say it and everyone is going to be upset at hearing it. Sure, this is what we all signed up for, but I don't think any of us ever thought that we would be in long enough to make it to a war. All I can do is silently pray that our exodus can wait until we've made it through the holidays with our families. My exhaustion and fear overcome me, and I fall into a deep sleep. My dreams tonight feel so real, but the whole time I'm aware that I'm dreaming, yet I'm trapped within them and unable to wake myself...

I've announced to everyone that we're going to have to go to war when all hell breaks loose. Emma Leigh launches herself at me, landing her first blow to the side of my face. I am knocked to the ground and having trouble moving, it feels as though I am being held down, but I can't see anything on me. I wonder if she drugged me, then I lose consciousness. I come to and I am in a dark room. Nothing and nobody around me. I am tied to a chair, arms behind me and my chest and legs bound to the chair so that I am left with no range of motion. Whoever brought me here has also placed curtains on either side of me, so that I can only see directly in front of me. I feel like a horse wearing blinders.

I stop myself from screaming, trying not to bring attention to the fact that I've come to. I need every second that I can get to come up with a plan to get myself out of this mess. I will never have enough time, though, whoever tied me up did so in a manner that makes it impossible to get out without some kind of blade. Even if I had one the first hurdle would be freeing my hands, which I've been working at since I came to, to no avail. Fear starts to set in, realizing that I am truly stuck here, when I hear a door open from behind me, I can't see who enters. They did this on purpose. They want to put as much fear into me as possible, and it is working.

Normally I can remain calm in situations like these; it isn't the first time that I've been trapped but it has never been to this extent. The footsteps are getting closer and are now on my left side, but I can't see who it is due to the curtains. Then, another set of footsteps start from the same door that the first person came through, except they are walking to the right of me. I am about to be ambushed, I am completely defenseless, and everything is about to get much much worse.

Before I can register what's happening there are two forms standing in front of me, both wearing ski masks. All I can really make out is that one is male and the other female. The female moves forward and strikes me across the face, with force. The male laughs as she strikes me again and again. Once she steps back I have a moment to assess my injuries, my nose is likely broken, and I can feel blood trickling down my face from multiple spots. Whoever this is, is making this personal. The female stares me dead in the face as she removes her mask. A gasp escapes my lips, *Emma Leigh,* and she begins laughing maniacally.

The next hit is worse than any physical one that Emma Leigh delivered. The male removes his mask and it's Bentley. I can't hide the hurt on my face. He starts laughing right along with Emma Leigh. They begin to kiss, and I can't help but sob, this is the worst kind of hurt that I could ever feel. Two very different types of betrayal, both painful. I am shaking and crying so hard that I wake myself up. I realize that the inability to move in my dream must have been due to Jethro trying to snuggle, his body spread on top of both of my legs. I shake the feeling, Bentley would never, but Emma Leigh I'm not sure about anymore. I quickly fall back into a dreamless sleep, exhausted from the nightmare.

CHAPTER TWENTY
PREPARING FOR BATTLE

The holidays come and go, bringing us a new year and new rumors about The South and The Trio's latest schemes. Everything that the Adlers said at dinner seems to be coming to fruition, leaving the inevitable now unavoidable, but at least we've been training harder than ever because of it. As my eyes adjust to the light of day I think about what it would be like to have a normal night of sleep, not one that's interrupted by terrible thoughts and plagued by nightmares. It's exhausting and makes me feel like I didn't actually sleep at all. I wish that we could go back in time, even to just before the break-in. I miss not having to worry about the war that's right in front us. Just the thought of having to go to Headquarters today is exhausting, I'm not ready to potentially announce to the team that we'll be deploying, pending Hudson's input on the matter. I can sense it though, today's the day, we've put it off as long as we could, but we need to get moving before things get further out of hand.

I quickly ping my brother to see if he's up yet, so that we can discuss everything before actually heading to Headquarters this morning.

Hey…mind stopping by my apartment this morning before we head in? Want to go over something with you.

Hudson wastes no time responding.

<u>Huddy</u>
Yup.

Within minutes Hudson is knocking on my door and heading in, completely ignoring my existence and greeting Jethro instead. Once they're finished with their love fest Hudson takes a seat on the couch with Jethro next to him, who is quick to lay his head in Hudson's lap begging for more ear scratches. Hudson, of course, obliges.

"So, what is it that's so important that you couldn't wait to talk to me until we got to Headquarters?" His tone is serious and irritable, especially for someone who has a dog laying in his lap.

I stay standing, leaning over the back of a chair that faces Hudson, "Well…I think it's time that we mobilize. Today."

Hudson stares at me, almost through me. I think he knew exactly why I was calling him here early and what I wanted to discuss with him, but I think that it's still hitting him hard. Our lives are about to change entirely, and it may not be for the better. This is what we signed up for, though. We had the choice to choose any other profession, even though we were requested to join this one.

We knew the risks and decided to join anyway. Now is the time to prove our worth to not only those that put us in these positions, but to ourselves that we are worthy of being here.

"I knew it. I knew the second that the Adlers started talking about all of the rumors that they heard that this was coming…at least we got through one last holiday with the family." He won't even make eye contact with me.

"Do you disagree with me?" I wish Jethro was next to me to offer some comfort.

"No, I think that the time is now. It just sucks that it got here so soon. I was kind of hoping to retire before anything like this happened." We both have to laugh. For me, at least, this morning is a laugh or cry type of morning. With my brother here, making jokes, it is easy enough to choose laughter. Later, when I'm alone, it might not be as easy. Although there won't be much time alone anymore.

"Our best bet is to be as quiet about this as possible; less chance of anyone following or ambushing us."

He finally looks at me, but I wish he hadn't because if anything breaks me this morning it's going to be the way he's looking at me now, "You don't have to explain yourself to me, Margot. I knew this was coming and today is as good a time as any. I'll let you do the honors of letting the team know." *Gee thanks.* Before I have a chance to respond Hudson gets up and heads to the door. "I'll see you in a little bit, Margot."

He leaves so quickly, he doesn't even give me a chance to respond. He's clearly upset about our sudden departure, but at least he agrees with me, it makes all of this a little easier. I take my time getting ready and grab Jethro, so that we can go into Headquarters together. Everyone else seems to have had the same idea this morning, as all of us are showing up late together. Since everyone is walking in together I decide that now is a perfect time to call the meeting, better to just rip off the bandage.

"Good morning, everyone. If you all could please meet me in the conference room, once you get a chance to put your stuff down. We're going to have a quick meeting before we start our day."

Everyone looks at me while nodding their heads in agreement and seem as though they're trying to read my mind and find out what exactly the meeting is going to be about. Bentley looks at me the longest, with a look of worry and wonder, as though he's trying to pick the thoughts from my brain. I wish that I had thought about telling him this morning before announcing it to the entire group. He holds my gaze for what feels like minutes before heading off to drop his things in the garage. I quickly follow, doing my best not to look suspicious.

I shouldn't be doing this, I'm supposed to be everyone's leader, but I don't think that I will be able to bear the look on his face if I tell him in front of everyone. Yes, he's one of my soldiers, but he's become so much more than that recently, especially with the amount of time we spent together, secretly, over the holidays.

If I don't have much time left, I am going to do what I think is right, regardless of what others think. It's like he senses me, Bentley dips into a corner of his office where people walking by aren't likely to see us. I follow.

"Margot? What's going on?" He's worried and not even bothering to hide it.

"Bentley, we're moving out today…" His face says everything: worry, anger, sadness, anticipation.

"Wow. That's one hell of a way to start a morning." He kind of half laughs as he says it, almost sounding as though he's trying to hide what he's really feeling. I don't blame him though. He grabs me and pulls me close to him, holding onto me as though he's a child holding on to their security blanket. I am grateful for whatever this relationship we have is. Although it makes going to war that much more difficult, I still struggle to admit to myself whatever this is and now I'm going to have to work harder to keep it from everyone else as any personal time is about to go out the window with this mission.

I push myself back to face him and decide that we've already pushed our luck this morning, so why not push it a step further? I place a quick kiss packed with longing on Bentley's lips. "I have to get going, people are going to get suspicious, and I have a meeting to run. Act surprised please!" Bentley is standing there smiling like a fool, but says nothing as I leave, at least I could improve his mood some.

I walk with my head on a swivel to the conference room, double-checking that no one saw Bentley and I together as I'm still not ready to admit to anyone what this is, including myself. I find Theo waiting in the conference room alone. He doesn't say anything as he studies a plan that he brought with him. Slowly, everyone else starts to trickle in. The last two to enter are Emma Leigh and Bentley. Emma Leigh looks like it's a personal offense to her that I've called a meeting this morning. Bentley still looks flustered from me kissing him after delivering life changing news. I try as hard as possible not to laugh at the expression on his face and the way he looks at me as he takes his seat. His smile is sweet, yet mischievous, holding a secret only the two of us know. I bite my lip to keep myself from smiling back, this is meant to be serious.

"Good morning, again, everyone. We've been talking about this war for a while now, and now is the time that we start making moves. Tonight, after dinner, we will be making our way out of town to head south." There are several gasps, but I continue to push through, "The plan as of right now is to head to The District first to get a feel for what's going on there before heading to The South and engaging." Everyone looks completely shocked, even Bentley is doing a good job at faking it. Although I think he's still truly shocked. No one makes any kind of comment though.

I continue, "I know that this is a bit of short notice, but we're going about it in this way to make sure that our enemies have less of a chance to follow us or attempt an ambush. We'll go ahead and take a half day here at Headquarters, once everything is ready to go here we can head out. This way everyone has a chance to go home to pack up and close up their apartments." I take a deep breath, since I know this is the part I'll struggle with the most. "Go ahead and notify your families that we'll be leaving on a mission, without giving any specifics. We'll have a small sendoff gathering outside of our apartments to say goodbye to everyone. Scratch that, not goodbye, just see you later." Still, no one says anything, only silent nods. Even Auriella, who is typically among the toughest, looks as though she's holding back tears; I see Felix reach for her hand.

"Alright, well, that's all I have to say on the matter. Hudson, anything from you?" He shakes his head, looking as anxious as those around him. "Okay, well with that everyone is free to go. I'm going to meet quickly with the leaders of the Beta, Omega, and Reserve teams to let them know what's going on. Come find me if there's anything you need." With that everyone gets up, their chairs screeching against the floor is the only sound penetrating the silence of shock as they head out.

I make my way over to Felix, with Jethro, before I make my way to find the other leaders. I think I had made the decision long before now, but today is the day that I solidified the decision. Jethro is coming with us. Typically, my parents keep Jethro when I have to go away for work, but not this time. I can't burden my parents with an extra soul to worry about if everything hits the fan and they have to get out quickly. I think about the impact it could have on Jethro too, if my parents were away when disaster struck he would be all by himself, and I can't do that to him either. When I rescued him from the edge of the forest, after being abandoned as a small pup, I vowed to him that that would never be his fate again.

Bringing Jethro with me isn't something that I'm taking lightly, which is why we have to visit Felix. Everyone very quickly became a fan of Jethro, so it's not a surprise that the moment Felix sees us approaching his station he stops what he's doing to greet him. This seems like it's going to be a much easier question to ask than I thought it was going to be. I feel bad asking Felix for extra help at the last minute but seeing his reaction to Jethro I know that he's not going to mind at all.

"So, what brings the two of you to visit me? I thought you were going to meet with the other leaders?" Felix is now sitting on the floor petting Jethro, craning his neck to talk to me.

"Well, Felix, I have a pretty large favor to ask you."

"What is it? Do you want me to keep Jethro forever? 'Cause I will." I quickly plop to the floor and hug Jethro around the neck, pulling him away from Felix.

"No! You can't have my dog!" Felix laughs, still petting Jethro while I'm hugging onto him.

"Alright, well then if it's not that, then what is it? It must have something to do with this good boy, or else he would be napping in a chair somewhere." Felix laughs to himself.

"You're right about it involving Jethro. I have decided to bring him with us, but I want to do this in the safest way possible, he needs protection of sorts. Could you help me with that?" Felix's eyes light up, like a child who was just given a new building brick set to put together. Felix hops up and runs over to his workbench and comes back with a sketch pad and a fabric tape measure. He gets right to work, taking Jethro's measurements and then sketching something. Every time that I try to take a peek at what he's doing he moves the sketch pad away from me. *Ugh.*

Without saying anything to me, Felix jumps up, taking his sketch pad with him to his work bench. "Uh, Felix? Update?"

Felix barely looks up from his work, "Not yet just leave Jethro with me and go have your meeting with the others. I'll have some things for you to look at once you're back."

I give Jethro a few scratches behind the ears, "Stay here boy, I'll be back." Jethro takes this as his cue to lie down and take a nap. For only being about two, he sure does nap a lot. I look back to him once I make it to the stairs and he's already sleeping. I shake my head and laugh while pushing my way into the staircase and heading up. It doesn't take me very long to find Kitty, and to my advantage she's actually walking along with the Omega captain, Darnell, and the Reserve captain, Mau. I've met Darnell on several occasions, and he is always very friendly, full of passion and energy. Everyone loves that about him. Mau is newer, so I've really only interacted with him once, but I've heard good things about him from Bentley and Lee; they occasionally get together for poker nights with folks from all different teams and departments. As I get closer Darnell already has his hand up waiting for a high five, a

Darnell signature move. I wave at Kitty and go in for a perfect high five with Darnell before diving into the real business.

"Hey guys! I've got a bit of news for all of you." I take a breath, the more I say it the more real it becomes. "The Alpha team will be setting out tonight. The plan is to head towards The South and figure out the rest of the plan as we go, based on our findings as we start moving. As of right now the plan is for the remaining teams to hang back until I give the say so. Obviously, when it is time for you to mobilize your teams, you're going to want to choose several people to stay back at Headquarters to protect it and to be able to provide us with remote support." I can feel the anxiety welling up inside of me again.

Kitty always looks so strong and fearless, but this seems to have caught her completely off guard. She looks as though she's struggling to comprehend what's happening. Another case of someone new to this role not realizing just how quickly everything can change. Darnell looks as though his gears are already turning, I can tell he's thinking of plans and who is going to be in charge of staying back. Darnell's been here almost as long as I have, so he's had ample time to prepare for this kind of news. I'm unable to read Mau fully since I don't know him well, but he looks eager. Probably excited for a chance to prove himself and the potential to be moved to a more involved team as a reward.

Kitty finally speaks up. "So, what are we supposed to do about our special projects in the basement? No one has interviewed them in a while. Are you going to try to get any more information out of Wesley before you leave?" Maybe this is why she looked concerned when I told them, it's like she's realized that we're not going to need her help directly for a while. Her first major achievement here was cracking Wesley, but now we don't have much of a need for him anymore. It's true, after our last interview with Wesley, we've left him be, knowing we've likely gotten all we're going to get from him. It probably has her thinking that we don't have any need for her either, which isn't true at all, and I need to reassure her of this.

"Good question, Kitty. For now, he's going to stay where he is, Victoria too. This way we have a pawn to use if needed, but I don't think that he holds any importance to The Trio. I think he was just a piece in their little game, to be used and thrown away afterwards. But, if we have anything we need answers to, that we think he might know, you'll be our first call to question him." I can see the tension leaving her body. "I'm sure we'll also need you to question some folks once we get closer to The South, but right now I'm not sure and don't want to risk anyone else until we know for sure what we're dealing with."

Kitty seems to perk up at this. I remember what it was like being a female leader, so young. It's hard trying to bring yourself up in the ranks and earn respect, especially when so many look at the military as a man's world. In our history classes we spoke about this a lot, it's not something new to our time. In the old United States, there was a time when women weren't allowed to be a part of the military or even vote, they were looked at as lesser, frail people. It's difficult to think about someone allowing something so outward to impact their judgment on another human being, from gender to color and every other difference in between that makes each of us. At the same time, it helps to understand how that same country became so divided once again. If you're able to think less of a person based on something so superficial, hate becomes easy. The, unfortunate, natural next step.

Every day I am thankful that I live in The East. Women are in power, just as much as men are. The color of your skin doesn't make a difference either, nor does the religion that you follow, or any other difference you might have whether it be physical or otherwise. A lot of people that think the opposite of this live in The South. You won't see many people in positions of power if they don't fit the mold decided on decades ago. The North and West believe in a similar way to The East, but you'll never see The North advocating for the mold to be broken. Whereas The West focuses too much on breaking the mold and not being prepared to pick up the pieces.

I break free from my thoughts, "Do any of you have any questions?"

All of them shake their heads, "Alright, well if you think of anything let me know. Otherwise, I will keep you all posted, and let you know when it's time for you to head out."

I walk away with a sinking feeling in the pit of my stomach, hoping that I will get to see them again, praying that nothing bad happens to them as a result of this war. That we can all come back here together and continue to grow our teams and our careers. I quicken my pace to widen the distance between us, hoping to block out my thoughts of the possible outcomes that may come over the next few weeks, months, or even years. I distract myself by making my mind busy, thinking about the possible solutions that Felix has come up with, I quicken my pace and make my way over to him.

As I get closer to Felix's workstation I can't believe my eyes, he's made Jethro his very own armor! Jethro looks as though he's wearing a full dark green camouflage spandex suit with a zipper going from his neck down his belly; it covers every inch of him minus his mouth, eyes, ears, and business. Whatever this is, Felix has designed it so that Jethro will still be able to eat, drink, and use the bathroom while wearing it. His ears must have been too difficult to cover, but they do look really cute sticking out.

"Felix! What is this contraption you have Jethro in?" Felix pulls back a little bit, looking nervous as though he thinks I'm about to tear his efforts apart.

"Well, I made Jethro armor, but wait, it gets better." Felix pulls out a pair of goggles, smiling like a fool, and places them over Jethro's eyes. "His suit is made from a tight woven material that is actually bullet and blade resistant, his goggles are made from something similar. This way he's still able to be mobile, while also being able to bite and defend himself if needed, even though his suit should do the trick." He says this in such a nonchalant way, like anyone could create doggie armor in such a short amount of time.

I can't resist, I throw myself toward Felix and give him the biggest hug, he awkwardly returns it. I can feel the tears coming, so I quickly let go of him before I start sobbing. "Thank you so so much, Felix! This is amazing and you have no idea how much this means to me!"

"Of course! I'm glad that Jethro can come with us. I think he's going to be great for morale too. I made him a couple spares as well, even though they're able to be washed, just in case. I took him for a walk in it already to make sure going to the bathroom wouldn't be an issue either." His smile stretches from ear to ear, "He's ready to go, an official member of the team." Felix points to Jethro's chest, he even included our official division logo along with his name, just like on the chest of our uniforms.

"Thanks again, Felix. I owe you one!" Felix hands me a bag full of spare uniforms for Jethro before we leave.

Jethro and I walk off to see where we can help with packing, Felix stays behind to finish packing up his things. Everyone admires Jethro's new outfit; I can tell that Jethro is comfortable in it and enjoys all of the attention. We make our way over to the garage where several team members are converging, probably learning about the vehicles we'll be taking. For this mission we will be taking four vehicles. Two are RVs, the first is for sleeping and meeting in its fully equipped kitchen. The second RV is meant for all of the technical equipment and where surveillance can be set up along with any of our weapons. Our last two vehicles are more practical for when we're on missions, one that is meant for speed, and another that is meant to take into battle as it has armor surrounding it and is fully stocked with weapons, including rocket launchers that come out from the sides and the sunroof.

Everyone either skips lunch or eats while working in order to get out of here as quickly as possible. We all finish up a little after lunchtime and head back to our homes to pack up our own personal belongings, extra clothes, and to close everything up since we don't know how long we'll be gone for. As I look around my apartment it takes a lot to stop myself from completely breaking down, thinking about every possible outcome that today's decision could bring, but I can't allow those thoughts to win.

I gather up all of my things and even grab myself several books as though trying to convince myself that this is all going to be okay and maybe I'll even have time to read. I make sure that Jethro has plenty of food, his bed and some toys, so that he has some comforts from home as well. Once I'm finished I sit down and breathe, I need a moment. While petting Jethro's ears my brain starts to run through everything I'm feeling; excited that we may be able to put a stop to all of this nonsense once and for all. There's a sadness that washes over me as well about leaving my family, I'm nervous about how all of this might go. I shake the feeling and say a little prayer before getting up to head out, as I can hear footsteps of my teammates walking past my apartment heading outside. As the footsteps stop there's a small knock on my door, I open it to find Bentley there, he pushes inside shutting the door behind himself with his foot. He takes no time dropping his things, pulling me into an embrace and quickly kissing me before running back out of the door to join the others. My hand brushes my lips, still burning from where he kissed me. I give my home one final look before heading out to join the others, at least my potential last memory of this place is a good one.

"Alright, Jethro. Time for us to go, next time we're here the war will be over." I really hope that I'm not lying to him.

As I make my way outside I feel another wave of emotions hit me. Everyone's families are standing outside in the parking lot waiting to see us off. Each person here seems a bit emotional, and rightfully so. As I walk by other families to get to my own I can hear bits and pieces of what other families are saying, but I'm so focused on getting to my own that everything sounds like a loud hum. When I get to my family Hudson is already there and my mother is crying but doing her best to hide it from us. I'm glad that both of my parents and Eloise were able to make it. As we all hug and say our goodbyes, my sister turns to Hudson and I to give us one final goodbye.

"You guys be safe, okay? I'll miss you." She gives both of us a tight hug at the same time. "Goodbye!"

As I hug her back I whisper to her, "Don't say goodbye Eloise, that's much too final. I prefer *'see you later'*, we'll all be back together soon."

Eloise gives me one final squeeze, "See you later, Margot." And makes her way to the car, my parents following behind her still shouting to us that they love us and that they're proud of us.

My see you laters are over, so I decide to make my way to the vehicles where we'll all get our assignments for which we'll be riding in. Before I can get there, I'm intercepted by Bentley's mother. Mrs. Adler is standing in front of me looking at me for a brief moment as if studying me before taking me in for an embrace. I've never hugged Mrs. Adler before, even though I've known her for as long as I've known Bentley and maybe that's why she chose to hug me today. She whispers just a few words to me before following her husband and younger son back to their cars.

"Take care of my son."

I wonder if she pulled anyone else aside. *Oh!* It hits me. It wasn't a teammate that saw us that night through the backdoor, it was Bentley's mother. I look at Bentley who looks slightly embarrassed, while also trying to hide a small smile, only the right corner of his mouth is turned up. His mother means the world to him, so her approval of me must be important too. At least my last memory of The East is a happy one, but hopefully I'll be back here soon to make many more.

CHAPTER TWENTY-ONE
ON THE MOVE

M y heart is racing as we all join together, Mrs. Adler just made whatever the relationship that Bentley and I have very real. Until now no one else has acknowledged this relationship, because we haven't told anyone and no one has caught us, I haven't even truly acknowledged it myself. Even when Theo had been close to discovering Bentley and I, I was able to sidestep the conversation by telling him truths about my relationship with Bentley while conveniently leaving out just how close we actually are. Bentley and I haven't even confessed anything to each other, guess I'll have a little bit of time on our ride to The District to decide whether or not I want to bring this up to Bentley. I don't have time to worry about this now though, it's time for us to get moving. Right now, every second counts.

"Alright, team. We're going to divide everyone up for the trip. Typically, it would only take us about ninety minutes to get there, but today we are going to detour in case anyone is following us. The car assignments will be as follows: Emma Leigh and Theo will ride together in the tech RV, Lee and Auriella will ride together in the hospitality RV, Hudson and Felix will be riding in the armored vehicle, and Bentley and I will take Jethro along with us in our additional car." Lee gives me a look of irritation probably thinking I put him and Auriella together with a purpose that isn't work related. Honestly, the only thing that crossed my mind during this pairing was hoping that maybe they could come up with some additional creations during their ride.

"I'd like to stagger our departure times by about five minutes, starting with Hudson and Felix. After that it'll be Auriella and Lee, then Emma Leigh and Theo, then Bentley and I will bring up the rear since it's easiest for us if we need to catch up to anyone. Does anyone have any questions or anything?"

Everyone shakes their heads and begins to make their way to their assigned vehicle. Hudson holds off from walking to his vehicle with Felix. I'm not quite sure what he's doing as he moves towards me and quickly gives me a hug.

"See you later, Margot. Be careful and don't do anything stupid trying to be brave." He gives Bentley a fist bump and Jethro a pat on the head before heading towards his vehicle. We've been on many missions and in several battles together, yet Hudson has never hugged me before any of them. While it's a nice gesture it also makes me even more anxious about this war, because that hug was his way of telling me that he is anxious too. *Just breathe, Margot.*

Surrounding each division is a perimeter of nothingness. From any exit point of a division it takes about thirty minutes to get to a main roadway that will take you to the next division. Here there is nothing but crumpled buildings and overgrown greenery, that is slowly swallowing up the old buildings. The only sign, besides the worn-out highway, that there had once been a time when everyone that lived here was connected and not separated by miles and miles of nothingness. We start our journey by heading towards The West in order to shake anyone that may be following us, to have them think that we're heading towards The West rather than The South. The hope is that they'll think this isn't a mission of importance and leave us alone.

Traveling to another division for war is something that we've never done before. If there was ever need for a discussion with another division it was done in the No Man's Land perimeter around our division, or over video conference if the division wasn't as close by. Those kinds of things were typically reserved for politicians anyway. If our President ever traveled to another division for a meeting they'd take their special guard team with them to defend them. We have spent a lot of time in a section of No Man's Land bordering The East, defending our division from those trying to invade. A lot of places that we pass by in No Man's Land look familiar but also bring back memories of battles fought with The Trio by our sides. This time we aren't stopping in No Man's Land to defend The East with The Trio but going out of our comfort zone to confront them.

The landscape out here, past the section of No Man's Land that borders The East, is much different than anything I've ever seen. None of us have ever ventured this far out of The East, so this is a first for all of us. The houses here aren't that different from the ones that are in parts of The East. It's as though someone built a bunch of the same houses and plopped them down everywhere; it reminds me of the gingerbread houses that we decorate at Christmas time, everyone gets the same structure, it's just the decorations that vary slightly. Now they are crumpling and have an overgrowth of trees, grass, and vines creeping up them. It's interesting looking at the places people had lived before The Great Divide, realizing that they must not have lived much differently from us. I even spot a house that, from the outside, looks identical to my parent's home. It's a surreal experience.

As we travel further down the abandoned highway that leads to The District, in a roundabout way, I start to notice that there are people here and there that seem to be inhabiting these crumpled homes. I don't recognize these people, and it makes me wonder where they came from and if they're headed somewhere else or have chosen a home between divisions to live. Bentley must have the same thought, because after not having said a word to each other yet during the ride, he finally speaks up.

"My dad told me that he heard from someone that recently moved to The East that there were people leaving their divisions to join ours but had stopped here to take refuge and avoid capture during their journey." His grip tightens on the steering wheel,

"They must be surviving on the land, because there's no way that they've been able to get into any of the other divisions to get any supplies"

I can't imagine living somewhere where this is the better option. "Wow, why don't they just make their way to The East, rather than living out here? We're usually pretty quick and understanding about letting people in, so long as they can pass the background checks." Compared to other divisions, The East is one of the easiest to migrate to, only requiring a background check that takes a few weeks. The West is of course the easiest, because they don't really have rules, people come and go as they please. The North is a bit stricter than The East about taking people in, but they still allow some people in after extensive paperwork and waiting periods. They even require a work agreement if you join them, but it can take around a year for a decision to be made. The South is the worst about allowing people in. Their process takes years, during that time people live on the outskirts being attacked and sometimes starving to death due to not being close enough to any food sources. Apparently, the land outside The South is barren, nothing like the lush area we're driving through now.

The District is open to anyone who wants to come in, but the price for entering is high. Entering means that you are on your own and that you are opening yourself up to any potential harm that may come from living in a place that is basically lawless. The District is a scary place, and most people don't go there willingly, it's their last choice. Yet, somehow, it's where we are headed at this very moment. I look up from my thoughts and I'm able to see some of the tall buildings and bridges in the distance, landmarks of The District. We are getting close, and these are most likely going to be my last moments with Bentley before this all begins.

I put my hand on Bentley's leg, prompting him to briefly take his eyes off of the road to look at me. The way that he looks at me is warm, a half-smile with a touch of sadness. He puts his hand on top of mine as he looks back to the road, his hands probably rougher than usual from the overtime prepping and training for war. "Bentley, I don't think I'm ready for this."

Once again Bentley takes his eyes off the road, this time taking his foot off the gas, to briefly look at me, studying my face. "What do you mean, Margot?"

"This war. I just wish that it wasn't something for us to go through. I wish one hundred years ago they could have lived together peacefully and not torn apart an entire country over differing opinions. Now we're stuck fighting a battle where the people who started it are now dead! Yet here we are stuck cleaning up their mess." I take a deep breath, like a yawn, to stop myself from crying. "I could be spending my time with Jethro, or reading, or just enjoying our time together and maybe going on an actual date."

Bentley squeezes my hand as if he's trying to ease my stress. I noticed that with my rant came the tightening of my hand on Bentley's thigh, probably a bit too tight, and him squeezing my hand was to gently ask me to stop doing the same thing to him. I release the grip that I have on Bentley, and he releases his on me. "Aren't you the least bit upset about any of this, Bentley?" I'm barely hiding the irritation in my voice. He should be upset too.

"Of course I am, but me being angry about it isn't going to go back in time and change how things in the past got us to where we are now. I can't control the actions of others, only the reactions that I have towards them." *Wow*. The things that drew me to Bentley are so much deeper than what's on the outside. Sure, the cover of his story is a great one, but it's the words on the pages that keep me interested and wanting to know more and how this story ends. So many times, I've seen him either make a joke or go straight to using his fists to solve problems, but then he says things like this. The insight he has is something that draws me toward him even more, knowing that he can have these kinds of deep conversations.

"You're right Bentley, and once this is all over you can take me on a proper date." I look around to make sure that none of our other teammates have looped back for some reason to be near us, and kiss Bentley on the cheek. I can feel his cheek under my lips moving, as his mouth forms into a smile. As I sit back in my seat Bentley abruptly pulls the car over on the shoulder, causing me to sit straight up in my seat, my whole body tenses thinking that something has happened and we are in danger. I look around though and don't see anyone anywhere. Bentley has now unbuckled his seatbelt and is leaning over the center console to grab my face and kiss me.

I've been kissed before, I've been kissed by Bentley before, but this time is different than any kiss that I've ever felt. I love Bentley, and I have for a long time, but I don't think I'm ready to face what kind of love exactly it is that I feel for him. I don't want to rush anything just because of this war. I'm not even ready to admit to myself about how I truly feel about him, so I know I'm not ready to tell him. Telling him, telling myself comes with the potential for horrible consequences that not only impact me, but my entire team as well. *Shut up, brain, just enjoy this.*

Bentley releases me and stares at me, smiling inches from my face. He leans in and presses his nose to mine. "That's going to be much more difficult with others always around, especially your brother. But I promise you, Margot Briar, once this is all over I'm taking you on a proper date. I want you. I want us. I don't want to continue to hide it. From anyone."

I smile, unsure of what to say. He kisses me once more before putting his seatbelt back on and making his way back onto the road, his smile glued to his face. I can't hide my smile, or my flush face, either.

We only drive for about ten more minutes before we're roughly ten minutes outside of The District, at a small park surrounded by trees, technically still in No Man's Land. Everyone is already at the designated meeting spot by the time that Bentley and I arrive, which was the plan since we were the last to leave; although we arrived a few minutes after we were scheduled to, due to our little pit stop. We're supposed to stay here until sunrise and then make our way into The District. This gives everyone a chance to have a meal and rest before taking this on, we even have the opportunity to shower if we'd like. The hospitality RV has already been expanded so that we have access to a full kitchen, and everyone has their own bed among the many bunk beds. Lee even went ahead and put a bed in for Jethro as well, he'll be near the front door to alert us of any intruders or approaching enemies.

Bentley and I get out of our vehicle with Jethro to make our way over to the others. Tonight, we will be sleeping in shifts, and everything will be done in pairs. If you are leaving the RV you are to have someone with you. Hudson and I decided this a long time ago when we started going to battles, the buddy system has saved lives before, and we aren't going to stop using it now. The person that you buddy up with can change day to day, but it is pertinent that you are *always* with someone else. You need someone to watch your back.

I greet my team, "How was everyone else's rides here? Hoping that no news means good news?"

Lee steps forward, clapping Bentley on the back, "Everything went well. Everything is set up, and we can start cooking dinner soon, if anyone is hungry."

"Starving!" Bentley yells.

"If I don't eat soon, I might start punching things." Hudson makes his way towards Lee. At this Lee wanders inside, followed by Auriella to start working on dinner. Lee has always been in charge of making meals while we're out on missions, he's always enjoyed cooking. He even worked part time for my Dad at the restaurant for a while and he learned a lot over the years. Some of the other people here, if put in charge of making our food, might wind up poisoning us all.

Everyone slowly makes their way inside. Today is a seasonably warm day for winter, but it's still only fifty degrees outside. Everyone's belongings were packed into this RV so it's easy to find more comfortable clothes to spend the rest of the evening in. Once inside I find myself a sweater to cozy up in.

Once I'm changed I settle into my bunk to try and figure out who is going to be taking which shifts for the night. As I start writing I immediately put myself on a shift with Bentley but quickly erase it because people might start to get suspicious if we are paired together for both the ride here and the shift tonight. To make it less obvious that I've not put Bentley and I together again, I decide to switch everyone around. This way it looks like I'm trying to mix up the pairings, so everyone has a chance to have different partners. I finish writing down the schedule and rip the page from my notebook to hang on the interior of the main RV door.

10pm-12am : Theo and Hudson
12am-2am : Bentley and Lee
2am-4am : Auriella and Emma Leigh
4am-6am : Margot and Felix

With Hudson and I being Major Generals of the team I think it's important that he and I be the first and last watches, this way if anyone needs to wake us up before or after our shifts we will hopefully at least have had a decent amount of sleep at that point. Although, I don't know how much sleep anyone will be getting tonight. I struggle to sleep whenever people are on watch, as we prepare for a mission, especially due to the location of my bunk. While on watch the pair spend thirty minutes inside and then the next ten minutes outside rounding the RV, continuing this pattern until their shift is over. My bed is near the door of the RV and a window. To top it all off, I'm at the front near the cabin door, where they sit while watching from the inside.

I've always been a light sleeper, and being here with the level of anxiety I am already feeling isn't going to help me tonight. Hudson's bunk is right above mine and I know I'm going to have to listen to his snores all night long, while he sleeps unbothered. The man could sleep through a wailing fire alarm that was taped to his chest. *Must be nice.* As I go to get my food, I decide that though it's cool outside it might be nice to head out there to eat since it feels a bit crowded in the RV with everyone awake. I grab an extra sweatshirt to throw on top of my sweater and head outside with my plate of food with Jethro in tow.

As I make my way to a camping chair that we already have set up, I hear the door of the RV open and shut again. I sit down before looking to see who it is, Bentley. He's really pushing our luck today as he comes to sit next to me.

"Gotta be quick, since Lee is coming out too, but how come you didn't pair us up together tonight for watch shift? Would have been nice." He looks both confused and hurt.

I whisper quickly to him, "I'm trying to make it look like I'm not constantly pairing the two of us together. I don't think it's a great idea to start a war between you and my brother as we're heading to a war of divisions."

Bentley opens his mouth to say something back, probably a smart remark, but I'm saved by Lee coming out to join us. I dive into my food.

"Hey, Lee. This dinner is great! Thank you!" I say as I hold a fork full of macaroni and cheese up to him, cheersing his culinary wizardry.

"Thanks, Margot, glad you're enjoying it. Hopefully you're enjoying it even more than you did putting Auriella and I together for the ride." He shoots me a side eye as he sits down beside me, "I'm on to you Margot."

I laugh at him, "Lee, you have to believe me. I didn't put the two of you together so that there might be some kind of love connection." I roll my eyes, "I put the two of you together in hopes that you might come up with some new genius idea while you were talking on the ride here. Honest."

Lee takes a moment to consider and then looks at me with a smug look, "Well your plan failed Margot. The girl sure does like to talk, so we did talk the entire way here. By we, I mean her. She didn't stop for a breath the entire ride here and I barely got a word in with her. Nothing important either, just her telling me her life story and now I know way too much about her." Bentley is silently laughing on the other side of me; I can see his shoulders bouncing.

"Are you really complaining that you had to spend the car ride listening to a pretty girl talk?" I rub my temples in irritation. At least he didn't end up with Emma Leigh who was probably irritated the entire time.

"You're right, Margot, I'm sure Bentley felt the same way about getting stuck riding here with you." I give Lee a warning look, hoping that he can't see that I'm blushing. Bentley, on the other hand, is sitting there stunned and unsure how to react. If he laughs it off too hard then it'll look suspicious and if he says nothing that's suspicious too. He has to answer like he would have a couple months back.

"Lee, you and I both know that Margot is all business. She literally talked my ear off about strategy the entire ride. *I* had to ride with one of our bosses." Lee starts laughing, because even though we are all friends technically Hudson and I are still their bosses. Bentley played it perfectly.

Lee lifts his glass towards Bentley, "Cheers man, since you're fully briefed on the plans you can be the one that runs into battle first." Both Lee and Bentley are laughing, it makes my heart happy to hear two of my friends laughing about something so ridiculous yet so serious. I miss this being our constant, rather than the seriousness that we're currently stuck in.

The next hour goes by quickly and then it's time for everyone to head to bed before the first shift starts. As I predicted, sleep doesn't come easily. Theo and Hudson are up first and don't talk much, but whenever Hudson decides to start speaking his voice carries through the entire RV. I only get about an hour of sleep before Bentley and Lee take over. As much as I want to sleep and respect their privacy I can't help but listen in, especially when I hear Lee mention my name.

"So, the ride here with Margot, honestly how'd that go? I know she freaked out on you the night that we were at your parents' once we'd chosen the new recruits. She still upset and being weird with you?" Bentley is pausing *way* too long before answering.

"Uh, not really. She mostly has been back to normal. Maybe Hudson said something to her or something." Bentley's answer lacks any type of confidence.

"She's always so serious, probably just needs someone to show her a good time and improve her mood." *Rude.* This time Bentley is definitely taking too long to respond and then starts laughing. I guess he decided that not saying any words was the best way to go about responding, without blowing our cover. They begin talking about video games and I allow myself to drift back to sleep.

Even though Auriella can be chatty I somehow sleep through her and Emma Leigh's shift and get woken up by my alarm to join Felix on watch. Emma Leigh must not have been up for conversation, leaving Auriella to sit with her thoughts in silence. I drag myself out of bed, knowing that today is going to be a long day. I creep past Jethro who is snoring, sprawled out on the floor to meet Felix at the front of the RV. He's already there looking fully awake eating a granola bar. As I take my seat he doesn't say anything to me but offers me a granola bar and juice.

"Thanks, maybe this will help me wake up a little bit. Did you get much sleep?"

"Yeah! I passed out the moment that we all went to bed and got up with my alarm. These beds are great! Reminds me of my childhood." These beds definitely aren't comfy. He must be a heavy sleeper like Hudson who can sleep anywhere on anything.

"I didn't sleep much at all, so at least one of us is well rested. What did you mean that it reminds you of your childhood?" I bite into my granola, hoping it'll help to fuel me.

"Right, we haven't really talked about personal stuff, what with planning for a war. Well, as you know Auriella and I are twins…well, twins run in the family." He pulls up a picture of his family on his phone to show me, "We're the oldest, mom and dad went to have one more and ended up with another set of twins. Things were tight for a little while before my parents bought the house that they live in now. For a couple of years, the four of us shared one bedroom with two sets of bunk beds in it. The younger set of twins are also a boy and a girl, so I shared with my brother, Lewis, and Auriella shared with our sister Delia." I have to think hard, I vaguely remember seeing the rest of their family at the sendoff, but all of that seems like a blur now.

"Oh wow! I didn't realize there were four of you, and that there were more twins! That's wild! Your parents must have been a bit shocked." Right now, the thought of one child is daunting.

"Oh yeah, they said no more after that…didn't want to risk going for the trifecta and having a third set of twins. But it worked out well. It was nice having another set of twins around." He certainly is chipper for it being so early.

"I can only imagine. I had my own room for a bit, but then when my sister came along I had to share a room with Hudson so that she could have her own room for a nursery, but when we all got a little older she and Hudson swapped rooms so the girls could be together. It was nice." Felix just smiles and nods at me as he starts to eat yet another granola bar.

Listening to Felix talk about his family makes me realize how little I know about my new teammates beyond the most basic level of information that I could find on a resume. Sure, I could tell you their strengths and weaknesses, but I couldn't begin to tell you what their dreams are or even something as basic as their favorite color or food. I lose myself in thought, so Felix and I finish our watch in silence, because before I'm able to bring up another topic the sun is beginning to rise.

It is time to start waking up the others, to pack up and make the short ten-minute drive into The District. Today is the first day of our mission and from here on out the war can begin at any time, whether or not we are ready for it. Hopefully this will be the beginning of the end of an era.

CHAPTER TWENTY-TWO
ENTERING THE DISTRICT

I allow Felix to go ahead of me to start waking up the people further back in the RV, I start at the front, and we'll meet in the middle. I go to Bentley's bunk first, skipping over Hudson's. I can't help but skim my thumb across his face when waking him up. As he opens his eyes he smiles up at me and places his hand over mine, closing his eyes once more while taking the moment in. I smile back at him, but I'm quickly snapped back to reality. I can hear others moving, he quickly kisses my palm before I pull my hand away and continue making my way over to wake the others. My hand almost tingles where he kissed me and my smile is far too big for this early in the morning.

Once everyone is awake we begin packing away our things, so that the RV can be closed up for driving. I use this time to take Jethro outside and have a few moments to myself. I break our buddy system rule knowing that Hudson will be pissed if he finds me out here alone, even though I think Jethro should count.

My alone time is quickly interrupted by Felix running up alongside me. He's carrying something, but I can't quite tell what it is.

"Felix, what's up?" Jethro trots back to investigate as well.

"I forgot to tell you that while I was making Jethro's armor suit I went ahead and made him this as well." He's holding some kind of rolled up mat in his hands, and I have zero clue what it could be for.

"Uh…what is it?" Jethro sniffs at it curiously.

Felix holds his creation up proudly over his head, allowing it to unroll. I'm still not sure what it is that I'm looking at. It just looks like a green textured yoga mat to me; I feel bad not knowing what it is, since Felix is clearly excited about it. Felix must be able to see the confusion in my eyes, because he proceeds to explain, "It's a potty mat for Jethro. I figured that there might be sometimes that we're unable to let him out to go to the bathroom. This way he can go in the RV in a specific spot that looks and feels like grass. We'll be able to wash it off in the shower too." Felix is probably one of the nicest, most thoughtful people that I know. Not only has he gone above and beyond in creating Jethro's suit, but he also went out of his way to make this too.

"Thank you so much Felix. I really appreciate this, and I know Jethro is going to too." Felix goes to give Jethro a pat and Jethro returns the favor by jumping up on him, paws on his chest to lick his face. We both have a little laugh.

Felix and I head back to the rest of the group once Jethro is finished. The RV is ready to go, and everyone is standing by the vehicle that they arrived in yesterday, since we will be keeping the same driving pairs to make the final drive into The District. I thank Felix once again as he throws the potty mat into the hospitality RV as Jethro and I make our way over to Bentley. This time we won't be staggering our departure, since it's such a short drive and we want to make sure we're all together heading into The District. It's very likely that we could be attacked on our way in and every second counts in this instance.

The ride towards The District is a tense one, but Bentley uses it as an opportunity to return the favor and places his hand on my thigh for the duration of the short ride. Only five minutes into our ride I begin seeing large buildings, huge empty homes. These homes are bigger than any I have ever seen before, they look as though someone came up with one idea for a mansion and plopped it down one next to another. None of them have too much space between the next one, it's like the person that was building these houses wanted to cram as many people as they could into one small space.

Then, in the distance, I can see a tall white building with a pointed top. I remember learning about this in my history class, but I can't remember its actual name, just that some referred to it as 'the big pencil'. It's amazing that out of all the buildings this one seems to be one of the only ones that really doesn't have that much damage to it. You would think that a building so far into the sky would be the first one that people would want to take down.

Especially since this large building is seen from far away and acts as a landmark so that anyone, including your enemies, can find you.

The closer we get the more monuments and buildings I'm able to see. The first that I see once we enter The District's boundaries is a large Sophia Marie statue. She is the last known President of The United States before The Great Divide. She was voted into office as the events that lead to The Great Divide were beginning. Some even say that she was the last straw that led to the divide; people couldn't handle the fact that there was a female in charge of their country. She was the first, and it threw people into a tizzy. She barely made it through one term before the country imploded on itself, but she stuck it out until the very end. I've looked up to Sophia Marie since learning about her during school. I was drawn in by her bravery and admire her perseverance. It's not very well known what happened to her after The Great Divide, the most recent rumor that I heard is that she finished her life off the grid, that she escaped to another country as a refugee to try and did what she could while also keeping herself safe. Unfortunately, a woman in power was something that so many wanted to destroy, this still rings true in The South.

In The East women are given the same respect that men are, but it's my understanding that it's not like that in other divisions. In The South, women are viewed as less than in many ways. They do not have any positions in power, and there are very few women that end up in their military; even those that do are typically put into demeaning positions. This makes it all the more confusing that Lena wanted to go and join them, she must have her reasoning though, even though I will never agree with her leaving. Having learned about these things always made me feel more grateful for living in The East and the opportunities that I was able to have, even being a woman.

As we enter The District, I start to see the people that I'd only ever heard about. I know you shouldn't judge a book by its cover, but these people scare me. Each of them looks unfriendly. One man in particular catches my attention. He's wearing some kind of tattered trench coat, made up of many different fabrics that look like they came from many different garments and were sewn together out of necessity. The moment that I realize I have been staring too long the man pulls his coat to the side to reveal a gun on his hip, an obvious threat just for looking at him. I quickly snap my head back to the front of the vehicle, with a small gasp.

My gasp is loud enough for Bentley to take notice, "What's going on, Margot?" *Everything.*

"I'm quickly learning that the things we've heard about this place weren't just rumors and scary stories that you tell your children, so that they don't run off and try to join The District. It's dangerous here and we're going to need to keep ourselves on the defensive the entire time we're here." I begin cracking my knuckles due to my anxiety, "We're on their territory now, and to make matters worse we don't even have a map of this place. All they have to do is lead us further in and they can trap us. We don't know where we are, and we definitely don't know how to get out if they take us off this main road."

I can feel the anxiety inside of me building more and more, thinking of all of the bad things that could possibly happen to us here. We haven't even made it to our final destination on this mission, and this could easily be where it all ends. My heartbeat is beginning to race. I start to think about my parents potentially not only losing one of their children, but two. How would they even handle losing two out of their three children? Or what would Hudson or I do if only one of us made it back to our parents. Then, Mrs. Adler's final words hit me. *'Take care of my son.'* I must do whatever it takes to make sure that Bentley makes it home to his family. As my breath quickens it takes everything I have to shake myself before I put myself into a full-blown panic attack, this is not something that I want Bentley to witness. It's something I keep private, even from my siblings.

I make it a point for the rest of our trip through The District to not make eye contact with anyone. If I even see anyone out of my peripherals, I make sure not to look in that direction until they're out of sight. We don't have an exact map of The District, we only knew how to get to it, but not how to get to the exact location we were looking for. Before leaving we had heard that we would find the "leaders" of The District in the biggest of the white buildings. If anyone knows what is going on in their division, it will be them. Hopefully we will be lucky enough that they will be willing to help us.

This trip is different from leg one, Bentley and I barely holding conversation, the both of us are too far into our heads, taking in everything that's around us. We've never seen The District before, except for in pictures in our history books, and all of those are pretty outdated. The pictures and stories made this place seem much milder than it actually is. I can't help but compare it to my home in The East. Sure, many homes are falling apart and covered in vines, but that's the worst of it. Here there is spray paint on everything, different sayings and threats directed not only at groups of people, but calling out individuals as well.

Underneath the spray paint there are boards that are clearly in place of windows that have been shattered. Not only are the boards covering places where windows belong, but they're being used as makeshift doors and walls as well. Occasionally I see a child playing outside, but they don't have toys like the kids in The East do. These are toys that look like they've been passed down from generation to generation and probably should have been replaced by now. There's a girl, probably about five, carrying around a teddy bear that's missing both legs and an arm. His fur looks like he's been loved for a long time and has been through a lot with each person that's loved him.

A few paces in front of her I see a boy who is a bit older, maybe her older brother, around about ten or eleven. He's carrying what looks like it might have been a basketball at some point. Not only is it flat, but it is also clearly dry rotted and doesn't have a bit of bounce left in it. He's riding along on what looks like an improvised skateboard; there are four wheels screwed onto a piece of wood. The piece of wood isn't shaped though; it's a square plank that looks like it might have been pulled off of one of the dilapidated houses.

We didn't have a lot growing up in The East, but part of me feels bad for ever complaining about what we did have. It's not fair that they are living with next to nothing and we grew up barely over an hour away and had so much more than them. Anger towards the people that put us in this position overtakes me. I feel angry that these kids' parents felt that they had no choice but to come here and · have their children live this way, or that they were forced to come here by their division. It's not right and seeing this lights the fire under me even more to fight and win this war, allowing everyone to have a better life.

I look at Bentley, who quickly wipes a single tear that's rolling down his cheek. He must be thinking similar thoughts. I put my hand on his leg to let him know that I'm here for him, even though I know he's not going to want to talk about this. I wouldn't be me if I didn't try and talk about this with him.

"Are you alright?"

He looks at me without turning his head from the road, placing his hand on top of mine, "I'm fine."

Neither of us are willing to talk about this, I can understand what he's feeling. Often I get too far into my own head, and the thoughts become overwhelming, I find myself suffocating in my thoughts. I don't want to burden Bentley with my feelings, I don't want him to worry about me, this is already going to be a heavy trip. For now, I will keep calm, but eventually I should get all of this out, no matter how uncomfortable it makes me. Right now, there are bigger things to worry about.

Suddenly all of my thoughts vanish as I see the large white building that we were told to look for. It's surrounded by iron gates, and it's the most massive home that I've ever seen. The gates look as though they no longer serve their original purpose, there are breaks in it and large chunks of the fence where there is no fence at all. This is our destination, it has to be. I look at Bentley, he's spotted it too. His grip on the steering wheel has tightened, I wish that he would talk to me about how he's feeling. We park on the street all getting out of our vehicles, minus Jethro, and begin walking towards the gates.

As we get closer I begin to see figures walking across the lawn of the big white house, toward the gates. Clearly these people have formed a team together. Unlike our team, their team looks to have a large age range. While the youngest looks to be about eighteen, the oldest looks to be somewhere around sixty. Since The Great Divide, The District has been the place where people who have nowhere else to go end up, unless you choose to live in one of the uninhabited areas, in isolation, and live off the land. It makes sense that their leaders and military are made up of a wide age range of people. Here it seems you have the opportunity to make a name for yourself, no matter your age. Other divisions have the idea that once you reach a certain age you are no longer useful to society.

Boy, are they wrong, Theo's grandfather for example is someone that I've always admired; he has so much experience, that is something that can only come with age. Even in retirement he still does so much.

As I take a moment to look at each of these people, it hits me; I know one of the people walking towards the gates. He's taken his place at the front of the group of people. He must have become their leader rather quickly. Maybe this connection will help them decide if we're going to work with or fight against each other. Even though he's been living here in The District, likely for several years, he's still just as handsome as I remember. Here being attractive isn't a first priority, but the way he looks seems effortless. I'm in complete shock. I look over to Bentley and it's clear that he has noticed him as well. He draws eyes to him.

He and Bentley were in the same Graduation class, but that doesn't necessarily mean that they knew each other. But, when it came to him, everyone in The East knew exactly who he was. How could they not? His face was plastered everywhere for months, and even after that he was the talk of the division until the following year's graduation. Before us stands Lincoln Hart, the standout from Bentley, Lee, and Hudson's Graduation. There have always been rumors that the pressure of being the standout was too much for him and that he had ended up here. I never knew whether or not to believe it though, because after what we had been taught, who would want to willingly come here to The District?

Everything is getting ready to change. All I can do at this point is pray that we don't have to add him to the list of people we'll have to fight, that came from back home. Beginning a battle is bad enough, having to fight with someone you know or have some kind of connection to, makes it that much worse. If the time comes I will have to put these thoughts to the back of my mind, protecting my team comes first. Something has to be done to make this world right and stop The South and The Trio from completely taking over. It is time to make the first stand. The people who caused this chaos aren't here to fight the battle, and now it's time for us to pay the ultimate price for their actions.

ACKNOWLEDGEMENTS

As I write this, I have tears in my eyes, I can't believe I wrote a book…and people are actually reading it! *The Great Divide* has been an idea in my head for years, and I am grateful to finally bring the thoughts in my head to you. *The Great Divide* has been three years' worth of pulling all of the ideas that I've collected on sticky notes and in the notes app on my phone. Writing late at night while babies slept or early mornings before heading to my nine to five. To the moms out there, take the chance, chase your dreams. The dream is to continue bringing you into more of the worlds that I've created, so continue to follow me and my story for more updates. Book two in *The Great Divide* series is in the works and I'm hoping to have it in your hands sooner than later. This book is to those who supported the girl with a dream to be an author. To the books and their authors that inspired me and always give me an escape from the crazy world we live in.

Thank you to my husband, for supporting my dream to write this story and put it out there to the world, and for letting me mess up all the settings on his computer chair while working on formatting. Thank you to my family who has promoted me and continued pushing me even when I was ready to give in. Thank you to my best friend for letting me send her each chapter of this book in their rawest forms, giving me honest feedback and support along the way to keep going. My real-life filing cabinet and Kitty. Thank you to the friends who offered to be my beta readers and gave me much needed critics. To my friends and "book auntie" who allowed me to send them endless formatting ideas to help me get my thoughts out of my own head and work through what would look best for you, the reader. Thank you to my cover designer and fellow author, poet Angelika Brewer, @signed_a.b. Thank you to my sister for the midnight panic calls and helping me work through formatting. Thank you to my friend/IT support for getting me through formatting and everything involving a computer that makes my brain melt a bit. Thank you to the teachers who pushed me to polish my writing and encouraged me to read. To my grandparents who always showed up to cheer me on, to Pop Pop for always reminding me to "take care of yourself".

Last, and furthest from the least to my babies who push me to be the best version of myself and push me to live my wildest dreams. This is for you, my peanut and my bubba. Never let anyone stop you from following your dreams and reaching for the stars. I love you both "too much".

If you've made it this far, you're probably my mom or dad. To the both of you thank you from the bottom of my heart. Thank you for pushing me to follow my dreams and never allowing me to settle. Love you guys.

www.ingramcontent.com/pod-product-compliance
Lightning Source LLC
Chambersburg PA
CBHW030240120726
47903CB00005B/1556